STEAL THE SHOW

ALSO BY THOMAS KAUFMAN

Drink the Tea

STEAL THE SHOW

A Willis Gidney Mystery

THOMAS KAUFMAN

MINOTAUR BOOKS

A THOMAS DUNNE BOOK

New York

This is a work of fiction. All of the characters, organizations, and events portrayed in this novel are either products of the author's imagination or are used fictitiously.

A THOMAS DUNNE BOOK FOR MINOTAUR BOOKS.
An imprint of St. Martin's Publishing Group.

STEAL THE SHOW. Copyright © 2011 by Thomas Kaufman. All rights reserved. Printed in the United States of America. For information, address St. Martin's Press, 175 Fifth Avenue, New York, N.Y. 10010.

www.thomasdunnebooks.com
www.minotaurbooks.com

Library of Congress Cataloging-in-Publication Data

Kaufman, Thomas.
  Steal the show : a mystery / Thomas Kaufman. — 1st ed.
      p. cm.
   ISBN 978-0-312-54632-8
   1. Private investigators—Fiction.   2. Washington (D.C.)—
Fiction.   I. Title.
   PS3611.A843S74 2011
   813'.6—dc22

2011007073

First Edition: July 2011

10 9 8 7 6 5 4 3 2 1

For Katie

ACKNOWLEDGMENTS

Many thanks to the folks who helped me with this book. From the community of writers: George Pelecanos, S. J. Rozan, Steve Hamilton, Robert Randisi, John Lutz, Robert Ward, Marcia Talley, and the late Walter Wager. From the publishing side, my editor Toni Plummer; publicist Bridget Hartzler; and Doug Grad, the world's best agent. Other folks were kind enough to supply hard information which I quickly subverted for my own use: Sari Horwitz and Scott Higham of the *Washington Post;* Terry Ryan, retired, Montgomery County Police; Tony Avendorph of Tony Avendorph Associates; Anthony Brigidini, Detective, D.C. police; Dr. David Hayes of the Mayo Clinic; Bill Burr of NIST; Wendy Aylsworth of Warner Bros. Technical Operations; Chuck Goldwater of Cinedigm; Alonzo Crawford, Howard University; Peter Banks of The National Center for Missing & Exploited Children; Ed Read; Patty Zubeck; and Maggie Magill. Then there are the brave souls who read early drafts and survived: Willard Carroll, Michael Cuddy, Kate Dell, Larry Klein, and Matt Nicholl. Special thanks to Laurie Webb for her amazing and insightful comments.

Last, I'd like to thank the late Ruth Cavin, a great editor with the uncanny ability to spot diamonds in the rough or, in my case, zircon. We'll miss you, Ruth.

STEAL THE SHOW

I reached through the jagged glass panel, then cut my hand unlocking the door.

It was a missing person case that had brought me to this ruined house. The house was in a row of boarded-up houses, the type that once held the glow of gaslight, where refined young ladies practiced piano while waiting for their beaux. Now the streets were dark, the only sound the thump of rap as cars with blackened windows rolled past.

Sheets of graffitied plywood had sealed the front door. I'd been about to work the back door lock, when I heard a baby cry.

No, that's wrong. A baby screamed, a mounting kind of scream that started me shaking. I threw my shoulder at the door and the baby stopped—for a moment—then screeched with new desperation.

No one answered the door, or moved the dirty gray towel to see who was there. The towel did nothing to stop the sound of the screams, or the faint whiff of smoke.

I rattled the knob and the baby's cries grew desperate, more animal than human. Just like the cries I'd heard years ago, the night Bockman's burned down. I kicked out the door's glass panel. The glass cut my hand when I snapped the lock open, then I heard a thud. The crying stopped.

My turn to panic. I shoved the door open. On the floor was a black baby with a pink-and-white bib, strapped to a high chair. She lay senseless in a puddle of blood.

It wasn't hers. It belonged to the dead white woman sitting in a chair by the table. Her body slumped, looking almost relaxed. Pale hands rested on her knees, palms upward. I stepped around the body, unhooked the high chair's belt, its plastic snap sounding loud in the tiny kitchen. The baby was so light as I lifted her out and into my arms. The pulse in her throat was strong and steady. I got her back to my car and drove away from there.

PART ONE

CHAPTER 1

The day Rush Gemelli came into my office, I hadn't had a job in weeks.

Back then I worked out of the second floor of a two-story building on F Street. The first floor held a wig and corset shop. The rent was cheap because the building would be gone inside a year. Just about every building on the block was making way for more Gap stores and Starbucks. Looking out across Ninth Street toward the Smithsonian American Art Museum, I wondered if they would also have to move. You could fit a pretty big Starbucks there.

The museum had a sculpture out front that was nine feet tall—a mustachioed vaquero riding a big blue bronco. The bronco had its front feet planted while the rear feet kicked high in the air. The vaquero gripped the bronco's reins in one hand and waved his gun above his head with the other, his face split with a crazy smile. At least he was having fun.

Me, not so much. I own a small copy of the vaquero, and I'd spent a chunk of that morning squatting with my eyes at desktop level, lining up my miniature with the original outside. Since getting my PI license, I've discovered that it does no good to worry when your phone stops ringing. Work will pick up, you tell yourself. Still, after a couple of weeks of no calls, I was ready for anything. If King James had called me for a new translation of the Bible, I'd have taken a whack at it.

I set the vaquero aside and pulled out the plastic baby doll from the bottom of my desk drawer, along with a fresh diaper. Good time to practice.

The hard part is getting the little sticky tabs that hold the diaper in place without trapping your thumbs. I had just managed to tape my right thumb to the doll's left cheek when I heard feet pound up the stairs.

I shoved the baby—with my thumb still attached—into the top desk drawer, then grabbed a yellow legal pad and leaned back in my chair. A pose of casual elegance—my feet on the blotter, the pad in my lap, jotting notes to a nonexistent case with my left hand while I tried to free my right.

A bald head peered inside and said, "You the detective?"

"I'm the detective." I was trying to work my thumb loose from the diaper.

"Oh man." He sighed. "I'm Rush Gemelli."

I waved him in. "Have a seat, Mr. Gemelli."

He gave another quick glance around my office, then approached my client chair the way Dannemora inmates had approached the electric one. After taking a deep breath, he forced himself to sit. Then, with no prompting from me, he launched into his story.

Which was strange. That he needed no prompting, I mean. Most clients would rather skip in front of a train than tell you why they trudged up the stairs. His story was strange, too—about a warehouse in Alexandria, Virginia, that needed breaking into.

"I don't do that kind of work." I felt disappointed. You go weeks without a client, it really hurts to turn anyone down.

"You're kinda choosy about your business." He swept his

hand, taking in yellowed walls that had been white around the time of Clinton's inaugural—his first one. Woodwork that had been enameled over so many times, none of the windows closed completely. The wall opposite my desk was bulging toward us, as though some giant insect were burrowing through from the other side. Whatever it was, it seemed to have plenty of patience. "Besides, from what I've heard, busting into places is up your alley."

"These days, I'm staying out of alleys."

"Look, Gidney, this warehouse is a Mid-Atlantic hub for pirate films and software." He pulled blueprints and diagrams from an ancient briefcase, then spread them out on my desk. "I got everything you need to know—about their security, alarm systems, everything." For a moment he grew excited and forgot to sneer. "It's safe, I guarantee it. And if you nailed these sleazes, you'd not only be helping me but also the FBI." He added quickly, "Job pays a thousand."

My normal fee is $350 a day, plus expenses. Gemelli was offering more than he should have, and I think he knew it. "Money's not the problem," I said. "But let's suppose that your information is wrong, and the warehouse is legit. In which case, I'm breaking the law and hurting the FBI's feelings." I liberated my thumb and shut the desk drawer.

"The FBI would say you're a hero." He wrinkled his nose. "Do you smell talcum powder?"

"No. The point is, I'm not doing it."

The sneer returned. "Would it ease your conscience to know why I'm asking?"

"Sure, tell me why I should commit a felony for you."

"Not for me, for my father. He's head of MPAC, the Motion Picture Alliance Council."

"How nice for him."

"Yeah, well, not lately. You read the papers, everyone thinks Hollywood's to blame for anything bad that happens. He's got congressmen blaming the industry for every wacko with an Uzi who takes out a preschool."

"Gosh, that sounds just awful for your dad."

Gemelli nodded. "The religious right—he's getting heat from them, too. Over sex and nudity and adulterous flings."

"Those are a few of my favorite things," I said.

Gemelli acted as though I hadn't spoken. "Now he's under fire because of pirated movies. The industry is losing over two billion a year, they figure. And he's gonna lose his job unless he shows he has a handle on things. So, you get the evidence of the pirate ring, and he takes the credit. It'd buy him some time."

"So he asked you to see me?"

Gemelli looked pained. "Christ no. He can't ever know I was here. My dad's a great guy, Gidney, but he keeps his own counsel. Always has, even at the White House."

That's where I knew the name. "He was adviser to the president, a few administrations back?"

Rush looked pleased. "Senior adviser. They call him 'the Elephant' because he never forgets a favor." Here he paused and tried to look intense. "Or a slight."

I clutched my chest and fell back in my chair. "Call an ambulance," I gasped.

He shook his head. "Look, I need help. And word is, you're good."

"Sorry, I'm keeping my life straight." I succeeded in looking modest. I *had* to keep my life straight so I could adopt Sarah, the baby I had found. And while I could be wrong about this, I suspected that committing felonies would not endear me to D.C. Adoptive Services.

I held out my hand. "Good luck to you and your father."

Gemelli fished out a business card. "You change your mind, call me."

Tapping his card on the blueprints, I said, "Don't you want these?"

Gemelli shrugged into his topcoat, which could've been carbon dated back to the Bronze Age. "Copies, keep 'em, you might change your mind." Then he clumped down the stairs. From my window I saw his bald noggin come out of the building, glance skyward even though it wasn't raining, then head for the Gallery Place Metro. I stuffed the card with the blueprints inside my desk. I could have saved myself a hell of a lot of trouble if I'd shredded everything and given Rush Gemelli a tiny confetti shower.

CHAPTER 2

An hour later, I parked outside a brick building on Second Street Northeast, a few blocks from Union Station. Late September in D.C. The rain was forcing us to forget our summer drought. The streets were shiny, and clouds bearing down promised more, making the morning sky dark.

Every day for the past two weeks, I'd been in a classroom here, my rear parked on a hard wooden chair. Today marked my last child-adoption class. I had taken ten—count 'em, ten—and I was glad I'd soon be free of this white room, its uncomfortable chairs, and Ms. Ferguson.

Ms. Ferguson, our instructor, was the only person I'd ever

seen who could stand stock-still for hours while she spoke. There are African tribesmen who take a drug when they hunt, rendering them motionless for hours. But I think Ms. Ferguson came by it honestly.

No matter. Today I'd be assigned a caseworker, and soon I'd be Sarah's adopted father. Which was good—Sarah was running out of time. So far, she had survived D.C. Adoptive Services. But in two weeks, they'd move her from the nursery into the barracks. That's where she'd meet other kids, kids up to twelve years old. Only a handful of them would be abandoned infants like two-year-old Sarah. The rest would be drug dealers, mental cases, and a sprinkling of sexual predators for good measure. O brave new world . . .

Why mix all these kids together? For the District, it's a matter of space and money—they don't have much of either. And it doesn't help that a judge is always ordering one or another of these kiddie asylums into receivership, or sentencing a higher-up for embezzlement. Besides, who really cares about these kids? Who would want a child seen as damaged, simply by being born in the wrong place? Me, that's who.

So I shifted in my chair, ignoring the pain in my backside, and waited for the last class to end. The Garfinkles sat across from me. I could feel their anxiety as Ms. Ferguson *finally* handed out our FR-43s. These forms would tell us if we'd cleared our background checks with the D.C. police, the FBI, and the National Child Abuse Registry. We would also read the name of our caseworker, the D.C.-appointed professional who'd work with us through the whole process.

As Ms. Ferguson went around the room, the door opened and the caseworkers filed in to meet us. The Garfinkles took their paper and scanned it quickly. They both exhaled together, their arms around each other. I raised my eyebrows at them, and David Garfinkle said, "We thought we'd get—our luck has been lousy up till now, I figured we get this nightmare caseworker we'd heard about." He grinned at his wife. "But our luck has turned."

She smiled at him. "Finally."

Ms. Ferguson completed the first aisle, then turned and headed my way. Each couple getting their paperwork smiled, they'd found their way out of the labyrinth. Ms. Ferguson dropped my form in front of me. My palms sweaty, I scanned the results of my background check. I wasn't worried about the FBI or the Child Abuse Registry. But I had grown up in D.C.—and passed through the very institutions I wanted Sarah to avoid. Also, my childhood had been, well, less than ideal. My first arrest came around age six. So I knew something was bound to pop up. The question was, How bad?

But amazingly, my D.C. record was clean. Some kind of clerical error no doubt. I wasn't going to point that out to Ms. Ferguson. I thought things were cool as I turned the page. That's when I saw the word *DENIED*, stamped in red ink. A different kind of bureaucratic blunder. Normally, I would have taken it in stride, but not with a two-week deadline looming for Sarah. A scraping of chair legs on the linoleum floor signaled that the other prospective parents had stood and were speaking earnestly with their new caseworkers. Then she approached me. "Mr. Gidney?"

"Yes?"

"I'm your caseworker, Florence Walters."

A pencil-thin African-American woman in her late fifties, with skin the color of cinnamon. She held out a dried hand. I shook it gently, hoping it wouldn't crumble. She was five feet tall, and if she topped one hundred pounds, it was by virtue of the thick lenses of her glasses. She raised her chin, peering at me with magnified brown eyes. A faded floral pattern covered her dress, which ended mid-calf, exposing a lovely stretch of baggy stockings, ending with flats that showed serious heel wear on the inside of each shoe.

All I had to do was notch up the charm—she'd go running for a revised form. "I think there's been a mistake on my application," I said, smiling and showing her plenty of teeth.

Florence Walters peered down, her brow wrinkled, as though seeing this kind of form for the first time. Then she looked up at me. "There's no mistake," she said.

"Well, see, there is, because I'm trying to adopt this girl and some bureaucrat used the wrong stamp on my paperwork."

"Mr. Gidney, *I* stamped your form, it was *not* a mistake." The Garfinkles looked at us.

"Well, can you tell me why you stamped it 'denied'?" I kept my voice even. Having dealt with D.C. bureaucrats all my life, I've found it does no good to antagonize them.

"Of course. Your application has been denied, Mr. Gidney, because, in the opinion of D.C. Adoptive Services, you are not a good match for this child."

My heart started racing. I glanced at the Garfinkles, their eyes telling me not to panic.

"But I saved this child's life."

A small shrug. "Yes, well, that really has nothing to do with the matter at hand. You've made an application, it's been denied."

I felt a stab of anger, tried my best to ignore it. "I'm going to appeal this decision."

She reached into her pocket and gave me her card. "That's up to you, of course."

"And I'm getting a lawyer."

"You'll probably need one. Good day, Mr. Gidney." Then she turned and walked out. I noticed the room had grown quiet.

Everyone was staring at me. The Garfinkles came over. David put his hand on my shoulder.

"Remember that nightmare caseworker I mentioned?" he said.

CHAPTER 3

The Garfinkles walked me out, feeling guilty for fobbing off their bad luck on me. I could've told them that I recognized the luck as my own, but I wasn't feeling that generous. With the lunchtime traffic whipping past, they advised me to find a good lawyer.

I thought of Stayne Matthews. Substitute *devious* for *good* and he was perfect. I thanked the Garfinkles, then called him from my car. Miraculously, he answered.

"Going for the common touch, answering your own phone?"

"My girl's left for the day," he said.

"And *my* girl's been left to the mercies of D.C. Adoptive Services." I told him about finding Sarah and trying to adopt her.

When I finished, he said, "Willis, my boy, I admire your intestinal fortitude." He ramped up what he called his "closing-argument voice." "Not every man would try to adopt an abandoned baby— a baby of color, I might add. That's the kind of civic-mindedness we need today."

"Could we save the bullshit for court?"

"Of course. As I see it, you have two choices. Number one, you could look into adopting a different child, maybe one from a Third World country—"

"I'm not comparison shopping here."

"Which leaves number two: We appeal the decision." Like any good lawyer, Matthews explained what he would do, calmed me down, and said he'd get right on it. Then he talked about my chances and his fee. It seems these two were closely linked. "I'll get an idea of our position, then give you a buzz around six. And Willis? Stay out of trouble, okay?"

"Sure." No problem. The way things were going, I'd never work again. Oh, I'd had some dribs and drabs, referrals from McClure Downing, a big firm too busy for the little niggling jobs they tossed my way. Lifesaver jobs, just enough to keep my business afloat. But Matthews was expensive, I'd need more than a lifesaver. I'd need an ocean liner.

I spent the next hour camped in my office chair, calling insurance companies—*Hey, Pete, how are you? . . . Great! Yeah, I've been really busy too, but I just wanted to call and see what's up!* When I got tired of that, I studied Gemelli's diagrams and blueprints. I decided a person would have to be crazy to break in, and I knew just how I'd do it.

By 5:15, I was home, glad to climb the narrow stairs to my second-floor apartment on Fortieth Street, a mile north of Georgetown University. I keyed my door, visions of junk food dancing in my head. Would snarfing a Ho Ho before nuking a burrito be déclassé?

The door swung open and Lillian McClellan sat at the dining table, tinkering with some piece of programming code on her laptop. Like me, Lilly was a freelance contractor. Unlike me, she was busy, writing software for dot-coms and government agencies. She held up a finger in a "Just a second" gesture, typed one more line, snapped the case shut, and slipped it in a carryall the size of a mailbag. She did that thing with her hair, swinging the black-and-tan dreadlocks from her face. She came close, stood on tiptoes, placed a hand behind my head, and kissed me.

It wasn't one of those perfunctory 1950s TV sitcom peck-on-the-lips kisses, either. This felt like a fork in an electric outlet. She fried me, then broke the embrace and looked up at me.

"Hi," she said.

"Like a kite," I agreed. She grinned, and her cheeks dimpled. The dimples went well with her faded denim blue eyes and café au lait skin. When she looked at me, I felt something that was new, and yet somehow familiar.

See, I've lost a part of my childhood. Nothing major, just the first five years or so, I don't know why. Some quack once told me my lack of memory is symptomatic of PTSD. Or maybe, during those first years, nothing interesting happened. That changed when Lilly came into my life. It's hard to describe, exactly. Have you ever read about Helen Keller? She'd lost her sight and hearing at age eighteen months. Then, at age seven, when Anne Sullivan came into her life, Keller said she had an epiphany—she experienced the sweet return of reason, something she barely remembered from those first months of her life.

That's what it was like with Lilly—I experienced the return of something precious, a feeling that I had nearly forgotten. I tapped her shoulder bag. "How's the big project? Got your code working?"

"Getting there. Speaking of working, how's the detective business?"

"Feh." I hung my wet coat on the back of a chair.

"Things'll pick up. Today was your last adoption class, right? You really going through with it?"

"That a problem?" I tried to sound casual. Lilly hated the idea of my adopting a little girl. Which struck me as unfair, since she'd been one herself. Over the past two months she'd gotten edgy, watching me get my apartment ready, installing safety plugs on the electric outlets, not to mention the toys and books I'd bought. This was stuff I'd had to do, so the when the DCAS folks inspected my place, they could report back that it was "a safe and healthy environment" for Sarah. She'd told me I was making a mistake, but that she was just curious enough to stick around and see how things turned out. I hoped she meant it. I couldn't bear the thought of losing her. Not that I had come right out and said so.

She shrugged. "Oh, Jan called. Emily's birthday party is, like, tomorrow. Can you believe she's five already? We're bringing pizza."

"Just pizza?"

"Uh-huh. Janet's getting hot dogs, caramel popcorn, candied apples, ice cream, soda pop, layer cake, of course, strawberries dipped in chocolate. . . . I think that's it. Jan said she's leaving the rest of the menu up in the air."

"Which is where the food will be, an hour after the kids eat it."

Lilly picked up a gift-wrapped package. "I bought Emily this diary kit. She decorates it herself. And I just got this for me." She showed me a little spray bottle—perfume?—then spritzed her wrist and held it under my nose as my phone began to ring.

"Willis Gidney." Definitely not perfume.

"Willis, my boy, it's Stayne."

"Hold on a sec." I muted the phone and wrinkled my nose at her. "Okay, I give up. What *is* that? Essence of Love Canal?"

She grinned a little wider. "Antipheromone spray, a lab in California makes it. Trying it out for my meeting tomorrow."

"Terrific." I unmuted the phone and Lilly pretended not to listen. "What's the word, counselor?"

Matthews said, "The word is *appeal*. We need to have a hearing with your caseworker's boss."

"When?"

"Day after tomorrow at two-forty-five. Meet me in the DCAS lobby, on Third Street. By the way, this is going to mean more hours on my part. I'll need a small retainer."

"How small?"

"Well, let's see. After today, six and a half hours, that's thirteen hundred."

"Christ. How much more?"

"Probably a lot more." I could almost hear him dry-washing his hands.

"You're a shark."

He chuckled. "Stop, you're embarrassing me." His tone got lower and friendlier. "By the way, I'm representing some young ladies in a class action against Hooters. I could fix you up, unless you're still dating the bag lady?"

I said good-bye and put down the phone. "He thinks you're a bag lady."

She smiled. "Nice. But it sounded like bad news for you."

I thought again about Gemelli's offer. One thousand dollars. Not bad for an evening's work, even if the work wasn't quite legal. "You know that movie on TV tonight?"

"*The Lady from Shanghai?* What about it?"

"I think you're watching it alone."

"Where'll you be? Doing a little target practice?" She stretched out the *r* in *target*.

"No, breaking into a warehouse."

She came close and spoke with mock disbelief. "You rather do that than, like, spend an evening with me and Rita Hayworth?"

I held her in my arms. "Not much choice."

We kissed again, then she rested her head against my chest. "Need some help?"

I gave her a squeeze. "Definitely. But not with the warehouse."

"I don't like you breaking into places."

"Relax. I won't be walking into anything I can't handle."

CHAPTER 4

The Rottweiler heard me coming, the metal cleats on my shoes clicking on the concrete. His clipped ears edged forward.

Good. A deaf dog would've meant trouble. He stared at me through the fence, as quiet as the night around us. No barking, no flashing of teeth. He just stood there, frozen, waiting. It was much scarier that way, and instinctively he knew it.

He tensed when I opened my backpack. I snatched a gray plastic box the size of a garage door opener and pointed it at him. His head tilted a bit as he tried to figure my game. I pressed a small button. The Rottweiler fell over sideways, out cold. Well, he'd looked a little tired.

A runner's store had sold me the box, a nice little device that sends out an earsplitting shriek. Earsplitting for dogs, that is. A handy gadget to keep dogs in the park from chasing you. And now that I'd altered its circuitry, it was even handier.

The warehouse stood in a row of identical buildings in Alexandria, Virginia, near the train tracks and close to Washington National Airport. At night the neighborhood was quiet. Nothing moved. Beyond the low, flat rooftops across the Potomac River poked the top of the Washington Monument.

Next problem—the fence. Twelve feet high, topped with a spiral of razor wire. I could have cut my way through, but Rush Gemelli had wanted no traces of breaking and entering. I took a quick look around. Apart from a rusted-out Chevy missing its front wheels, the streets were empty.

Out came the roll of lightweight titanium mesh. My cleated shoes made scaling the fence easy. At the top I unrolled the mesh, then clambered over the razor wire without shredding myself.

Down the other side, I stuffed the mesh in the backpack and exchanged the cleats for sneakers, which were considerably more quiet. I edged past the Rottweiler, found the wire lead he spent the day tied to, and hooked him up. Hard to say how long he'd nap, and I hate unpleasant surprises.

The alarm box was right where it was supposed to be. The company that made it has a helpful tech support section on their Web site—including schematic diagrams. I'd checked it against the information Rush had given me. Next came the portable soldering gun and a Y-shaped piece of wire I'd made earlier, the copper ends of which I attached to a circuit board deep inside the box. Now I could unlock the door's three locks without any distracting alarms.

Three locks. Whoever paid for the alarm and the Rottweiler and the razor wire had been anal retentive enough to lock the door three times. It promised something good on the other side.

The locks were easy—I went through them in under ten minutes. Back in the day, when I'd worn rubber gloves, I'd still have been fumbling around. I'd switched from gloves to a quick-drying liquid polymer, which I brushed on my fingertips. They kept their sense of touch without leaving any telltale prints.

The thing with rubber gloves—they give you a false sense of security. I knew this guy, a B and E artist who always wore gloves. One night he set out to pilfer a mansion, the owners of which were out for a surprise party. So, of course, they came home hours early, and the surprise was on him. Now, when he tears through the back door and out the yard, he snags a glove on the fence. The cops come and lift a whole set of his prints—from the *inside* of the glove. Besides, I hate the way rubber gloves look. They just scream "I'm a burglar." I placed my hand on the warehouse doorknob, took a breath, turned it, and opened the door a crack.

The gloom of the warehouse was pierced by the flashing green eye of the disarmed system's keypad. I didn't walk in, not just yet, because if I had, I would have stepped on a weight sensor beneath the floor, which would have made all my precautions worthless.

I gripped the top of the door and pushed off, swinging past the floor sensor. Then I dropped softly—catlike, you might say—to the other side and pushed the door shut.

And that was that. I was inside. Not for the first time, I wished someone had come with me. I'm not a show-off , but it's nice to have someone along to ooh and aah. Unfortunately, B and E is either a solitary affair or done with a bunch of hard cases who aren't given to expressions of wonder.

After a few minutes of searching, I found a labeling station, equipped with an industrial-size container of Super Glue, sheets and sheets of labels, a scanner, and a color printer. I also found twenty-six disc burners running off copies—most likely illegal.

Twenty-six burners? This was pygmy piracy. Small-time stuff, but maybe enough to help Rush. I wasted a moment watching the numbers on the blue LED counters tick past. These machines were forty minutes into whatever they were copying. I didn't know how much longer the discs would run before someone showed up. I planned to be long gone before then.

I scribbled down some of the serial numbers from the backs of the disc burners, then ejected a few samples of the pirated videos. If Rush didn't want them, Lilly might. But I doubted it. The market for pirated videos was exclusively new films. For Lilly, Hollywood stopped making movies around 1961.

With the discs stuffed in my backpack, I checked everything, making sure all was as I'd found it. As I strolled to the door, I thought about the drive home. WPFW would be finishing their "Rhythms of the World" program, and then Rusty Hassan's "Jazz Overnight." Or I could pop in an old Orioles game; I had a bunch of them burned to CDs.

I felt the satisfaction of a place well burgled as I approached the door. Just then it swung open. The silhouettes of two men pointing flashlights and guns, and one of them shouted, "*Fleas!*"

CHAPTER 5

I don't care how tough you are, or how tough you think you are. When someone points a gun at you, your stomach drops. Along with your self-esteem. It's bad enough when a pro holds the piece, but so much worse when it's an amateur. Or two.

And then that crack about fleas. Did they think the Rottweiler had infested me? Or vice versa? Before I got a chance to ask, one of them growled, "Keep still."

Then, as an afterthought, he asked, "What you want here?"

He spoke in the voice of a young man, eighteen or twenty. Sounded Asian. And nervous. But his gun hand was steady. So was his partner's.

Smiling in a disarming way, I said, "I was looking for a copy of *Dead of Night,* but I'd settle for *How Green Was My Valley.*"

"Keep your hands up," he said. He pronounced "your" like *yoll.* So when he said "fleas," he probably meant "freeze." Nice deduction, Gidney. As they came closer, I could see the flashlight glint off the barrels of their guns. Glocks. Which meant they could shoot me twenty-eight times if they really wanted to. They stepped on the weight sensor and the keypad started beeping. The second kid punched some buttons. The alarm stopped.

While the first kid steadied his gun on me, the second tucked his gun in the front of his belt and came toward me, holding his flashlight in one hand and reaching the other out for the gun he expected me to have. I hated to disappoint him, but I wasn't carrying a gun. I hadn't thought I'd need one.

This kind of situation, you watch the opening moves. It's like chess. Right at the start of the game, you can tell what kind of player your opponent is by those first moves. For instance, when the nearer kid closed in on me, he stepped between me and his buddy.

That's a terrible opening move.

I snap-kicked him in the chin, not hard enough to knock him out, just enough to leave him wobbly. He teetered on his heels as I grabbed his still-outstretched left hand with my right to steady him, then plucked the gun from his waistband.

Then I noticed that the kid's head had moved into precise alignment with his buddy's behind him. How often does that happen? More important, when it does, you take advantage of it. I nailed him again, a good kick with a lot of hip behind it. His head ricocheted back and *chunked* into the face of his buddy. They collapsed nicely on the floor.

No shots had gone off. Which was good news because, as I bent to pluck the gun from the other kid, I saw through the open doorway a car parked outside, near the sleeping Rottweiler. Two guys in the car were having a lively conversation. It was too dark for them to see what had just happened, even if they had been looking. Time to go, Gidney.

Grabbing hold of their baggy green army jackets, I dragged my two new friends away from the door and into darkness. This was easier than it sounds. Together, they couldn't have weighed much more than two hundred pounds.

I needed to get the hell out of there, but not the way I'd come in. A minute later I found a conveyor belt leading to a small door cut into the rear wall. My only option was to clip my way through the rear fence, then circle around to my car. The small slatted door rolled up, showing the empty loading dock. Perfect. But to keep my retreat quiet and bullet-free, I needed to immobilize my little Asian buddies. I didn't want to inflict multiple concussions on these two—they probably needed all the brain power they had. The labeling station had what I needed. When I returned, the kid I'd kicked was still out. But his friend wasn't. He glared at me, his face bloody, eyes as black as his hair.

I pointed the gun at him. "What's your name?" I said.

"Fuck you."

"Mind if I call you Ph'uck? Strip off your buddy's shirt."

He looked at me in disbelief. "You some kind of pervert?"

I showed him his gun. "Absolutely." Once he finished with his buddy, I told him he should do the same. He told me his name a few more times, but the Glock persuaded him.

"On the floor, back-to-back with your buddy."

He shot me a look of pure hatred. "You gonna regret this."

I cocked the gun and pointed it at him. "Just do it," I said.

Once he was down, I took the container of Super Glue and sprayed a liberal amount where their pale backs met. In seconds, they were bonded together. I backed away, squeezing my girth through the loading dock door, saying, "Don't do anything 'til I get back."

CHAPTER 6

I called Rush on my way home. He said he'd have his contact at MPAC get the cops over to the warehouse right away. I doubted Ph'uck and his friends would still be there, but I told Rush there were some half-tough characters with guns, so he'd tell the cops to be careful.

After a sleepless night—another in a series of nights so long that dreams were something I dreamed about—I found Sarah in the big dayroom of D.C. Adoptive Services, playing with a toy train. She hadn't noticed me. I stood there for a moment, watching. Her lower lip was stuck out in concentration.

Then she looked up and saw me. And when she smiled, her face radiated love. What a rush. No one had ever looked at me that way before.

Officially, I wasn't allowed to visit her every day. That was okay because, officially, the big, bright, drafty room we were in didn't exist. The policy of D.C. Adoptive Services dictated that no infants be cared for. Certainly not a roomful of babies mewling and puking in their cribs. And if they *did* allow for such a room, they would never, ever allow non-DCAS personnel inside. An invasion of the babies' privacy, they'd say. Right.

The real reason? They didn't want anyone to see the conditions under which their smallest charges lived. It's true, a person who didn't know the system might be shocked. Not me. As a reluctant expert on DCAS, I thought the nurses did a good job.

Sarah held up a toy train. "Wiss, you," she said.

"Oh, it's my turn?"

Sarah grinned. She knew I could do it. Now, I have to tell you, I didn't see myself as a natural for being anyone's dad. Away from Sarah, the doubts burned right through me. But when I was with her, she made me feel as if I really could do this. As if her child's wisdom told me something I never would've guessed about myself. I was making the kind of sound I thought a little train would make, when I heard a voice with a thick Jamaican accent. "And here I thought only the criminals returned to the scene of the crime."

Looking at Sarah, I said, "Is that some kind of island thing? Talking nonsense all the time?" Nurse Eunice Edgerton came around, a canvas Diaper Donnie bag rustling as she moved. Sarah looked up at her, smiling.

Eunice said, "You came through this same place, right? Child, if that ain't a crime, I don't know what is."

"Just why are *you* still here? D.C.'s got mandatory retirement for nurses over a hundred."

She leaned down to pat my cheek. "I'm too mean to retire, dear."

"Okay to take the baby outside?"

She stood, looking stern. "Now, you *know* that's against the rules."

Sarah had lost interest in the trains and was now studying a pink plastic heart.

I said, "How could it be against the rules? Sarah's not officially here, and neither am I. And what about that?" I pointed at the pink heart. "Wasn't here yesterday and I didn't bring it. Against the rules for nurses to give the kids toys, isn't it?"

Eunice gave a look around. The glance was so quick, so practiced, it would've been easy to miss. She looked back at me. "You two stay close, you hear me?"

"Just outside the door." I took Sarah's hand and we pushed through the doorway. Outside, we found a tiny patch of grass that someone had forgotten to pave over. Sarah didn't care that the grass was still wet from the rain. She found a yellow leaf and showed it to me, looking proud, as though she'd made the leaf herself, after much personal sacrifice.

"Oh, it's beautiful," I said. She smiled, turning the leaf and hugging it. She was two feet tall, and so perfect. She had big brown eyes, soft brown skin, and quite a few teeth that were new. Eunice said that Sarah was a tooth genius, a future Supreme Court justice.

Time with Sarah meant we'd inspect every blade of grass and leaf and ant. Nothing was too ordinary. With Sarah, I lived in the moment. What a concept. It reminded me of taking LSD when I was nine, back at Bockman's. Eddie Vermeer had traded some PCP with a new kid. Of course, Eddie didn't really have PCP; it was probably weed killer. And who the hell knew what the other kid was passing off as LSD. But we were zonked for hours and hours. I remember watching the crows perched atop the cyclone fence, how their cawing delighted us.

In the middle of the crow concert, Eddie said he'd never realized just how beautiful Bockman's was. I laughed so hard, I fell down. Something very powerful about existing in the moment on that day, just like this morning with Sarah. With her, I felt in the Now, and it was intensely beautiful.

Then Eunice came to the door. Her expression was hard to read. "Willis, bring that child in. Now." This did not bode well.

I took Sarah's hand as we followed Eunice to the office. She shut the door, handed Sarah a juice box, colored markers, and paper. Sarah sat on the floor and Eunice told me take a chair.

"What's wrong?" I asked.

Eunice shifted in her seat. "Well, we're not supposed to talk to nonpersonnel about it—but Sarah's status has changed."

"Come again?"

"Her DCAS status. She can be adopted."

"I know that. I'm the one who's adopting her."

Sarah shook her juice box, then squeezed it, squirting a stream of apple juice onto my shirt.

"You don't understand." Eunice handed me a Kleenex. "Before, when your form was in, no one else could file on her, okay? But something happened. Sarah's status changed."

"Florence Walters." Her name tasted like copper pennies in the back of my throat.

"Who?"

"The caseworker who rejected me." You'd think DCAS would be cool, having one of their success stories—me—adopt a kid from the next generation. I felt something, looked down. Sarah was drawing wavy lines on my jeans with a black marker. I picked her up and put her on my knee. The top of her head smelled like macaroons. "So how does that change anything about Sarah?"

"Don't you see? Sarah—anyone can file to adopt her now."

"Has anyone asked?"

"And how would I know something like that? But, Willis, you're so involved. Maybe too much. I've seen adoptions fail. It can mess you up bad, child." She looked at me, expecting something. I didn't know what she wanted me to say. "Sometimes

27

you gotta think about yourself, don't be all—" Her eyes got teary. She turned away, grabbed a tissue. I looked at the pamphlets on the rack by the door.

"These dusty old buildings," she said, wiping her eyes. When I turned back, she was perfectly composed. "All right, dear. Now you better scat, we got things to do."

I set Sarah in her crib. She suddenly smiled and tossed the pink plastic heart at me. I tried to catch it, I grasped at it, but it slipped to the floor, where the pink casing broke. Sarah started to cry, fat tears rolling down pudgy cheeks.

I wanted to stay, to comfort her, but instead I handed her off to Eunice. I felt bad about it, but I had to meet with Rush Gemelli and collect the cash to pay the lawyer to grease the wheels to adopt my Sarah. It was like a Mother Goose story. And if I didn't get going, I'd miss my meeting. Then the tale would have one hell of an unhappy ending.

CHAPTER 7

A block from my office was the Zamboanga Café. There're two things I love about this place. The first was Chella, a Bockman's alumna and the Zamboanga's owner. And the second was its complete lack of atmosphere—high ceilings with bare fluorescent lights, the house specials hand-written on stiff manila paper thumb-tacked to the walls, and five creaky booths that looked out the plate glass window onto F Street.

Chella smiled at me while she poured coffee for me and Rush

Gemelli, then put the check between us. Rush tapped his fingers on the tabletop—without any discernible rhythm or pattern, I might add—waiting for her to leave. I don't think he even saw her. His loss.

Once Chella went behind the cash register, I pulled out five of the seven video discs I had taken from the warehouse the night before and slid them across the table. Gemelli was delighted. I thought he might even chortle in his joy.

He slid the discs into his cracked leather briefcase, then took out an envelope. I counted ten one-hundred-dollar bills. "Your warehouse security information was wrong."

He blinked behind his horn-rimmed glasses. "How wrong?"

I stuffed the bills in my pocket. "Very. Like the part about no guards. A carload of kids showed up, they had guns."

"Well, shit, you can't blame me for that."

"Perfectly safe, you said."

"According to my source, man. Blame him, you gotta blame somebody." He set down his cup carefully, took a paper napkin from the dispenser, and began to fold it in half. "So. Business slow for you?" He kept his eyes on the napkin.

"It's been slower," I said.

He looked up from his napkin, his brown eyes enlarged by his horn-rimmed glasses. "You don't like me much, do you?"

"I think you're wonderful. But I'm not breaking any more laws for you."

"You're an inspiration, Gidney, a saint. Look, my dad's gonna do a press conference at MPAC this afternoon with Tony Corona." Corona was a news anchor, a square-jawed on-camera idiot who always carried Corona cigars in his shirt pocket, just in case you were trying to forget his name. Rush said, "Dad'll talk about the pirating operation in Alexandria, then showcase

29

this new antipiracy technology. Your name's on the security list, my source inside's got you cleared."

"Your father told you this?"

"Fuck no, man. I told you: He doesn't know I'm helping him." He looked up. "I'd like you to be there—at MPAC, I mean."

"Did you hear me a moment ago?"

"Hey, Saint Gidney, there's nothing illegal about TV interviews." He turned the napkin, folded it again. "Christ, you got a problem earning some cash? I want you to get with MPAC, be an adviser, whatever. You free this afternoon?"

"Never free, but always reasonable," I said. "If I were interested."

He frowned at the napkin. "Look, just go there, okay? Make contact with my dad."

"Why would I do that?"

He spoke quickly. "Why? How many times I gotta tell you? I want you working with my dad, Gidney, look out for him. I'll get you more leads. This way, I can help the old man without him knowing."

I looked at him for a moment. "This isn't my first day on the planet."

"The fuck does that mean?"

"It means that over the years I've developed a kind of internal bullshit meter. Right now it's pinning." He blinked at me from behind his glasses. "You're not telling me everything," I said. "You said I'd find a hub of film pirating. Twenty-six burners—that's not a hub. Not even a spoke. You know, a less trusting sleuth might have felt set up."

"Why would I do that?"

"Who knows? Maybe you were testing me. Or you're incompetent. Either way, it's good-bye." I got up.

"Okay, you need to trust me, I get it. Take a look," he said, sliding a green folder from his briefcase. "You think the cops'd be interested in these?"

Still standing, I opened the folder and saw a poor-quality color photo, the type lifted from a videotape. The photo showed a man, his back to camera, and a dog, with a fence between them.

Shit. The next shot showed me straddling the top of the fence with a piece of steel mesh underneath. Christ, my ass was the size of Quebec. Must've been the camera angle. The third photo showed me picking the locks to the warehouse. I sat, put the photos back in the folder, and picked up the catsup bottle, just to keep myself from strangling him. "That Chevy across the street, the clunker with no wheels."

Gemelli grinned. "Man, I thought for sure you'd spot me. So, what do you think?"

"I'm thinking how far I can push this bottle up your nose."

"You're pissed, that's understandable."

"You said this would help me trust you," I said, tapping the file folder. "It's not working."

"Maybe this'll help." He pulled out a tiny videocassette and slid it toward me.

"This the tape you shot?"

"Yeah." Gemelli smiled. "See, I could go to the cops with this, but I'm handing you the original, Gidney. And this," he said, pulling a second envelope out of his pocket. Inside were ten more portraits of Ben Franklin. They *did* look kind of cozy, all lined up together like that.

Gemelli said, "A retainer, okay? Something big's gonna go down at MPAC."

"Like what?"

"All I can tell you is, it'll make or break my dad. I'll hire you, starting today, through Sunday night."

"So you won't tell me why, but you expect me to walk in cold and get a job with MPAC? Just how am I supposed to do that?"

"You're resourceful, you'll think of something. I'll pay eight hundred a day, plus expenses."

Enough to pay off Matthews, enough to breathe easier for a few weeks.

"Cash?" I asked.

He nodded.

"Next time, you should lead with that." I put the bills in my pocket.

Gemelli's egg-shaped head bobbed, the fluorescent tubes above gleaming off his dome. "Cool. See, I knew you could trust me."

"Trust? Let's talk about these pictures. They came off the video. You printed them out yourself."

"So?"

"So that means you loaded the video onto a computer first, in order to print out the stills. Which means these"—and here I shoved the folder back at him—"are not the *only* copies, are they?"

He held up his hands. "Trust, babe. It's a two-way street."

CHAPTER 8

This was the first time I'd ever had a client blackmail me.

Maybe I should've felt flattered. Instead, I wanted to find Gemelli's computer and do to it what he was trying to do to me. I left the Zamboanga with him, hoping he'd lead me to his car. His license plate would get me his address. Instead, Rush walked to a Metro stop. He smiled when he said good-bye, and I wondered if he'd guessed what I'd had in mind.

On the way to MPAC, I stopped at Stayne Matthews's Cleveland Park office. Stayne came around the desk with pleasure. Not to shake my hand, but take the white envelope Rush had given me. The warm track lights gleamed off Stayne's perfectly coiffed albino-white hair. His pink bunny eyes gleamed and his nose twitched in pleasure while he counted the fifteen hundred dollars—his kind of lettuce.

An hour later I crossed Seventeenth Street, near Lafayette Park, and walked past a satellite TV truck that was idling outside the MPAC building. The building looked like rows of mud-colored cement boxes, one on top of another, with a mud-colored grid in front as an embellishment. You see these types of nondescript, 1960s buildings all over D.C.—as if every architect in the city had fallen asleep and been taken over by alien pods. Pods who hated style, of course.

I was wearing my blue blazer, a blue oxford shirt, tan cotton slacks and cordovan Rockport shoes. The well-dressed sleuth. Lilly had picked out the clothes. I'd complained that they felt new and scratchy. She said I ought to have a least one good outfit. Maybe she was right, I could tell the security guys were jealous.

They got more jealous when the elevator doors opened and a blond woman in a green sweater smiled and shook my hand. She had a nice smile. I wondered if using it were part of her job description. We rode the elevator to the second floor, then walked through a long, narrow hallway. Black cases of TV gear nearly blocked our path, but we made our way around the lights and cameras. The young woman deposited me in the conference room, gave me the smile again, said I should wait here, then left.

The carpet had a few shallow craters, probably from the legs of a heavy table. The MPAC staff must've cleared the furniture to make room for some interesting gear. At the far end of the room was a white screen, and pointing at it was a large dark green projector that had on its side the name *Julie* in raised script and, beneath that, *4K Ultrashow*. Next to the projector, a big gray box whirred contentedly. Some fat black cables went from the box—a computer server?—to the projector.

Technicians set and pointed lights, cameras were wheeled into place, and sound guys were tweaking their mixers. No one gave me a second look. In the next room, two men sat in high-backed directors chairs under very bright lights. The younger man—Tony Corona from SatNews—was closest to the doorway. He made a show of frowning at his type-written pages.

The older man was Chuck Gemelli. The Elephant.

The resemblance between Chuck and his son Rush was clear enough, but instead of being pale and bald, Chuck Gemelli had a sun lamp tan and sported a comb-over of hair that looked like steel wool. I introduced myself while a makeup woman fussed over him. Gemelli nodded at me. His smile stretched wrinkle lines from chin to eyes. A nice smile if you ignored the eyes. They were ice blue and guarded.

The makeup woman shielded them with her hand as she sprayed his hair. From behind her hand he said, "Are you with the projection people, Mr. Gidney?"

"Actually, I'm not." This was the tricky part—on the one hand, I didn't want to admit I'd found the tiny pirating operation the night before, because that would make me guilty of B and E and totally kill my chances of adopting Sarah. On the other hand, if I didn't mention the warehouse, Gemelli would think I was just a keyhole-peeping hack trying to hustle a client.

But on the *third* hand, if I couldn't get on Gemelli's staff, his

34

son would turn over his incriminating video to the cops, which would *also* destroy my chances of adopting Sarah. I needed the job, if only to buy some time.

So when the makeup woman's hand came away from his eyes, I said, "Mr. Gemelli, I'm a private investigator, and I'm here because I love the movies. When I read about those film pirates threatening the industry, well, I knew I had to meet you. I can help you, and your investigation into film piracy." I handed him one of my new cards, the one without the slogan "Mayhem a Specialty."

A worried-looking kid with glasses burst through the door and said, "We go live in two minutes." The makeup woman clucked. Tony Corona stood and looked at her. "Problem?"

"No. I'm just trying to get Mr. Gemelli's skin tone right."

Gemelli's skin had a grayish pallor. The whites of his eyes looked a bit yellow as well.

"See, I grew up loving the movies," I said. "To me, the movies *are* America." I smacked my fist in my hand. "Mr. Gemelli, I'm a huge fan. And I'm an experienced investigator. I've got the talent, and I've got the motivation." Hey, not bad. Sounding like a sincere Tom Cruise. Without the high squeaky voice, of course.

Gemelli leaned back, tilted his head to better take in my girth. The smile still in place, he said, "A *huge* fan? Well, no one could argue that."

Just then, a tall skinny guy swaggered into the dressing room. Mid-forties, with a face the sun had darkened and wrinkled, making him look older than he was. He wore a western-style string tie, a silver belt buckle, and fancy boots. Gemelli gave him a nod. "Longstreet, your section need any outside help?"

"Can't say we do, 'cause we don't," Longstreet said. With his freckles, apple cheeks, and sandy crew cut, he looked as though he'd stepped out of a Norman Rockwell painting. Except for the eyes. Rockwell never painted eyes like those.

In his midwestern drawl, Longstreet said, "Truth is, another fella'd just get underfoot." He glanced my way. Now his eyes had an amused look to them.

The worried-looking kid shoved his face through the door again. "One minute," he pleaded.

"I'm not looking to replace anyone," I said. "But it might help your investigation—to have someone local."

"Thanks but no thanks," Longstreet said.

Gemelli stood. "I agree. We don't need your help; we don't want your help." They began moving toward the conference room. Looking over his shoulder, Gemelli added, "If we need someone to go diving Dumpster, we'll call you."

CHAPTER 9

Corona and Gemelli parked themselves beneath the bright TV lights. There were three cameras. One was positioned to capture a three-shot of Gemelli, the projector, and Corona. The second was aimed over Corona's shoulder at Gemelli, and third was placed at the reverse angle. I thought about Rush's camera, of him e-mailing the cops the pictures of my caboose perched on the warehouse fence.

Once Corona and Gemelli were on their marks, a sound technician rearranged their ties, clipping on tiny microphones, the cables of which ended in little black boxes—wireless transmitters. Someone shouted, "Ten seconds" and someone else shouted, "Lock it down." Everything stopped while Tony Corona—lantern jaw, serious expression, and earpiece in place—awaited his cue from Sat-News. A floor director stood by the center camera, held out her hand, then silently counted down on her fingers. Three, two, one.

The red light on top of one camera winked on, and Corona gazed into the lens. "Thank you, Bernard. We're here in the Washington headquarters of the Motion Picture Alliance Council, discussing film piracy with its president, Charles Gemelli." Corona turned to Gemelli. "So, has MPAC had much impact? Deterring theft of movies worldwide?"

Gemelli flashed his false smile. "Yes, Tony, it has. Only last night, we busted open a pirate ring operating in a warehouse just a stone's throw from our nation's capital. The FBI confiscated illegal discs and software with a street value of over one million dollars."

A million? Well, who could blame him for a little exuberance.

"But that's just a drop in the bucket, isn't it?" Corona said.

Gemelli notched down the smile. "Unfortunately, yes. We estimate worldwide losses exceed two and a half billion a year." He looked uneasy. Sweat beaded up from beneath the makeup.

Corona gave a stern nod. "But film piracy is about to become the stuff of history books, is that right?"

"We hope so, thanks to this." Gemelli patted the top of the server. "Up to now, movies have been sent one of two ways. The old way was to ship a thirty-five-millimeter print, weighing hundreds of pounds and costing thousands of dollars. More recently, studios send out movies on hard drives, to be loaded into the projectors of your neighborhood theater."

"Do a lot of theaters use this newer technology?"

"Yes, it saves the movie studios *and* the theater owners a lot of money. Here's how it works—the movie is first encrypted as a digital file. Then it's shipped to the theaters where it's loaded on a server like the one you see here." A cameraman reframed the shot to include the whirring gray box. "Now, each projector has a unique identity, embedded as an RMA code on its circuit board. Once the server acknowledges the projector's identity, the server decrypts the movie and loads it into the projector's memory. Then the movie is ready to show." Gemelli smiled, oozing an oily charm. He reminded me of a used car salesman, minus the sincerity.

Corona said, "So projectors now have their own identities. Sounds like sending movies on hard drives is the way to go."

"Yes and no. Shipping hard drives is risky, they're small, lightweight, and make great targets for pirates."

"Even though the files are encrypted?"

"Given enough time and computing power, the encryption could get hacked. Believe me, it's a serious problem."

"So satellite delivery is the answer?"

"Partly. True, it removes the risk of a thief snatching a hard drive and cracking its encryption. But sending movies via satellite takes time, about six hours. Movies contain a huge amount of data. You need that much, to project at four K resolution. That six-hour window gives the thieves a fat target, almost as risky as shipping hard drives."

Gemelli's words came out okay, but something was wrong. I saw the sound tech frown at his meters. Then he took off his headphones. He listened to Gemelli talking, then put the headphones back on, comparing the real sound with what he was getting. Whatever he heard, it made him shake his head.

Corona said, "But now you've got something new, bankrolled by top-grossing film director Roger Franklin Quell."

"That's right, Tony. This weekend, Mr. Quell and I will give D.C. audiences a glimpse of the future. Working with engineers at the National Institute of Standards and Technology, we've developed a new kind of algorithm, light-years ahead of what we've seen before. Imagine transmitting a movie in four K resolution in a matter of minutes."

"A burst, in other words."

"Exactly. But that's just the first part of our plan. The second part is a new type of asymmetric code. The projectionist inputs the code using this keypad." Gemelli pointed at a numeric pad mounted on the projector, like the kind you'd find on an ATM. "This code opens a much larger, asymmetric key, which gives permission to the server to decrypt the movie before the projector can download it."

"Sounds foolproof."

"Absolutely. This technology will virtually eliminate the black market in stolen films."

Corona flashed an even smile, his teeth reflecting the bright lights. "It must be something special, for Quell to bring his two stars with him."

Gemelli's smile looked ghastly. "Well, I think Corbin Brooks and Sondra Stoddard would be the first to say that Roger Franklin Quell's plan is the real star, when the three of them premiere *Explosive Rounds* this weekend."

That was it, what Rush Gemelli had meant when he told me something big was about to happen at MPAC. Brooks and Stoddard were two of Hollywood's biggest stars. Their films made billions worldwide. Just by mentioning their names, Chuck Gemelli created a buzz in the room.

Corona said, "So this coming Sunday, Roger Franklin Quell will have two premieres—his new film, *Explosive Rounds,* and this new anti-piracy technology. Which excites you the most?" This was Gemelli's cue to pick up the ball and score. Instead his eyelids fluttered and he began to fall back against the projector.

I told the floor director, "Pull the plug."

She looked appalled. "There's another minute."

"Suit yourself."

She saw it was too late to stop me—she gave Corona a frantic cue.

He caught it and fumbled through a quick impromptu ending, the red light on the camera switching off just as I caught Gemelli before he hit the ground. I eased him down as a group formed around me.

I ignored them. Longstreet looked confused but kept them at bay while I yanked the transmitter off Gemelli and threw it away, microphone and all. I placed my hand on his chest, felt a small lump over his heart. I ripped open his shirt and saw the scar.

Someone shouted, "Call nine one one." Gemelli's heart stumbled like a sprinter over a block of concrete. I patted his pockets, then found a capped plastic bottle. I recognized the scored pink pills before I read the label—amiodarone. One of my foster fathers had taken them. Guy was totally freaked by anything electronic. Every time his wife used the microwave, he went to the garage. Come to think of it, he had the yellow eyes and gray skin too. I slipped a pill into Gemelli's mouth. Someone handed me a glass of water and I held it to his lips.

Gemelli's eyelids flickered as he swallowed the pill. Then he took my hands in his. "No ambulance." His whisper was hoarse. I had to lean in close to hear him.

"You sure?"

He nodded. "A little arrhythmia. From that transmitter. The doctor said not to carry a cell phone." He took a deep breath, released it slowly. "He never said a thing about wireless microphones."

He took another breath and sat up. "I'm okay. Do you have your driver's license?"

"What for?"

"For payroll. I can use a man like you. Assuming you still want the job."

I sat on the floor beside him. Now *I* was out of breath.

"Okay," I whispered back, "but next time, at least tell the sound techs you've got a pacemaker."

CHAPTER 10

Once the SatNews team cleared away, Longstreet had me sign a W-9 form for payroll—another first, getting paid twice for the same gig. After he visited his office to file the form and check messages, we walked a block to the Carlton Hotel.

I love the Carlton. These days it's called the St. Regis, but no matter—for me, it was and shall always be the Carlton. With its large rooms, soft beds, closets, pantries, and basement hallways, a kid could have a blast hiding out there. Which is exactly what I did for three weeks, during an early escape from Junior Village. The Carlton was like a second institution to me. The lobby bathrooms impressed me, they had white cloth hand towels. I used to steal ten at a time.

And now, suddenly, here I was, sitting in the bar with a tie around my neck and a drink in my hand—like a jump cut from a movie. Impersonating a grown-up. I worried that once the staff noticed, they'd chase me away with pitchforks.

Longstreet sat across from me, fiddling with his string tie while the waiter served our drinks—Wild Turkey on the rocks for Longstreet, black coffee with a shot of rum for me. Once the waiter left, Longstreet set his drink down and said, "So. You mind tellin' me what the fuck happened back there?"

The guy had a voice like an airline pilot's—tough, in charge, no bullshit. It was a voice you could trust right away. It was unapologetic, the way it dropped its g's, as if telling the world this was who he was and he didn't care who knew it.

"I have no idea." I blew across the coffee cup, determined it was still too hot to sip, and dunked in my first biscotti. Where there's a will, there's a way.

Longstreet's country-boy looks barely hid his impatience. "What did Gemelli whisper to you, when you were leanin' over him?"

"He asked me to take my knee off his chest."

Longstreet tried to look stern, which couldn't have been easy for him. He bobbed his head when he spoke and his walnut-size Adam's apple bounced in his throat. "Let's understand each other. I don't wantcha on the team, I said as much to Gemelli. But he's the boss." He took out his cell phone and put it on the table. "I got Gemelli's number on speed dial, I can call him with one push of a button." He held his finger over the phone. "And I got no problem callin' him, sayin' he made a mistake with you. He'll argue, but in the end I'll win and you'll be out on your ass. So when I ask you a question . . ." His pilot's voice warned about bumpy weather ahead.

"Okay, take it easy." I dipped biscotti number two. "Well," I said, "I'm a little embarrassed for the guy, but when he was on the floor, he said he was sorry."

"For what?"

"He was embarrassed, I think he had some kind of panic attack." If Chuck Gemelli wanted to keep his pacemaker a secret, it was okay with me. I tried the coffee again. Just right. "You making any progress, finding film pirates?"

"Some. Funny, I saw him do a TV gig in L.A., at a film-piracy conference. Woulda guessed he had more experience with interviews."

"Me too. Are the other pirate operations in D.C.?"

Longstreet signaled for another drink, then leaned back as the dark-coated waiter returned. Other waiters and waitresses glided past, serving drinks to the lawyers and lobbyists who made their deals while the Carlton made a profit.

The bar smelled of old leather and polished wood and expense accounts. High-tech jazz drifted from hidden speakers in the carved wooden ceiling, fourteen feet above us. Our table sat in the corner, between the fireplace and the bookshelves. When you walked in, you noticed the bookshelves right away—tiny yellow lights lined the shelves, casting an orange glow on impressive leather-bound volumes like the *Iliad* and *The Rise and Fall of the Roman Empire*. But from a different angle, you could see the bindings were only that—bindings. The pages of text, the substance and wisdom of these writers, had been cut away to save space, leaving only the illusion of stored knowledge.

It was very D.C., and somehow comforting in a bizarre way.

Longstreet sipped, then wiped his mouth with the back of his hand. "The other pirate operations, that's what we gotta find out. And just maybe a local fella could help. Even a PI who's got a low-rent office on Ninth Street."

"You checked me out?"

"Hey, I was FBI. I got *some* investigative skills." He grinned. "In a backward, countrified kind of way, of course."

"When you say 'countrified,' it sounds like Oklahoma City."

"You got a good ear." Longstreet set his glass down, making

a second circle of water, which linked with the first. Looking at the rings, he said, "I called D.C. cops, talked with a fella named Heinrick. Said you were a capable investigator."

"Nothing about my good looks?"

Longstreet frowned. "He also said you're a pain to work with, you don't follow directions, you make jokes that aren't funny, and that you got a really high opinion of yourself. His recommendation means you cleared the first hurdle."

"Thought I'd cleared that when Gemelli hired me."

"All you did was get on the payroll." He leaned forward. "And look, if that's all you want, fine. I'll getcha a desk, you can fill out forms and stuff envelopes. Is that your style?"

It wasn't, but more important, Rush had hired me to do a job. If he discovered I was sitting out the game on the sidelines, I'd be finished. I said, "You kidding? And deprive myself of seeing how an FBI agent works?"

"*Former* agent, as of a year ago. But my buddies at the Bureau say there's a gang in D.C. makin' illegal dupes and sendin' 'em to South America and the Ukraine."

"A D.C. gang? Sounds ambitious."

Longstreet smiled and shook his head. He looked so folksy, with his crew cut and all-American features, that I had to resist the urge to tell him to run for Congress. "Shit, it ain't hard to dupe a buncha discs. I mean, we're livin' through a digital revolution, ya know?"

"Sure."

"And this gang's probably spittin' distance from the capital. Maybe a local could help us figure the players. You got more gangs in D.C. than flies on a pig."

"Who owns the warehouse?"

Longstreet's eyes took on a shrewd look. "Who said anything about a warehouse?"

"Gemelli did, to Corona."

"We spoke to him, the owner, he's retired to Ocala and knows squat."

"And how many machines did you find?"

"Twenty or thirty."

"Big operators, they'd have two or three thousand."

"Maybe they got several locations, minimize their loss if they get busted. Could be there's more'n one gang doin' it. Maybe two or three gangs, maybe more. Who knows."

"You want me to nail them all? Give you a discount for a group arrest?"

"Gidney, in the words of Elvis, I want a little less conversation and a little more action." He stuck his phone in his pocket. The meeting was over. "You got till tomorrow. Report to me at the Uptown Theater, seven P.M. Security detail for Quell's press conference." He gave me his card.

"Think globally, arrest locally," I said.

Longstreet stood, threw some bills on the table. "Hell yes. Do that and you'll be earnin' your pay."

"Let's not forget about the fame and glory."

He grinned. "Let's never forget about that."

CHAPTER 11

Longstreet had given me a day to prove myself, and I needed to stay in Rush's good graces. So every minute counted. I would've started right then, that night, but I couldn't—tonight was Emily's birthday party. I wanted to go, though I was feeling apprehensive. I'd never been to a birthday party before.

I'd never even thought much about birthdays, but I supposed I needed to start. Sarah would want parties, right? Even though she was a foundling, so no one knew exactly when she was born. Same as me. But she deserved *something*. I left the bar and checked out the Carlton's men's room, proud of myself for not stealing their cloth towels. Too bad Florence Walters wasn't witness to this, it proved I was parent material.

Why do we even bother with birthdays? I mean, you're a year older, so what? They should make a law—if you've accomplished something with your life, made a real contribution, *then* go ahead, celebrate. It's not like an five-year-old has really *done* anything. The Australian aborigines don't celebrate birthdays, which shows how good sense and civilization don't always go together.

On the other hand, the aborigines think dried caterpillars are a delicacy.

Jan and I had dated as teenagers. Despite my best efforts, things hadn't worked. Then I kind of lost track of her. When she resurfaced, she introduced me to her partner, Janet. I thought she meant Janet taught architecture with her at George Washington University. But once they started smooching in front of me, I deduced she had used the word *partner* in a different sense. At first, I was happy for them. Then, when Jan gave birth to Emily, a kind of jealousy started creeping in.

I grew up without a family. Foster families, those I had a lot of, but it's not the same. Jan and Janet understood, and did their best to make me a part of their small tribe. So that's the first reason I wanted to go to the birthday party.

The second reason was Lilly—she'd be at the party too, helping Jan and Janet decorate the house, tie balloons outside, get the food, all that stuff. So of course I was going. Any time with Lilly was time well spent.

And come to think of it, I had a third reason—Terry Price. I'd recommended him to Jan and Janet because Terry had the best magic show in D.C. I just had to get to their house before he left. Even when his act was over, Terry had a habit of making items disappear.

The air was warm and the sky was gray as I crossed H Street, past the statue of General Lafayette and the protesters who camped across from the White House. I started my car, then listened to Bill Evans as I took Sixteenth to Massachusetts, past the statue of Winston Churchill, whose right hand was raised in a V for Victory. To paraphrase the great man, I was ready to meet the birthday partiers; whether they were ready for the ordeal of meeting me was an entirely different matter. I turned onto Jan and Janet's street, then slowed, looking for parking. My phone started chirping.

"Gidney? Did you make it? Are you on Dad's staff?"

Apparently Rush was the kind of guy who never said hello or asked how you were. Probably saved a good two to three minutes a year that way. "Hey, Rush? Your dad's a piece of work."

"Tell me about it."

Did Rush know about the pacemaker? "First he said Longstreet was all the help he needed. But then your dad had a change of heart. I think he picked up on the pace I was making with the investigation."

"Good. So you're on the team?"

So maybe Rush didn't know. "Longstreet gave me the secret decoder ring and everything. So how about handing over that hard drive?"

He laughed. "So you can quit? You think I'm an idiot? Just fucking remember—we want Dad looking good, okay?"

CHAPTER 12

I pulled alongside Jan and Janet's home, a tiny row house that had shrunk when Emily entered the world five years ago. I parked right behind Lilly's silver Volkswagen Beetle. My car was a rusted-out Plymouth Duster. Our cars looked a little odd side by side. But then, so did Lilly and I.

Silver balloons bobbed from the ends of ribbons tied to the front door light. Seemed like a lot of trouble. I could hear kids squealing before I opened the door.

Inside, a thousand children ran riot with Emily their leader. They were like a breaking wave, flowing around me. I managed to wade into the kitchen. The smell of cardboard pizza boxes and tomato sauce surrounded the women working there. Lilly was resplendent in her baggy, faded clothes, helping Jan scrape pizza crusts into the sink while Janet planted five candles into a large cake. Someone had spent a lot of time on the cake. It said *Happy Birthday, Emily* in cursive, and there were clowns and balloons.

"And one to grow on." When Janet saw me, she said, "Hey, stranger," and kissed my cheek. "You're late. Busy day foiling the bad guys?"

I gave her a squeeze, found two slices of pizza that looked un-molested by tiny hands, and started munching.

Lilly said, "You missed the magic show."

"The Great Effluvia was awesome," Janet said. "You've known him a long time?"

"Forever. Where is he?"

"Packing up in the den. He asked that room be off-limits so he could prepare his show."

"I'll go say hi." I finished the pizza sandwich, then intercepted Terry Price—a.k.a. "the Great Effluvia"—by grabbing the coattails of his tux before he could head out the door. "Hey."

He turned, his long black hair swinging past his face, and attempted a smile. "Oh, hey, Gidney."

"Looking heavy, Terry."

"Heavy? Me?"

"You. Let's talk." Still gripping his tails, I pulled him backward to the den and closed the door. "Put it all on the desktop."

His smile was a caricature of innocence. "Say what?"

"Say 'what' again, Terry, and you'll be on the floor, looking up at me."

He held up his palms. "Okay, Jesus, take it easy." He began emptying his pockets. Out came rings, a watch, credit cards with Jan's name on them, and a wax block with key impressions.

"All of it." I've known Terry since we were kids at Bockman's.

Sighing, he pulled a flash drive from his inside pocket, placed it alongside his other stolen objects. "Okay, happy? That's it."

I picked up the drive. "Your greatest hits?"

"C'mon, Willis. This is good stuff. Bank accounts, Social Security numbers." He shrugged. "We're in the middle of a digital revolution, you gotta keep up with the times."

"Speaking of time, how about ten seconds before I throw you out?"

"Well, fuck you, too."

I moved toward him.

"Okay, I'm leaving, I'm leaving." As I followed him to the door, he said, "Hey, Gidney, you knew I'd, uh, help myself to a few odds and ends. Why'd you recommend me to these gals?"

"Because you're good, Terry. The best sleight-of hand artist I know."

He pushed his black hair back, and his smile returned, tentative but real this time. "No shit?"

"No shit. Just don't rip off my friends."

He shrugged again, the padded shoulders of his moth-eaten tux approaching ear level. "Hey, a misunderstanding."

I felt a little better as I came back to the kitchen, as if rousting Terry had given me a much-needed dose of reality in this parallel birthday universe. Janet switched off the lights. Lilly held the cake, her face glowing in the candlelight. She smiled up at me. "Ready?"

My throat went dry at the sight of her. "Sure," I said.

In the warm night air of early autumn, we herded the kids to a picnic table in the backyard; as the last fireflies of the season drifted above their heads, winking on and off. When Emily saw the cake, she squealed, and then her friends squealed.

Lilly carried the cake to the table. The wind stirred and the candle flames wavered but stayed lit. Everyone sang "Happy Birthday." Funny, I heard the song, but the words were stripped of meaning. Just open mouths, vibrations pouring out of them. The kids could've been singing in an alien language. In a moment, little antennae would sprout from their pumpkin heads. I promised myself that Sarah's birthday parties would be completely different.

Emily closed her eyes and blew out the candles. Everyone around me cheered. I had a sense of watching myself from above, the event unfolding around me. The air felt thin, as if the candles had burned up all the available oxygen.

While the kids snarfed down ice cream and cake—a singular moment of quiet—Lilly sidled up to me. "Hey, slim, care for a piece?" she said in a Mae West voice. She shoved a forkful in my mouth.

Dried caterpillars. I chewed, managed a smile. "I'm gonna head out."

She said, "You okay?"

"Sure."

Jan came over to us. "You'll stay for tea?"

"Not tonight, thanks." Lilly looked at me. "Big day tomorrow," I told the group, moving closer to her. I whispered, "See you at my place?" I really needed to be with her. She touched my cheek. I leaned down to give Emily a kiss. She batted her hazel eyes at me, making a silly face.

"Going so sooooon?" she said. Her friends giggled. I said good-bye to Janet, who was busy cutting seconds, then made it back to my car.

Driving home, I felt drunk. It was all I could do to stay on the road.

CHAPTER 13

I thought the thing on the sidewalk was a stuffed toy. Tiny motionless feet in the air, little face frozen into what looked like a frown. From the smell, I guessed it had been there all day.

In back of my building was the shed, where I got a shovel and a plastic trash bag, then used the shovel to lift the possum carcass and set it inside the bag. Back then, I lived in an apartment less than a mile from Glover Park. I saw possums and raccoons all the time. I'd even seen a deer nibbling leaves in my backyard.

I tied the garbage bag shut, put it inside the trash can, and placed a brick on the lid to discourage neighborhood critters.

Back in my apartment I put on Miles's *In a Silent Way*. I love the way it begins, and I started feeling better, especially after some Cherry Garcia and a cupcake and a bean burrito. A half hour later I was on the couch reading, when I heard Lilly at my door. I slipped the book beneath the couch while she hung up her green army jacket.

"I never saw you pass up a piece of cake before."

"I'm trying to hold on to my slim physique."

"That's my job."

Miles blew his horn, while Dave Holland put down a bass-line groove so that John McLaughlin could wail. I put my arms around Lilly and she pulled me over so I was on top of her, face-to-face. She placed her lips on mine, the smell of sandalwood wrapping around us like gauze. Some time later, she took her lips away. "Where did you learn to kiss like that?" she asked.

"I practice when I'm alone."

"Mmmm." She gave me a squeeze. "So. You, like, miss the magic show, you skip the cake, and then you split. What's up?"

"Someone had to bag the possum."

"You lost me."

"I stuck a dead possum in a trash bag."

"Well, I hope so. That it was dead, I mean. Here, in the yard?"

I nodded, shifting my weight off of her. She sat up, looking at me, drawing me in. I took one of her hands and kissed her palm, caught a glimpse of something. I turned her hand and saw the word *HATE* written across her knuckles, a letter for each knuckle. The word *LOVE* was on the other one.

I said, "I hope those aren't permanent."

"Just blue ink. It's from *The Night of the Hunter*."

"I know what it's from. This was for your afternoon meeting?"

"The head programmer couldn't make it, so now it's tomorrow. But *this* is tomorrow's outfit." She stood and did a parody of a model's runway walk, giving me the full effect—dark smudges under the eyes, a sports bra that flattened her breasts, and some pillows down by her caboose, making it look bigger than a foldout couch. "What do you think?"

"That you look like shit."

Here came the serious look. "Honestly?"

"Absolutely. You'd make the witch from *The Wizard of Oz* look like Miss America."

She smiled, her cheeks dimpled. "You're sweet. Should I use the anti-pheromone spray? Or is that, like, too much?"

"Well, let me ask—you ever worry that when your clients see you, they're gonna jump out a window?"

She shook her head. "You've never been a woman, Willis."

"True."

"Or a model."

"I tried once, but they told me I was too handsome. Said they'd have to fire all the other guys."

"Uh-huh. The point is, I have—been a model, I mean. You don't know what it's like, dealing with these men day in and day out."

Her face was inches from mine. "The thing about writing software? That's really great? I don't have to meet with anyone. That's when the problems start. I go to some office, the guys're too busy hitting on me to hear a word I say. Then I lose the account." She looked at me with those amazing faded-denim eyes. "You understand, don't you?"

I swallowed. "Of course. Of course I understand." She could have spoken Cantonese and I would've agreed with every word.

She went to the bathroom. Makeup-removal time. I think she took a secret pleasure in twisting the tricks she learned as a model to her own design. "You *say* you understand, but you hate me dressing like this. I mean, this is how I dressed when you met me, what? A year ago? And it's bothered you all this time."

"Not true."

"I just wanna go someplace, do my work, and not get hit on." Off came the bulky green sweater. "Why else would I bother? I'm just trying to look plain."

"You do," I said. "Extremely plain." Always supportive.

"You know I'm almost thirty? This is the longest relationship I've ever had." She scrubbed the ink off her hands. "We beat my old record by ten months. Doesn't it make you wonder?" She sponged the dark smudges and a number of years off her face. "Why are we still together?"

Simple—we were still together because I had never told her I loved her. Never mentioned that her eyes were lovely and deep, that her skin was like warm wind of a summer night, that her face would make Botticelli burn his brushes. And I had *definitely* never told her that I wanted to touch her whenever I saw her. I knew that, should I say these things, I'd be just another guy. Lilly would toss me into love's Dumpster.

She stripped the pillows from her backside, leaving only bra and panties. I was glad she'd added a few pounds since we met, she looked healthy and wild. I sighed. "What?" she asked, instantly suspicious.

"Just a little tired." Definitely the most beautiful woman I had ever seen. Our affair would have ended months ago if it weren't for my iron control.

"So what's the answer?" she asked, bundling her clothes. "Why am I, like, still here?"

"Isn't it obvious? I feel sorry for you. Otherwise, you'd be out the door."

She smiled, dropped her clothes, and we kissed. The seconds slowed, then froze in place, and I stopped thinking about Rush and the Elephant and Longstreet. I rested my cheek on the top of her head and breathed the sandalwood she wore in her hair as my fingers fumbled to unhook her bra. She said, "Willis, it's a sports bra. No hook."

"Just checking the stitching."

"So what was up with you at the party?"

"I'm a little old for ice cream and cake, don't you think?"

She looked up at me with a kind of lopsided smile. "Seen your refrigerator lately?"

CHAPTER 14

We caught the end of *The Girl Can't Help It* on TV, the part with the Platters and Fats Domino. Then Lilly and I made love, and I thought what I always thought when we made love—that we should be doing this a lot more often. Later I lay beside her. I stared at the shadows the streetlamp cast on the ceiling. Sometimes listening to Lilly's breath helped me sleep.

Not tonight. Overhead, a plane was landing at Dulles. Forty-three minutes later, a freight train rumbled past—over a mile away, but it felt loud enough to be in my backyard, the vibration rattling my apartment until the cups and saucers chattered like novelty windup teeth.

I groaned and turned over, trying to get comfortable. It was futile. No way was I going to sleep. I put on my robe and, in the next room, pulled the book from where I'd hidden it beneath the couch. *The Possum That Didn't*. Not sure why I hid it, except that Lilly unlocking the door had surprised me and I'd felt, well, a little embarrassed. It was just a kid's book, a fragment from my fragmented childhood.

When the book starts, the possum is happy. But some fiercely unpleasant humans mistake his smile for a frown, because the possum's hanging by his tail. The humans decide they'll cheer him up by taking him to the city, where everyone's happy.

Of course, no one in the city is happy, right? These misguided humans nearly destroy the little guy. At the end he escapes and finds his way back to the woods. The author, Frank Tashlin, was the same man who wrote and directed *The Girl Can't Help It*.

Funny thing was that, as a grown-up, I thought Tashlin made some of the best film comedies of the fifties, not to mention the Bugs Bunny cartoons he directed. But I'd had no idea he had also created this book. Then, as an adult, I was rummaging through Second Story Books' sale table and ran across it. Which just goes to show that your tastes are pretty much locked in by the time you're four or five years old. Kind of a scary thought.

I flipped through the pages for the zillionth time, wondering which gang—if any—could be duping movies illegally in D.C. For ten minutes I sat staring at the book's cover. It didn't tell me anything. Then I walked to the narrow kitchen to get a drink of water and looked at my reflection in the darkened back door window. It didn't tell me anything, either.

I thought about the possum in the trash can. Not much of a burial for him. Or her—I couldn't tell one way or the other. Then I remembered seeing a pouch. A her.

Robed and barefoot, I inched the back door open, so as not to wake Lilly, then made my way down the stairs to the shed. I figured I could find the shovel in the dark, just like I could find a soft piece of ground for a small possum-size grave.

When I came around to the front of the building, shovel in hand, I saw two familiar figures by the front door—Ph'uck and his buddy in their olive drab fatigues. They were huddled over a 9 mm pistol, trying to unjam its clip. Too busy to see me or hear the *whoosh* of the shovel's blade.

CHAPTER 15

Lt. Emil Haggler perched on the edge of a scarred and beaten desk. Above him the fluorescents leaked a sickly yellow color. The yellow made a nice touch, I decided. It gave a bleak tenor to the room, and matched the yellow-stained wall tiles.

Haggler broke the silence, his voice sounding like wood cracking. "Tell 'em they get one chance, that's it. Otherwise, they'll each get a tube of K-Y 'fore we ship their asses off to the FCI at Cumberland."

He turned from the interpreter to look at Ph'uck and his friend. I'd called Haggler after smacking them with the shovel and tying them together. Haggler had dumped them in D.C. jail's overnight tank, along with the winos, crazies, and street fighters. Soften 'em up, he said. I hoped he'd been right. I wanted to find out how these kids knew where I lived.

If their time in the tank had affected Ph'uck and his buddy, they didn't show it. They slouched in their chairs, army jackets on their laps, their long-sleeved shirts buttoned neatly at their wrists, looking into Haggler's craggy black face.

I didn't envy them. Haggler's face could be kindly as a church deacon's, but not right now. Now he looked like he was going to snap their heads off and string them to the rearview mirror of his car. Haggler held up a dark, meaty hand and ticked off on his fingers. "I want to know why they're after Gidney, how they found out where he lives, and the names of the other gang members." He spoke clearly to the civilian interpreter the cops'd hired—they had no staff who spoke Vietnamese. My two little buddies from the Alexandria warehouse had evidently forgotten all their English. The interpreter repeated what Haggler had said.

The two kids looked at each other and burst out laughing. Then they made a gesture at Haggler. It wasn't the peace sign.

Haggler smiled as though he'd made some progress, then his hand shot out and grabbed Ph'uck's wrist and yanked back his sleeve hard enough to pop his buttons. With the sleeve back, you could see the tattoo—a circle of chain with a flame inside. Ph'uck struggled to get his arm free but kept silent.

Haggler took a deep breath and seemed to relax. He rapped on the interview room mirror, then a uniform took the smirking kids back to the tank. The interpreter looked at us, then followed them out. The whole time Haggler kept his eyes on me. He leaned his chair against the wall so its front feet were off the ground.

"Aren't you ashamed, scaring them like that?" I said.

Haggler kept a straight face. "Don't know how I live with myself."

"You ever see ink like that before?"

"Sure. Virginia gang, the Dragon Boys."

"I've heard of them."

"Right, 'cause we got no shortage of gangs. The Crips, the Bloods, the Locos, the Pagans. Shit, we even got some Russians sneaking in."

"And the Dragons?"

"Extortion, kidnapping, drug dealing. Mostly Vietnamese immigrants' kids. They leave Nam and get here with no money, no English, no clue."

"I bet they fit right in."

"Yeah, for some reason, the other kids don't really take to them, so they stick together, form gangs. Little fucks like to hang out at the Eden Center in Fairfax, mostly prey on their own kind. I wish to hell they'd stay there."

"Why bother with the tats if they keep their shirtsleeves rolled down?"

"So no one gets a peek. Secret like."

Haggler brought down the chair legs and gave me a dead-eyed look, the very same look he used to give me when I was eight. He'd caught me stealing change from the pockets of my foster father, Shadrack Davies. Now it's one thing to pick your foster dad's pocket, quite another when the guy is also D.C.'s captain of police.

Shad was my last foster father. I'd had dozens. Maybe even broken a DCAS record, who knows?

My first linear memory as a kid syncs with my first arrest, when the cops caught me stealing money from a Metro farecard machine. I was about six or seven. They tossed me into Junior Village, a D.C. kiddie jail. Two important things happened to me there—I found that I loved to read, and I met Eddie Vermeer.

At ten years old, Eddie was a natural-born con man. He took an interest in me. We became partners, and Eddie taught me some excellent scams. We prospered.

Junior Village was poorly run, even by D.C. standards. A

District judge issued Junior Village a court order to improve. When it didn't, we got shipped to Bockman's—a larger and less friendly place.

Nothing stopped Eddie. He worked out a plan for me, for furthering my education. Through a hefty series of bribes, Eddie arranged my placement with a variety of foster families. I'd pick up whatever I could. Valuables, of course, but I was also there to learn.

It's amazing what a wide-eyed kid can absorb if he pays attention—research, a bit of legal training, even basic lock-picking. When I felt I'd gotten all there was, and it was time to head home to Bockman's, I'd break something valuable, or set fire to part of the foster family's house. It never failed.

The downside was, I never learned how to live with a family.

Now, I have to tell you, the whole thing with Shadrack Davies was a fluke. Shad had spotted me early on and, for whatever reason, thought there was something in me he could salvage. It wasn't Eddie's idea, me living with a cop. But once Eddie heard about it, he loved it. He told me to spy on Shad, learn how the cops worked. What better way to keep out of jail? See, with Shad I didn't *mean* to learn about right or wrong. I certainly didn't mean to learn about ethics. Christ, it's like some alien substance, once it gets on you, you can never get it off.

That last night at Bockman's, when it burned to the ground, Eddie and Shad both died. Eddie died going after twenty thousand we had stolen. Shad died protecting me.

Maybe Haggler was trying to protect me now. He pointed his finger at me like a gun. "So tell me—why were the Dragon Boys trying to shoot you?"

"Hey, there're four apartments in my building—they could've been after the retired guy downstairs, or the writer across the hall."

"Sure. Or maybe they were gonna nail the Pope and figured your apartment was the Vatican. What you working on, you'd piss off these animals?"

I wasn't going to tell Haggler a thing before checking with Rush Gemelli. And since I'd been breaking and entering—technically speaking, that is—I wasn't sure I'd tell Haggler anything at all, even with Rush's okay. "I haven't worked in weeks."

He nodded. "Now tell me you never saw them before."

"I was just about to," I said.

Haggler shook his head. "Sure glad Shad ain't here to see this, you lyin' to me and all." I noticed Haggler dropped a *g*. When that happened, it meant he was getting pissed off. His southern roots were showing.

"Here we go," I said.

He appeared not to have heard me. "I remember that road trip we took to Pennsylvania. It was summer, you were ten or so, and Shad drove us in his car to that jail."

"I remember the car." Shad polished it almost every Sunday afternoon for the nineteen months we were together.

Haggler nodded, his eyes losing none of their hardness. "You spent most the trip sleepin' in the back. I told Shad he was nuts, a black police captain takin' in a crazy-ass white kid like you. Told him, 'You wanna be a foster dad, get a black kid you got some chance with.' Guess he wanted a lyin' white boy instead. Wonder what he'd say if he saw you today."

"'Hey there, lyin' white boy'?"

Haggler shook his head. "How'd he stand you for two years?"

"Nineteen months. No accounting for taste, I guess."

"First true thing you said today."

I got up to go. "What'll happen to the kids?"

"Chip and Dale? Some suit'll come bail them out. They

should hit the street in an hour or so." He stood up and stretched. "Never mind, I'll nail the little fuckers soon enough."

"When?"

He looked surprised. "Why, after they whack you, of course."

CHAPTER 16

I got back to my place a little after nine that morning. Lilly had already left for her big meeting with the software mavens. It'd be cool if they offered her the job. I tried calling Rush, got his answering machine, so I left a message, took a shower, shaved, then saw my remaining clean shirt. It was new, and I hate new clothes. A legacy from my days at Bockman's, when I'd been given "previously worn" clothes to wear. As a kid, I dreamed about the day I'd buy new shirts and pants.

I finally did. I remember the first new shirt I ever bought—it took me ten minutes to figure out where all the pins were. When I put the shirt on, I took it right off again. I must've missed some pins, I could feel them sticking into me. Imagine my surprise when I found it was the shirt itself, the scratchy new fabric that felt so uncomfortable. And the pants? No way. Since then, it's been previously worn clothes for me.

My last clean shirt was silk, Lilly had given it to me at Christmas. It had a frantic design, lots of purples and blacks and greens. The fit was a little snug. I didn't so much put the shirt on as enter it, like a moth burrowing back into its cocoon. Then I clicked onto the Net and spent a half hour or so digging for information on Rush Gemelli. Always good to know your clients, especially when they blackmail you.

I found stuff about Rush's dad, most of it written like a press release and about as reliable. A lot about his business smarts, his days as CEO of various high-tech companies, and his wild campaign schedules, traveling through the South and Midwest, getting the president elected. I found a picture of Chuck Gemelli in the lobby of the Skirvin hotel. Then I read about his White House days. Gemelli's wife had died on October 10 a year ago. Rush was their only child. I also saw that father and son had owned a company together four years ago—EncryptU.com.

I Googled the newsgroups for EncryptU.com. One link lead to another. I found myself reading a thread from four years ago, about how Rush left the company, a few months before it went belly up. There were quite a few messages, people speculating as to why Rush had left. Most of them thought he was smart enough to have seen the train wreck before it happened.

When I went down the stairs to my car, I half-expected to see more Vietnamese kids in the bushes. Traffic was light—for once—down Wisconsin Avenue to Q Street, then across to Twentieth. I parked near McClure Downing, a big PI firm on Dupont Circle. They had an investigator I'd worked with before, Jones St. Pierre.

On the way to the fourth floor, I evaluated which lies and evasions I would parade past the receptionist, but when the elevator doors slid open, St. Pierre was by the front desk, reading her messages.

She saw me, smiled, and shook her head, her braided black hair moving across an ebony face. In a clipped British accent, she said, "Of all the PI firms in all the cities of the world . . ." She came forward and we hugged, then she took my hands and looked up at me. "What's new, gruesome? Don't tell me you're looking for real work?"

"I'd be in the wrong place then, wouldn't I?"

"C'mon back and spill your guts," she said, turning down the hall, the slit in her ankle-length black skirt showing calf-length boots and a fine stretch of leg. I followed her down the muted gray hallway, the carpet a darker gray beneath our feet, muffling the sounds in case anyone found them disturbing. The overhead lighting was so soft as to be shadowless. Nothing sharp, no contrast. Just shades of gray. Being there always made me feel ill at ease, vague and undefined.

When we reached her office, she gestured toward the client chair while she sat behind her desk, smoothing some nonexistent wrinkles on her lavender blouse.

"How can you stand it here?" I asked.

"You mean with no corset shop downstairs? It's a strain, but I manage. How's solo practice these days?"

"Fine. I need a little help, though."

"More than a little, love. But one step at a time." Her lips curved into a slight smile. "What exactly did you have in mind?"

"Ever hear of Rush Gemelli?" I asked.

"No."

"How about Chuck Gemelli?"

"Ah. The president's campaign manager, then senior advisor, several years ago. Now he runs the motion picture lobby, for a paltry one point five million a year. For how much longer is anybody's guess."

"What do you know about EncryptU.com?" I asked.

"Apart from having the most daft name I've ever heard?" She

shrugged. "Nothing juicy. Just another dot-com, a little fish that bloated, then floated."

"Father and son ran it?"

"Along with another fellow, I think."

"Who?" I asked.

"Ah." She smiled, a feline kind of smile and very white teeth. She swiveled in her chair, brushed away some braids, and typed on her computer. "You're looking good, by the way."

"Thanks, you too."

"Just good?"

"Jones, it's all I can do to keep from rolling on my back with my hands and feet in the air. You got anything or not?"

She wrote something down, handed it to me. Draper Kane, 888 Sixteenth Street, next to the Hay-Adams. I looked up at her. "Nice neighborhood."

"Well, his D & B rating was good until this past year. At that address, he must have a lot of overhead." She typed some more. "Apparently, his biggest client is MPAC. Cozy, isn't it? Anything else you care to know?"

"You hear anything about a gang duping videos?"

"Illegal dupes? For profit? No, I can't say that I have."

"Let me know if you hear anything, all right?"

"And exactly what would I get out of this?"

I spread my arms wide. "Another fabulous visit from me, of course."

She smiled. "How delicious."

CHAPTER 17

Longstreet had told me a D.C. gang was flooding the country with illegal dupes. So I went to see a man who called himself Griffin Blake, a drug dealer who worked out of a club, the Toucantina, at Fourteenth and Colorado.

I had been there before, at night. With its low lighting, smoky atmosphere, and selection of abused tables and chairs, the Toucantina had looked like a dump. Daylight was not as kind. For a moment, I stood in the doorway, seeing only the neon beer signs until my eyes adjusted. The smells of booze and sweat and fresh coffee covered me like a wet sheet. An ice machine *chunked* on, its compressor humming through the soles of my shoes. A few steps in and I spotted Dante, Blake's enforcer, slouched in a chair in the shadows with a book in his lap.

He glanced up at me as I walked in. "Wild shirt."

"Thanks."

"Somewhere be a '62 Chevy missin' the seat covers."

I bent down to see the title of his book. "*Modern English Syntax?*"

"Yeah, by this dude name of Onions." He snapped the book shut, then scratched the dark wool cap on his head. "English, it's one fucked-up language, you know?" He made a "Turn around" gesture with his free hand. I leaned against the wall while he set his book carefully on the wobbly table in front of him. The weight of the book nearly sloshed coffee from the full cup next to it. As he checked me for weapons and wires, I said, "I didn't know slam poets were careful about their syntax."

He finished and stepped back. "Hey, don' be callin' me that. I a rapper."

"*I'm* a rapper."

"You don' look like one. C'mon."

We went down a dark hallway to Blake's office, where I found Washington's most successful pot dealer jamming his suitcase with clothes and spiral notebooks. As usual, the reek of marijuana came off him in waves. Now, Blake was the kind of guy that, if you went to him with your hat in your hand, asking a favor, he'd tell you to take a walk. I wanted information. The only way to get it was to harass him. So I started by calling him by his real name. "Howdy, Buford."

Without turning toward me, he said, "Gidney, you call me that again, I shall instruct Dante to shoot you." He had a way of speaking, a kind of to-the-manor-born accent, that was as real as a three-dollar Rolex.

I looked at Dante. "You'd do it?"

He shrugged. "If I were bored."

"Nice use of the conditional tense," I said.

Blake said, "Dante, out." After he left, Blake looked at me. "You've ruined that kid. You started in on his language, now he's obsessed. I have to remind him we're selling pot, not poetry. Why're you here?"

I pointed at the suitcase. "Business or pleasure?"

He stopped packing, looked up at me. Or rather, looked at me with his left eye. The right eye gazed off at a tangent, as though part of him were there and part wasn't. "I'm flying to Amsterdam in two hours."

"Cutting it close. Dope dealer convention?"

"Marijuana design and distribution, if you don't mind."

"You get to write that off?"

"Did you come by just to annoy me?"

"A fringe benefit. I'm trying to get a line on a film-pirating operation working out of D.C., or thereabouts. Early this morning, I had a run-in with the Dragon Boys. You know them?"

"Vietnamese gang. Based in Fairfax."

"Uh-huh. They're involved in a small way. But I thought you might know of any film pirates doing volume business."

He blew out a lungful of air. "Gidney, you've got a handful of gimme and a mouthful of much obliged. Why should I help you?"

"Because I saved your life. That should count for something, though probably not much." Some men had killed Blake's partner last year, and he had been next on their list.

He pulled a home-rolled from his pocket. Probably had gone an entire ten minutes without a hit. "If I hadn't gotten to them, you'd be dead now," I said.

"Bullshit." Said through a cloud of smoke.

I snatched the lighter from his hand. He was so high, he barely reacted. Then I grabbed the notebook from his suitcase. *Now* he reacted. I flipped to a diagram of a molecular chain. "New design?"

"Yes, and it's private." He clutched at the book.

I dangled it out of reach while I flicked the lighter and held it to the edge of the page. "Tell me who to contact, where I can meet him, and when."

"Okay, okay. There's this little guy named Tuckerman, deals for the Palmer Park Roaches."

I stiff-armed him away from the book. "And he'd be good why?"

"He's spent most of his life in jail. Knows all the players in town. He'll be at the ball field at M and Twenty-sixth around noon. Can't miss him, scratches his neck all the time."

"Palmer Park? In PG County? The Roaches're into film pirating?" I asked.

"Who knows? They're into everything else." The fight had left him.

"You don't approve."

"They're amateurs."

I snapped off the lighter. "I know what you mean. Nobody specializes anymore. You look at today's crooks, it's a wonder any crime gets committed at all." I handed him his pages.

He took them, then another hit, his anger fading with the hovering cloud of smoke. He shoved the notebook into the mound of clothes in his suitcase. "But let me caveat you, Gidney. Take backup. The Roaches like to shoot people." Now he struggled with the shallow lid of the case, trying to force it shut.

"Anything else?"

His spindly, pale arms tried to press the suitcase halves together, his face white with the effort. He gave me the one-eyed look again, his gentleman persona peeling off like a rattlesnake's skin. "Anything else? Like a letter of introduction? Just go fuck off, okay? I gotta get this suitcase shut."

"Why don't you sit on it, Buford?"

"And you'll shut the latches?"

I went for the door. "I wasn't talking about the suitcase."

CHAPTER 18

Blake was probably right about backup. But try finding anyone good on short notice. My aikido teacher could really move, but he was on parole. Most likely wouldn't want to help me meet a few gang members. I turned onto Fourteenth Street, getting an idea. I mean, at the time I thought it was an idea. Looking back, I'm not so sure. A quick left and I stopped outside the Barnett brothers' garage.

The garage was in a dirty brick building, crowded by Whole Foods on one side and lofts/condos on the other. I pulled the handle to their front door, only to find it locked. Someone with a four-year-old's handwriting had scrawled a sign that said CLOSD 'TIL FERTHER NOTISE.

So I walked to the alley, hearing the *beep-beep* of a truck in reverse. Behind the Barnetts' garage was a car hauler unloading a black Lexus and a red Porsche. Both cars looked new. I went for a closer look, when a mountain wearing a camo jacket blocked me. "Jaysus, so it's himself, then?"

I looked up to Emmet Barnett, in the literal sense. He and his brother Slip were giants with the voices of helium addicts. They both had long gray hair and long gray beards that spread over beer bellies. If you took two of those ornamental gnomes you see on people's lawns and exposed them to radiation 'til they grew seven feet high and nearly as wide, you'd get the general idea.

I tried pointing around him at the luxury cars. "Kind of different for you, isn't it?"

Emmet put his hands on my shoulders and spun me toward the garage. "Let's talk." He gave me a polite shove, and it was all I could do to stay on my feet. I regained my balance by gripping the doorjamb on my way in, then said, "Oh my God."

It wasn't the push that made me say it, or the force with which Emmet had propelled me. No, it was the sight of Slip Barnett pinned beneath the front tire of a car.

"Hold on," I shouted. There was a jack nearby, and as I reached for it, Emmet's hand came down on mine. "And just what the fuck are you doing?"

"Saving your brother's life."

Emmet waved his hand at me. "Sure, and he's fine."

"He's pinned under a car."

"And don't you think I can see that?"

"Then help me get him out."

Emmet shook his head, his gray beard swaying. He grumbled. "This is bullshit." We got the jack in place and dragged Slip from beneath the car. He opened his eyes and looked at Emmet.

"How long?"

"Eighteen minutes," Emmet said.

"That's it?" Slip's voice was a roar. "And why the fuck did you not leave me?"

"Would someone please tell me what's going on?" I asked.

Emmet jerked his thumb at Slip. "He can't beat my record."

Slip's face went red. "And didn't I have you beat, except for certain meddlers sticking their nose in?" This last was directed at me.

Emmet laughed. "And doesn't the meddler look confused? Gidney doesn't know about the car that came down on me last week, I was there for twenty minutes. So is it any wonder that Slip's been trying to beat my record?"

The Barnetts were the kind of crazy they'd needed to be to survive Bockman's. So maybe that entitled them to a few peculiarities. Slip stood, a bit off balance, steadied himself against Emmet, who pulled a joint from his pocket. "Suck on this, loser."

Slip took the joint, then stumbled into his office. Their garage was the usual chaos. Grit and oil scrunched beneath my shoes, the astringent smell of primer opened my sinuses like needle-nose pliers, and the revving of engines vibrated through my body as though someone were shaking me. The car exhaust and spray paint created a blue haze so dense, I could barely make out the Barnetts' collection of Snap-on tool calendars and the photos of girls who graced them.

Slip threw himself into his chair, put his black boots up on his desk, and said, "So why the fuck are you here? On your way to a love-in, judgin' from that shirt."

He peered out the dirty window and grunted. "That rusted-out Plymouth, that piece of shit's your ride?" Two of his garage monkeys had popped open the trunk.

"Tell your guys to keep their hands off."

"All your cars are rusted out, Gidney, and have you ever thought why? Maybe you attract corrosion." He pivoted toward me. "Anyway, we'll not be dealing with you now, we're backed up three weeks."

"Things are busy," I said.

"And why shouldn't they be, praise God. This gang is getting us more cars than we can deal with, which means no time for the likes of you." He gave another glance at my car. "But I can't think of anyone who'd waste his time on your piece of scrap."

"Thanks, but I'm here for backup."

"And me balancing a car on my chest? I can hardly breathe.

72

It's my little brother you'll be wanting." He chin-pointed at Emmet, who was barreling toward us, a chrome car bumper on each shoulder. "Sure, and Emmet's the best man."

Without looking, Emmet swung the bumper and clocked one of his workmen square in the head. The workman dropped, scattering car parts across the floor. Emmet stopped, turned to see the inert body, and nudged it with his toe. "Hey," he said. "Haven't I told you, 'Duck or bleed'?"

Slip smiled. "Our little diplomat."

CHAPTER 19

It began to rain as soon as we pulled away. After three blocks, an interior fog had covered the windshield. I got a rag and was wiping the away the moisture when Emmet pulled out a joint. I glanced at him. "This is a nonsmoking vehicle."

"You've seen your exhaust, then?"

"I mean *inside* the car." He ignored me and lit the joint. "I said don't do that."

"Jaysus, lighten up, Gidney." He took an enormous drag, then filled the Plymouth with smoke. As he flicked ashes on the floor, he grimaced. "This shit is the worst. I hate to be saying it, but I got ripped off."

"Then why not flick it out the window?"

"Me, who doesn't believe in littering?" He managed to look hurt and belligerent at the same time. He leaned his huge torso back against the seat and a spring snapped. "Didn't you learn it's a sin to waste?"

"I don't want my backup stoned."

"And haven't I just told you this weed is shit? I take no pleasure in smoking it, but I have to get rid of it." He took another puff and shook his head. "I don't mind telling you—the guy that sold it to me is a fucking dead man. If I ever find him."

"*If* you find him? You buy it on eBay or something?"

"Nah, at a concert. I'm sitting next to a guy, he says let's split a joint, so I say sure."

"Just being neighborly."

"And why shouldn't I be? Well, this weed—it was great, making everything kinda cartoony." He glanced over again. "Like that shirt you're wearing. So I tell him okay, and he sells me a bag of shit, saying it's the same stuff."

I looked at him. "That's it? Who are you and what've you done with Emmet Barnett?"

"Didn't I say I was high?"

"You're pathetic. What's the guy look like? White? Black? Some unregistered color?"

"Didn't register with me. A local gangbanger. Apart from what you'll be paying me, that's why I'm here. Maybe I'll ask a few questions when you're finished. See"—and here Emmet managed somehow to turn in his seat so he was facing me—"I remember what he was saying to me as I walked away. He was saying 'Adios, asshole.' That's how I'll be knowing him next time." He took another toke. "Only then he'll be saying adios to *his* asshole."

Another block slid by. I wiped the now-smoky film off the windshield. There *had* to be an easier way of adopting a kid. I pictured Sarah in her crib, making those baby noises while she played with the toys I'd bought her. "Emmet, didn't you once tell me that we all live in a state of grace?"

He nodded. "We're all perfect, Gidney. Even you." He closed his eyes, leaning back and popping a few more springs. "Everything you do will be perfect."

CHAPTER 20

We peeled off of M street and parked on Twenty-sixth a few minutes after the rain slacked off. There's a baseball field, bordered by Beach Drive on one side and office buildings on the other. Two men stood near home plate, their canvas bags and bats resting on a wooden bench. They were changing their shirts, getting ready for a game.

A swirling cloud of blue pot smoke followed Emmet. My shirt reeked. Wonderful. Our feet squished across the wet grass as a plane made a lazy approach to National Airport. The rain had boosted the humidity, I could almost see drops of water hanging in the air. The ballplayers watched as we approached them. I pulled on my collar to peel my shirt away from my back.

The two players were both bare-chested and glassy-eyed, as though they could detect our movement but not much else. I stopped worrying about how my clothes smelled. One of them, the taller and more muscular of the two, looked Latino. He had black hair held back in a ponytail and there were two tears tattooed below his right eye—meaning he had done two stretches of hard time and wanted everyone to know it. But in case there was any doubt, he had the letters *FTW* above his left eye, which stood for Fuck the World. A philosopher. He slipped on a white baseball jersey with the word *Roaches* spread across the front in red cursive.

The short one was a light-skinned African-American. From a distance, his wall-to-wall tattoos had looked like a paisley body glove. Before he shrugged into a baseball jersey, I caught a glimpse of a death skull, snakes, guard towers, angry clowns, calendar pages, and a lightning bolt.

"Nice ink," I said. "You two part of the Palmer Park Roaches?"

The Latino said, "Why you say that?"

Emmet grunted. " 'Cause it's written on your shirt, Einstein."

"You actually have a baseball team?" I asked.

The short guy scratched his throat. "A league, man, twelve teams. Like networking." He unzipped a canvas bag and pulled out a plastic trophy. "We two-time division champs, we went to the finals in L. A. last year."

"A dope-dealing baseball league, how enterprising," I said. "Your name Tuckerman?"

He started to scratch under his chin once more, then dropped his hand to his side. "Never heard of him, man."

"Right. I got your name from Griffin Blake."

"Never heard of him either."

"He's heard of you. Said you might know about a film-piracy ring operating around here."

He laughed without humor. "Pirates? We look like pirates to you? Lemme learn you up, white. We baseball players. Paulo, the best hitter in the league. Got eighteen homers this season." Paulo had an excitable look to him. He'd slipped a baseball glove on his left hand and now he was punching it with his right. Emmet was two steps behind me.

Tuckerman let his fingers scratch his throat. "They think we pirates, Paulo."

Paulo punched his glove harder, glaring at me, working himself up to it.

I shrugged. "Sorry if you thought I said that. Have you heard of any gangs making pirate videos for profit?"

"I ain't heard shit, and if I did, why the fuck would I tell you?"

"Because you're enjoying the glow of my godlike presence."

Paulo moved. The punch that should've landed in his glove came whistling toward my head. I stepped left, letting his arm *swoosh* past, then pivoted and drove my fist as hard as I could into his side, about where his floating rib would be. Paulo staggered, then bent down, just in time to let his chin meet my knee. He dropped onto home plate just as my shirt ripped down the back. Goddamn it. I looked over at Emmet. He hadn't moved.

I wiped the sweat from my face. "Look," I said to Tuckerman. Then I turned around again. "Emmet, you okay? Pulse and respiration normal?"

He gave me a thumbs-up.

Jesus. I sighed, turned back to Tuckerman. "This is really simple. I ask you a question. You answer it. We go away."

Tuckerman was down looking at Paulo. When his gaze came back to me, I thought he might cry. "Man, Paulo the MVP. How we gonna win now? This a division championship *game,* man." He waved the trophy at me. "You coldcock my best hitter and you want *information?* Get outta here 'fore I cap you myself. Just get the fuck out of here."

"Let's give him a minute," I said to Emmet.

We turned to give him some space, but Tuckerman called after us, "Tha's right, get out of here. Sayonara, fuckheads."

Emmet stopped. He turned around. He started walking back to Tuckerman.

"Emmet," I said.

Tuckerman looked up at him, trying for tough. "Back off, motherfucker."

"You," Emmet said. "You ripped me off."

"Never seen you before, man, never wanna see you again."

Emmet's hand shot out. He could move when he wanted to. He grabbed Tuckerman by his baseball shirt and picked him up off the ground with one hand. He started shaking him. "I don't like people ripping me off." Emmet threw him down like pitching a grounder. Tuckerman tumbled to rest in the mud. "Just this once, I'll be letting you make it up to me." Emmet stepped over to the canvas bags and began ransacking them.

Tuckerman rolled to his feet, rushed him. Emmet didn't even turn around, just shot back his elbow and caught Tuckerman in the cheek. A small cracking sound and Tuckerman went down again. This time, he stayed there.

Emmet found a Ziploc bag stuffed with pot. He opened it, smelled it, nodded.

I shook my head. "You finished?"

"Almost." He put his old weed in the canvas bag.

We drove in silence for a few blocks. Emmet took out the bag to admire it some more. Then he began to roll a joint. "Hey," I said, "what happened to that state of grace we're all living in?"

Emmet looked at me, his bloodshot eyes small and gray in his too-big face. "You saw it yourself, didn't you? How he didn't want to exchange?" He spoke slowly, as though explaining something obvious.

"So?"

He lit up his joint. "Well," he said, sending a pungent cloud at me, "that wasn't very gracious, was it?"

I rolled down my window. "You notice the tats?"

"Sure I noticed."

"Those pictures of guard towers seem familiar to you?"

"Me, who runs a fucking garage? Why would prison towers be familiar?"

We drove on. I knew I'd seen those towers before.

CHAPTER 21

We parked behind Emmet's garage, but he didn't want to leave my car. He wanted to stay and argue about his fee as backup. I said he should get what he was worth, and he thought I should double it. Since two times nothing is still nothing, I didn't know what the argument was about.

I sped south on Fourteenth, my windows open to clear the pot smell. Stayne Matthews called to double-check we were on for that afternoon. Like I'd forget. I stopped by Caliber Clothes for some new old shirts, then parked near Georgia Brown's on Fifteenth.

Kane's office stood on a corner near Lafayette Park and, just a bit farther, the White House. His sixth-floor waiting room was all burnished steel and walnut. I was instantly jealous. I expected some pampered goddess to welcome me and, in a way, I got her. I just didn't expect her to be on a screen.

"Good afternoon, sir. Can I help you?" She had a lovely East Indian accent, black hair, and large dark eyes. She wore a sari the color of saffron, and most likely she was seven thousand miles away.

"My name's Willis Gidney, I'd like a few minutes with Mr. Kane."

"Do you have an appointment?"

Why do they always ask that? Wouldn't they know if I did? "No, sorry, but I'm working with a colleague of Mr. Kane's, Charles Gemelli."

She smiled. "I see. Well"—and here a smaller box popped up on the screen—"you can see for yourself that Mr. Kane's schedule is quite full. Maybe sometime next week?"

"Next week? Sure, that's—wait. What's that?"

She looked confused. "Sir?"

"There's some black smoke coming from the back of your—hold on."

I walked behind the monitor and yanked out the plug. Maybe the digital revolution wasn't so bad after all. I gave a discrete rap on Kane's office door, then opened it to find a man in a shirt and a tie and boxer shorts. He stood behind an ironing board, a cigarette in one hand and a plugged-in iron in the other. Behind was a cot, and a small refrigerator with a hot plate on top. The room smelled of sweat, smoke, and scorched coffee.

"Who the fuck are you?"

"Name's Gidney. I'm from MPAC, working with Chuck Gemelli."

"But you didn't bring me anything."

What did that mean? "Uh, no. Sorry."

"Oh. Well, come on in."

A screen came to life on his desk, and the dark-eyed woman popped up. "I'm sorry, Mr. Kane, but this man has no appointment. Should I call security?"

Kane shrugged. "No, it's okay."

"Yes, sir." The screen winked out.

He tapped some ash in a glass tray on his desk, then went back to ironing his blue serge pants. "What can I do for you, Gidney?"

"Background information, trying to find local pirating operations. I'd ask Chuck, but he's a little tied up."

"Tied up. Meaning the guy's salivating over quality time with Brooks and Stoddard." He blew out smoke. "Of course, any time with Sondra Stoddard would be quality time, am I right? What kind of background?"

"Encryption, for one thing. You guys had a business together."

"We've had a number of them. But you're talking about EncryptU.com, am I right? We went bust years ago."

"That was you, Chuck, and his son."

"Right. A bust—we lost everything,"

"Who came up with the start-up money?"

"I found a backer, that was my job. Rainmaker. Hey, hand me that can of starch."

While he shook the can and sprayed, I said, "Who put up the money for EncryptU.com?"

He smiled and shook his head while he ironed. "I don't see how that helps you with Chuck."

"All right, then who did the code writing?"

"Rush." He saw my expression and added, "Chuck doesn't know shit about that, he's a salesman."

"So neither of you knew about cryptography. Yet here you are, still in the same business."

"I'm a security consultant now. Chuck hires me to advise him." Here I got the big, confident, "You can trust me" smile, which would've worked a lot better if he hadn't been standing in his underwear. Also, Jones had told me Kane's gravy train with MPAC was over. "Sure makes life easier," Kane said, "I just tell people what to do. If I need someone to write code, I hire it out. There're guys in New Delhi that are good."

"Sounds like you know how things work."

He grinned. "I've been around."

I laughed, just one of the boys. "So I heard. Some wild times on the road, huh?"

"We got our share of pussy." He shook his head, smiling at the memory.

"It's hard to imagine, managing a presidential campaign. You must've racked up some miles. The president came from some-where down south, right?"

"Oklahoma."

"So you and Chuck must've spent a fair amount of time there."

Kane's eyes grew wary. "What's this have to do with MPAC?"

"I read that you were the guy who put out fires for the campaign."

He checked his watch—D.C. sign language for "This meeting is over."

"I've got to get going. You need anything else, shoot me an e-mail."

"One last question. Have you met Agent Longstreet?"

"Once. About a year ago."

"What do you think of him?'

He shrugged into his pants, got them zipped and buckled. "What's to think? Guy's ex-FBI. They're all cut from the same cloth, am I right?"

I punched in Rush's number as I walked back to my car.

"Gidney, what's up?"

"Two of our Vietnamese friends from the warehouse put in an appearance at my apartment last night."

"Christ."

"Yeah. Now tell me how they got my address."

"Not from me, man. Why the fuck would I do that? They came to your house? What'd you do?"

"Turned them over to the cops. I'm about ten minutes from your office, we'll talk." And lay the groundwork for a midnight visit—I was anxious to burn Rush's drive before he burned me with his photos.

He said, "What's to talk about?"

"How about me pissing off a police lieutenant named Haggler by withholding information."

"Why the hell did you hold out on him?"

"Because you're my client. The cops're going to want the name of your inside source at MPAC."

"Right, right, you did right. But we gotta keep quiet on this, okay?"

I got in my car and keyed the ignition, then pulled into traffic. "I plan on keeping my license. So if the cops turn up the heat, your name'll pop."

"All right, all right—you got other leads?"

"Draper Kane."

Rush snorted. "*That* asshole. Why's he on your list?"

"Because of the failed business you had together. There's motive, if Kane was angry enough over what happened. He has the know-how to launch that piracy operation. Funny, but when I told him I worked for the Elephant, he seemed disappointed I'd nothing to give him."

Rush barked out a laugh. "He's been sucking at MPAC's tit

for years. Guy's a glad-hander, totally useless. God knows why Dad keeps him on."

"About EncryptU.com—why did you leave your own company?"

"I hated the coffee. Look, Gidney, this's got nothing to do with me helping Dad."

"I'm just trying to understand the connection between you and Kane."

"Kane's a loser. Forget him."

I pulled up to DCAS Before I pocketed the phone I checked the time. Good, I wasn't late. Keep breathing, Gidney. I felt light-headed as I entered the lobby and thumbed the elevator button. I had to focus, concentrate on this meeting with Florence Walters and her boss. Walters was an old lady, feeble, on her last legs. I was young, quick-witted and wily. So why did I think it would all fall apart?

CHAPTER 22

I was trapped, suffocating in a drab fourteen-by-ten conference room at D.C. Adoptive Services. On the walls hung framed portraits of ancient purse-mouthed D.C. judges. They seemed unhappy I was there.

Sitting across from me was Florence Walters, also purse-mouthed and unhappy. And taking up all available space next to her was her boss, Oscar Penny, a big marshmallow-soft white guy in his fifties.

What was I doing there? I'd already survived this system—I'd escaped DCAS. Now it was coming after me, like the end of a bad horror movie. Sitting beside me, my lawyer, Stayne Matthews, looked crisp, his albino-white hair combed back off his forehead, his skin as white as a fresh blanket of snow. He shuffled his papers, giving me a fine view of his profile. It would be unfair to say he had a weak chin. Matthews had no chin at all.

The first time I met him, we shared a D.C. jail cell. Then and there he'd tried to hustle me as a client. I'd admired his complete lack of propriety. Besides, a lawyer who's spent time in the slammer is motivated to avoid it in the future.

While Walters summarized my case for Penny, Matthews made a small scraping sound, running his thumbnail across his slightly bucked teeth. He's got this nervous tic—he blinks his pink eyes constantly. When he looked at Walters, his bunny eyes magnified by his tortoiseshell glasses, Matthews had a surprised look, as though Farmer Jones had just found him raiding the carrot patch.

Matthews knows this. He is, in fact, one of the most cunning lawyers I've ever met. So it's no surprise he uses his bunny face time and again to flummox his opponents. Like now. I could tell Walters thought Matthews was a loser. The detached way she spoke, the canned phrases. She'd used this speech dozens of times. We hadn't rated a new one. Her words fell like dead leaves on the table.

"Everyone wants a healthy, bubbly infant," she told me. "We understand that." Back to Matthews. "But Adoptive Services has concluded that Mr. Gidney would not be a suitable match for . . ." When she couldn't find the case number, she simply said, ". . . this baby."

"Sarah," I said.

She looked up at me. "Excuse me?"

"Her name. It's Sarah. That's the name I call her, and she smiles when she hears me say it."

She gave me a sad look. "I'm sorry, Mr. Gidney, but she's Baby Doe until we place her."

When I'm around bureaucrats—and growing up in D.C. foster care, I've been around them a lot—I usually keep a tight rein on my feelings. But as I looked at Walters, bile surged up my throat. In a moment, my head would spin with pea soup flying out of my mouth. Matthews sensed this and said, "I'm surprised, Ms. Walters."

"What surprises you?" She spoke with near-perfect diction.

"Your conclusion." Matthews turned to Penny, the judge in this little mock trial. "We're simply appealing to get an extension. Mr. Gidney has obtained all the necessary clearances. He's attended five meetings outlining orientation policies and procedures. He's gone to each and every foster parent training class, that's ten classes over a two-month period."

Matthews hadn't even finished talking when I cut in. "I've done the research—I've got the paperwork—for her health insurance." Which was quite a trick, since I'd had none myself. "I'll pay for everything. Did Ms. Walters tell you I saved Sarah's life?" Matthews patted my arm, meaning "Shut up."

Penny nodded his big head, the picture of gray-haired wisdom. The only thing that spoiled the effect were the quick glances he stole at his watch.

Matthews said, "In other words, my client has done everything possible to adopt this little girl. Yet his appeal is being denied. It seems to me that perhaps he is being victimized."

A sliver of curiosity caused Walters to wrinkle her brow. "Just how is *he* a victim?"

"Because he's followed every guideline, attended every meeting, met every requirement. His application to adopt this girl—excuse me, to adopt Sarah—was rejected. And now you're refusing his legal right to appeal." Matthews reached into his briefcase to produce a stack of green folders the size of a Manhattan phone book. "Our research indicates there's a possibility of discrimination here." The folders made a satisfying *thunk* as they hit the table.

Staring at the folders, glassy-eyed, Penny asked, "What discrimination?"

Mathews said, "That simply by surviving D.C. foster care, Mr. Gidney has possibly, in your eyes, put himself among the broken. 'He can't be a good father, just look at how we raised him.'" Matthews rested his hand on the folders. "You'll see a long history of prejudicial action on the part of Adoptive Services, a pattern that begins eleven years ago." Now Matthews's pink eyes didn't seem watery at all.

Beads of perspiration hobnailed Penny's forehead. Coke sweat from our former mayor had never popped out so quickly. Penny gave a lightning-quick glance at his watch, then cleared his throat and said, "Um, that won't be necessary, Mr. Matthews."

"Mr. Penny, my client's right to appeal is at stake. We *must* be allowed the chance to answer the objections Ms. Walters is raising."

Penny patted the air between us. "No, I mean that I understand your position completely." He smiled at Walters. "I think, under these circumstances, we could allow Mr. Gidney an extension for his appeal."

Walters's lips puckered, like those of a church lady who overheard her pastor say there is no God. "Mr. Penny, do I have to remind you? Mr. Gidney works as a private investigator. His hours—and his livelihood—are uncertain. Now, how in good conscience can we consider him a suitable parent?"

Matthews said, "This is exactly the type of insidious discrimination I was referring to." He started to open the top folder. "I think you'll see there's been a history of this."

Penny had been fidgeting. Now he stood. "Mr. Matthews, while I'm not admitting to any discrimination on our part, I am willing to grant you an extension for Mr. Gidney's appeal." Here he looked at me. "But Ms. Walters has valid questions, Mr. Gidney."

He put on his jacket and moved so he could view his reflection in one of the framed judges' portraits. Adjusting his tie, he said, "Of course we're concerned with the baby's safety, the quality of life she deserves." He turned to me. "The question of your, ah, profession—well, it *is* troubling."

Before I could answer, he moved toward the door. "Another question—income. I've looked at your 1040s. I wonder how you expect to afford a child. But these are questions best answered after careful consideration, don't you think?" In other words, later. He was out the door. Walters glared at us as she gathered her papers, then left without a word. Matthews gave me a grin and began collecting his research folders.

"Penny was in a hurry," I said.

"You private eyes don't miss a thing, do you? He had a date with a young lady."

"How do you know that?"

"Same way I know her name's Alice."

"You arranged it."

He gave me a wicked smile, and for a moment a shark appeared from beneath his rabbit persona. Then he gathered his stack of folders quickly together, a rabbit in a hurry once more.

I pointed at the folders. "I'll pay you more next week. But all this research—you're killing me."

"Don't worry about it."

"Never knew you to give things away."

He showed me the pages within the folders.

They were blank. All of them.

"Oh," I said.

CHAPTER 23

My DCAS meeting went better than I'd expected. In other words I was dangling by a piece of dollar-store thread. Still, Walter's boss wouldn't let her set a match to it. Not quite yet.

By the way, I'm not an idiot. The stuff Penny had asked about, the stuff that he found "troubling?" I had it covered. I knew I'd have to work hard to support Sarah. Okay, fine. I was ready to do whatever I had to do. I'd found a daycare center in Glover Park, for times I was on a case. The center was expensive, but I liked the people there and felt Sarah would too. I'd save money by working out of my apartment. I'd even talked to Haggler's wife, Vera, on the down low, in case Sarah would need to overnight someplace. She said it was fine, but I doubt she'd told Haggler. I know I hadn't.

I stopped at 6th and F Streets to fortify myself with coffee and scones and chocolate-covered grahams, then headed to the Uptown. Clouds kept the sky dark, and that made the traffic slow on Connecticut Avenue. I stayed in the right-hand lane and made better time than the drivers who darted in and out of traffic. All the while thinking about Oscar Penny, and his saying that my lack of income was troubling. Tell me about it. I knew that adopting Sarah would put a crimp in my already frugal lifestyle. But I couldn't just walk away.

One Sunday, back when I was living with Shad, we went to a Safeway, and as we walked in, a woman came out the other door. Her bag ripped open and her groceries tumbled out. Shad bent down to help her. I was impatient, there was a kind of cookie I wanted, but I stuck with Shad, watching him help the lady but not helping her myself. Then Shad gave me this look. So I sighed, bent down, and helped her, too. We finally got inside the store, and when I reached for the cookies, Shad said, "You know that helping that woman was the right thing to do."

I groaned. "Yeah, I know."

"How do you know?"

We'd been over this so many times. "Because it was more work for me, that's how."

Shad nodded. "Most times, doing the right thing means more work for you. Even so, you still gotta do what's right."

I dropped the cookies into the shopping cart. "Is there ever a time when doing the right thing means less work?"

"It's possible, I guess." He'd smiled at me. "Bet you'd like that better, huh?"

No joke. I drove past the Uptown, u-turned, and parked near the fire station, figuring the best angle of attack to get Chuck Gemelli talking about Draper Kane.

A line of people snaked down the block, while workmen in white overalls rode a cherry picker to the roof. Against the night sky, other white overalls played with what looked like a satellite dish. Longstreet stood by the entrance, a smoking cigarette cupped in his hand, watching them work. Five D.C. cops walked to him.

He said a few words, nodded them inside, then approached me. "Willis." We shook hands. "Got any leads?"

"It's been a long, frustrating day. What's with the cops?"

"Extra security, ordered by Roger Franklin Quell."

"Where's the Elephant?"

"Inside, like a kid on Christmas Day."

"And Santa would be?"

He look surprised. "Quell, I guess. He's bringin' Brooks and Stoddard as presents." He took a last drag and flicked the butt into the street. "Wouldn't mind findin' Sondra Stoddard in my stockin'. Let's go."

The Uptown was a movie palace, one of those 1930's places just made for films like *Gone With the Wind* and *The Adventures of Robin Hood*. Now the Uptown had maybe the last big-screen in Washington. Everything else was mondo-plexes, movie houses with fourteen screens the size of postage stamps. I rubbed my arms. It felt almost as chilly inside as out. "They saving money on their heating bill?" I asked.

"Furnace's broken. They'll fix it before the premiere."

Great. Digitally encrypted movies and no heat. Soundmen with headphones and cables scurried back and forth, clipping yet another microphone to the growing hornet's nest on the podium, set front and center. Longstreet and I passed the first three rows of seats, reserved for print and radio journalists. The rest of the seating was for the crowd outside.

The techies were quiet as they went about their business. Bright lights from video cameras flipped on and off at random, casting giant shadows onto the screen.

Phone to ear, Gemelli saw us. He brushed past me, head down. I started to follow, when Longstreet put a hand on my shoulder.

"Hold up, cuz. This was your big chance today. You were gonna help us target the right gang. Remember?"

"I didn't get as far as I wanted. Talked to a guy named Tuckerman."

"Who's he?"

"A local gang member."

"Jesus, that's it?" He waited a beat, then shook his head. "Okay. Take a look around. Enjoy, 'cause it's probably your last night on this gig. Make sure you're back when Quell starts the ball rollin'."

I started up the aisle, trying to catch Gemelli. Then the doors opened and people flooded in. I felt like a salmon. Finally, I made it past the concession stand. Gemelli stood outside the glass doors, red-faced and shouting at Draper Kane, who was shouting back. I was too far away to hear them. By the time I reached the doors, Kane had taken off. The Elephant didn't see me, he brushed past as I held the door. I followed him into the theater. The Elephant kept quiet. "What were you arguing about?"

He shot me a look, and for a moment the mask dropped away. Whatever Draper Kane had said, he'd hit a nerve. Then Gemelli veered away from me, saying, "My son." He said it as though the notion of having a son was ridiculous.

I veered with him. "What about him?"

Gemelli stopped. "You are not here to investigate *me*."

"Part of my job is to ask questions. Sometimes they're personal. That's the way I have to operate if I'm going to help you."

"So long as they're not questions aimed at *me*. Kane is not involved."

"Maybe he should be. Maybe he could help you."

Gemelli snorted. "No way."

"Because of the business you and Kane had? Did the business fold because your son left?"

Gemelli picked a nonexistent piece of lint from his lapel. "I've got a question for you." He glanced up at me, his mask back in place, his blue eyes as soft as a hunk of concrete. "Now that you're officially fired. How do you expect to adopt a child with no job?"

CHAPTER 24

Chuck Gemelli smiled and walked away. Longstreet must've told him about Sarah. I ground my teeth together. Gemelli had just screwed me. He'd enjoyed doing it. And there was nothing I could do, except damage control. I'd have to ask Lilly to help me trace Rush. Destroying the blackmail photos was now my best bet.

I kicked open the door to the men's room, washed my hands with hot water to take away the chill, then gave the door a vicious shove. It hit something. A man's voice swore. I pushed the door more slowly, and saw him on the ground. "Sorry," I said, offering a hand up.

He slapped my hand away. When he stood, he was more than a foot shorter than me. He clenched his fists and tucked his chin and glared at me from the tops of his eyes. I think that was supposed to scare me. "You know who am I?"

Sure, I thought, the jockey who poses for those cute little lawn ornaments. "You're Corbin Brooks."

He bunched his jaw muscles and shoved past me into the men's room. Ahead, people jammed into theater seats, TV lights burned, and a tall man stood behind the podium, smiling and talking to a woman with hair so red, it looked to be on fire. The tall man nodded, then snapped his phone shut as he leaned in toward the redhead. His words, "They're ready in L.A.," carried over the nest of microphones.

The redhead wore a backless silver dress—it looked like a liquid mirror that had poured over her body and hardened. The dress wasn't any longer than it had to be. Amazing legs, ending in stiletto heels. I liked watching her move. But up close, it seemed her every movement was somehow choreographed. For her, this was just another gig, nothing more, like a carpenter driving a nail.

The cops let the media guys and gals stampede to the front, where they started snapping pictures of the tall man, Roger Franklin Quell, and the redhead, Sondra Stoddard.

Quell shot his cuff, checked his watch. Not every day you see an Osama bin Laden wristwatch. Quell leaned into the microphones, saying, "We're going to start as soon as we have *both* of our stars up here."

A wave of excitement rippled through the crowd. They started clapping again, louder than before. The audience held groups of black kids in baggy clothes, white Rasta boys with their hair in knit caps, kids in army fatigues that made me think of the Dragons. Near the front center sat a neat-looking man. Jacket and tie, presentable, his shaved head reflecting the video lights.

I turned and there was Brooks. He went past, his eyes scraping me with a hostile look. Then he grabbed Stoddard and kissed her. A bit aggressively, I thought, but the crowd loved it, everyone clapped.

Well, nearly everyone. The guy with the sweaty shaved head just smiled. A small, private smile. That bothered me. Brooks and Stoddard held hands and went to Quell's podium. I inched toward them, about four feet from the podium and two feet from the first row of chairs. Quell introduced himself as the director of *Explosive Rounds*. "The scenes we're showing will be a landmark in digital encryption technology—you'll all be part of history here tonight." Quell chuckled. "But before we begin, I'd like to introduce the stars of Sunday's premiere, Sondra Stoddard"—his words were nearly drowned out by shouting male voices—"and, back in his hometown, Corbin Brooks!"

Everyone stood and cheered. Sondra Stoddard moved to my left and struck a pose that would give a heart attack to a moose. Three rows back, a group of high school boys began whistling and stamping their feet. You could see the hormone cloud above them. But I wasn't looking at them, I was watching the guy with the shaved head. How could he be sweating in this icebox? I inched toward him, trying to time it just right. His right hand reached inside his jacket. When he stood, I moved. I grabbed his hand, pinned it to his chest through the fabric of his jacket—so whatever he had *stayed* in his jacket. He tried to twist away. I drove my knee into his stomach. His breath *whooshed* out, he bent over in profile, and I punched his nose straight across his face. I felt the nose break, then put my foot behind him and my hand beneath his chin and flipped him backward and down. He stayed there.

I bent down, carefully slid his limp hand out of his jacket, then pried the 9mm Smith & Wesson from his hand. For a second, the theater was completely silent. Brooks stood staring. Stoddard had her mouth open. Then the crowd erupted in applause, louder than before. I thought about clasping my hands above my head but settled for a steely nod. Class all the way.

The cops picked the guy up and carried him out of the theater. Quell settled the audience down as Brooks came between me and Stoddard, flexing his muscles and looking disappointed he hadn't had a chance to show how tough he was. Through clenched teeth he told me, "Keep your distance."

Stoddard's eyes flashed at me. I'd read about people's eyes flashing, but I'd never seen it before. Must've taken eye-flashing lessons in L.A.

She undulated toward me, linked her arm with mine, and came down so hard on my foot with her stiletto heel that tears sprang into my eyes. Smiling, she put her lips to my ear. "You cocksucking show stealer," she hissed. "Are you even *in* this movie?"

CHAPTER 25

My foot was throbbing, I could barely make it to my car. Somehow I heaved myself into the driver's seat. Was I even in this movie? And if so, who did I have to screw to get out of it?

I looked out the windshield at the Connecticut Avenue traffic, thinking about Gemelli and Kane screaming at each other. Anything that could change Gemelli's mask of a face was bound to be interesting. But what had they argued about? What was so important that Kane would confront Gemelli publicly? Was it Gemelli cutting off Kane's main source of income? Finding something juicy could buy me another day at MPAC, which might be enough time to stop Rush from doing something I'd regret. Kane's office files were worth a look.

I called him on the way, got his voice mail. At Sixteenth, I pulled over and looked up. Kane's office lights were dead. I'd seen a cot there, like the one I have in my office. Kind of made us brothers, in a way. I hoped he wasn't already asleep, I'd hate to disturb him.

The locks on the plate-glass doors out front were a colossal pain, but the loading dock was a breeze. Upstairs, I knocked on Kane's office door, just to cover my bases. Nothing. I got out my picking tools. Whenever I open locks, I think about Eddie Vermeer. As kids, when we found a likely spot, we played Pop That Lock.

First, we'd take turns inspecting the lock. Then Eddie would step back with his hand on his chin and say, "I can pop that lock in forty seconds." He'd give me this look, smiling and full of confidence. If he'd lived, he would've made the FBI's Most Wanted. Eddie was also my teacher, so when I said I could pop that lock in thirty-five seconds, he grinned a little wider. "Thirty," he said. I took a step back, as though carefully weighing what we both knew I would say next.

"Twenty-five."

Eddie made a sweeping "After you" gesture. "Pop that lock."

I could hear his voice now as I finished Kane's office door. I went through it in less than a minute. Rusty. I locked the door behind me, then beamed my flashlight at Kane's outer office— empty except for dust motes the size of bees. I smelled tobacco, plus something else. My Ruger 9 mm jumped into my hand. Outside, the rain started and tires hissed on wet pavement. The reception monitor was dark. I wondered if the dark-eyed woman was relaxing at home. What time was it in India? I opened the door to his inner office more slowly than the first, standing to the left of the doorjamb. No volley of bullets. Excellent. I realized I'd been holding my breath, and exhaled. I put my arm inside.

Once I'd flipped the lights, I peered around the corner. The ironing board was still up. The iron was cold. So was Kane.

He sat behind the desk. He seemed to stare right at me. I pocketed the Ruger, and felt his carotid artery. Nothing. A small-caliber entry wound at the base of his skull. No shell casings. His desk was unlocked. I went through his files, statements, charge slips. It confirmed only what I already knew—that MPAC accounted for 95 percent of Kane's money, until seven or eight months ago. Time to split, Gidney.

I'd just finished wiping my prints off the surfaces when I heard them—in the hallway, unlocking Kane's door. I ran to the window. Two patrol cars were waiting out front. More cops hustled into the building.

A perfect setup, and I had walked right into it.

PART TWO

CHAPTER 26

When the cops burst into Kane's office, I had my hands in the air. The male cop drew his Glock.

"I've got a gun in my left coat pocket," I said.

The woman cop snapped on rubber gloves and bagged my gun carefully, all the while giving me a hostile look. Cops don't like PIs, especially when they carry guns. It's illegal in the District, but even if it weren't, they still wouldn't like it.

The woman cop asked where the body was and if I'd touched anything. I pointed to the next room. She told me to sit in one of the waiting room chairs. While she took a look in Kane's office, her male partner tried to question me. A moment later, the woman, who looked to have a few years on him, returned and told him to shut up and wait for the 'tecs.

D.C. has a centralized homicide unit, so there are about forty-five to fifty detectives at any given time, investigating murders city-wide. I knew a lot of them, was friendly with a few, but there was only one I had a real problem with.

Naturally, that's the one who showed up.

Al Marziak was frowning when he walked through the door

to Kane's office. The female patrol officer said, "Hey, Detective, how we doin'?"

He didn't look at her. "You want the truth or a lie you can live with?" Then he saw me. "Well, well."

"Nice to see you too, Al," I said.

He stood there for a moment, looking me up and down. He was about my height, slim, black-haired, with a solid black eyebrow that ran across his forehead. Back at the Police Academy, he'd been nicknamed "the Unibrower." He took out his little notebook and shook his head. "Shame about the gun. You should know better."

"It's licensed in Virginia. So am I, I do a lot of work for a company there."

"Show me paper." I fished out my gun permit. "I didn't think you did a lot of work for anybody," he said, reading the permit. He gave it back. "I see your tailor is still the Salvation Army."

"You're looking good too," I said. "How's business?"

"Booming. Heard you worked a case last year, charged the guy a dollar. Lemme ask you—you get audited, you think the IRS will end up owing you?"

"Could we just do the drill?"

"Suppose you tell me how you happened to be here."

"I'm working for a firm, and Kane was giving me some information."

"What firm?"

"MPAC," I said. "They're lobbyists for the film business. Kane gave me background information."

"At eleven o'clock at night?"

"No, this afternoon. Then tonight, I was driving up Ninth and saw his office lights on." I was glad I'd taken the time to wipe my prints off the light switches.

"You must be tight with the guy, stopping by so late."

"Met him for the first time today."

"What did you and Kane talk about?"

"Data encryption."

"Uh-huh. That's all?"

"That's all."

"Then you happened to see his lights on, came upstairs, and found him dead."

"Right."

He rubbed his square chin with his hand. I asked, "We finished here?"

"Not even started. You say you're working for MPAC? Punching a clock? I seem to remember you were against salaried jobs. They took too much—what? Integrity? Loyalty?"

We both knew he wasn't talking about MPAC; he was talking about our time together as cops. We graduated in the same class, Emil Haggler had recruited both of us. Marziak stayed. I didn't. I said, "The smart move is to recuse yourself."

"From this case?" That got a rare grin. "The fuck would I do that?"

"Because we know each other."

He shook his head, motioned me out to the hallway. Marziak had a little voice recorder, which he ID'd with the date and time. Then we went through it—all of it—again. "So you drop in on Kane this afternoon—what time?"

"About two o'clock."

"Exactly what time?"

"Exactly two o'clock."

"Okay. You and Kane have a heart-to-heart about"—and here he checked his notebook—"data encryption, then eight hours later he's dead." He stopped writing and looked up. "See, it's the timing—you meet a guy this afternoon, now he's dead. Even you might've learned enough from the Academy to see why that would trouble me. The second thing, you're driving by and see Kane's lights on. Another coincidence."

"They happen."

"Not on *my* cases." He leaned against the wall. Totally relaxed, enjoying himself. "Let's start all over. I got all night."

CHAPTER 27

It was almost dawn before Marziak let me go home. Lilly had spent the night at her place. Given my frame of mind and body, that was probably a good thing. I stripped off my clothes and took a shower, hoping it would wash away everything—the dirt, the talk with Marziak, my own existence—as though the showerhead were a chrome god with the power to obliterate me. But it didn't. It never does.

I'd limped into bed—my foot had turned purple from Stoddard's heel—and had just pulled up the covers when the phone rang. "Damn, boy, you still asleep?"

"Detective Haggler." I yawned.

"Captain wants to see you. Your office, thirty minutes."

So I got dressed and, not for the first time, thought about the basic design flaw of the human body—that you could store a sleep deficit but not a surplus. I skimmed the *Post* as I slammed down breakfast. I almost missed the four lines on page three of the "Metro" section about a gang member who'd been shot the night before near Palmer Park. His name was Tuckerman, the gangbanger with the tattoos on his chest.

I'd just parked my bulk behind my desk when Haggler held the office door, so that Frank Heinrick could limp in on two metal canes. He was fighting a rare lymphoma. Right then, it was winning. A caffeinated snail could've beaten him to the client chair. I wondered how long ago they'd entered the building. Maybe Haggler had phoned my apartment from the lobby.

Finally, they were both seated. Heinrick took a breath, then regarded my office with mock admiration. "Lieutenant, we're in the wrong business."

"How's the chemo?" I asked.

"Peachy. I'm getting gift certificates for my friends. Are you busy just now?" He seemed concerned. "I hope you don't mind Emil and me dropping in like this."

"Why I have the office, so you guys could hang out." Actually, I had expected this visit. Heinrick was still the acting captain, but Haggler was taking on more of his duties. Which meant Haggler would be grooming Al Marziak.

"Where you working these days?" Haggler asked.

"MPAC."

"Yeah." Haggler took out a spiral notebook. "A lobbying group, run by Chuck Gemelli. Your boss had a business relationship with the decedent." He looked up at me. "That means 'dead guy.'"

"Marziak recorded my statement last night. This morning, actually." I looked from one to the other. "You're telling me to go through it all again?"

Heinrick looked at Haggler, and something unspoken passed between them. Haggler said, "If you want to."

If I want to. Interrogation as therapy. I leaned back in my chair and told them everything—almost. When I finished, Heinrick handed me a plastic bag with a gun in it—my Ruger—and said, "You like it at MPAC?"

I unloaded the Ruger and put it in my desk. "Just like Willie Sutton liked banks."

Heinrick nodded. "Sure, the adoption. That takes money. Kid's name is Sarah, right?" Heinrick had a facility for names. I found myself wishing he were my caseworker. "How's that going?"

"Fine. Thanks for asking."

"Tell us about Chuck Gemelli. We know Gemelli and Kane had a shouting match last night at the Uptown. You were there."

"I saw them argue, but I didn't hear what they were talking about." Which was true. It was after their shouting match that Chuck Gemelli had told me they'd argued about his son.

"And after? You were with Chuck Gemelli the whole time?"

"No, I left before they finished their test." I was lucky I could even hobble out of there. Again, I told the truth but not the whole truth—I'd lost sight of Chuck Gemelli before Quell addressed the crowd. Which meant that I didn't really know where either of the Gemellis had been when Kane got capped. Haggler and Heinrick glanced at each other.

Haggler said, "The Kane shooting—that have anything to do with your two little Vietnamese buddies, the ones who tried to break into your place?"

"How could it?"

"Well, think about it—two nights ago some shitbirds try to whack you, then yesterday afternoon you meet with Kane, and last night you find him dead in his office. You're telling me that's a coincidence?"

"I don't see how they're related." But he was right, of course. It was the timing. Just like Tuckerman getting whacked the day after I spoke to him. Probably best not to mention that.

Heinrick shot a quick look at Haggler. There it was again, something going on between them. I thought in another minute they'd start giggling. I said, "Anything else?"

"Oh, you mean about Kane." Heinrick spoke with elaborate innocence. "That's not why we're here."

I looked at them. "Excuse me?"

CHAPTER 28

Haggler said, "Someone wanted to find you, and we're public servants, right? We're just helping, making sure he gets to your office okay." He shot another quick look at Heinrick, then back to me. "That's some lady, Willis."

Before I could answer, my office door slammed open and Corbin Brooks stormed in, all five feet six of him. He brandished a rolled-up newspaper in his hand. "Get up."

I leaned back in my swivel chair. "Good morning, Mr. Brooks."

He came around my desk and leaned over me. Anger made deep lines across his face, and his breath came in short bursts. It felt unreal, like he was playing a scene. He had a kind of actor-ish quality—as though he were outside himself, watching. He jabbed me in the chest with the end of the newspaper, his eyes on me but aware of his audience. "I told you to keep away."

"From Ms. Stoddard? I have."

"Then explain this." He shoved the paper in my face. Page three of the "Style" section, a photo of Stoddard and me. It was the moment after Stoddard had harpooned my foot. She was smiling and I had tears in my eyes. Beneath the photo was some fluff about a local investigator—me—totally smitten by sexy Sondra Stoddard.

I said, "Nothing happened."

Brooks said, "Get up."

Haggler and Heinrick were grinning. I said, "I'm sure we can talk about this." Then Brooks grabbed my shirt. Was he going to yank me to my feet? Unlikely. So I obliged him and stood. He swung me around, slamming my back against the wall. "You," he said, "stay away from my wife, understand? She doesn't have time to waste on a . . . on a—"

"On a two-bit hawkshaw?"

"On a scumbag, a lousy scumbag like you," he said, pushing me again. Usually when someone pushes me, I push back. Harder. But I had two of D.C.'s finest as witnesses. They were enjoying this.

I backed away from Brooks, my palms up between us. "Hey, sorry. Still, I bet this happens to you all the time."

Brooks screwed up his face. "*What?*"

"Well, she's that kind of woman." He gave me this look of disgust—and something else. For a moment, his whole actor shtick just fell away, he was real—in a way he hadn't been a second before. Maybe he was actually concerned about her. Was that why this angry little guy was trying to push me around, warn me off in front of the cops? So I decided to push *him*. How far he would go?

Brooks stuck his finger in my face. "We're in town til Sunday. You so much as walk on her side of the street, you're going to jail. Got it?"

"Wow, you sound just like Burt Lancaster," I said. He glared at me, nodded at Haggler and Heinrick, then stormed out. I shrugged. "Maybe he doesn't like Lancaster."

Haggler said, "Hell, I thought everyone liked him."

Heinrick clapped his hands together. "Well, that was entertaining." He gripped his canes and got to his feet.

"Glad to be a source of amusement for you," I said.

"They say laughter is the best medicine." He hobbled to the door, then turned. "By the way, your story's on par with that guy's acting. But I'm cutting you a little slack. Until your story checks out or I pull your license."

"Why are you so good to me?"

He grinned at me, his face a death mask. "You earned it. This is the most fun I've had since hitting a dog on my way to work."

CHAPTER 29

The year before, I'd wanted to kill Heinrick with my bare hands. I'd found Sarah, and he took her away from me. Then Heinrick turned her over to the DCAS. I'd hated him for that. Now I almost thought he might have—just possibly—been right. Maybe it was part of living the straight life, you know? If you find a kid, you go through channels to adopt her. You don't keep her illegally, right?

I locked up and took my car across town. Chet Baker's version of "Dolphin Dance" came out the speakers. I'd been fired from the only job I had, two Vietnamese kids were trying to kill me, and a lava flow of legal bills was ready to smother me. Plus Brooks and Stoddard. Despite all of that, I felt good. Go figure.

When I walked into D.C. Adoptive Services, the rent-a-cops nodded hi. Why not? They'd seen me the day before yesterday, just as they'd seen me most every day for months now. I made my way to the dayroom, figuring I'd check in with Eunice before playing with Sarah. But now a nurse I had never seen before blocked my way with a suspicious look.

I smiled at her. "Hi there. I'd like to see Nurse Edgerton, please."

She didn't smile back. "Nurse Edgerton no longer works here."

"Well, maybe you could double-check. Her first name is Eunice."

Her suspicion grew a bit hostile. "Yes, I know. Nurse Eunice Edgerton. You are asking me if she is here and I am telling you she no longer works here."

I didn't say that Eunice was my friend there, that she was the person who bent the rules so that I could play with Sarah, that she was my unindicted coconspirator in keeping this child safe and happy while she was in D.C.'s baby prison. And now Eunice was gone? "She was here two days ago."

"Sir, I understand that. I am telling you she is no longer working here."

I glanced at her nameplate. "Well, Nurse Belt, can you tell me where she is now?"

"I really have no idea, *sir.*"

My skin started itching. The only line of contact with Sarah that I had was gone, missing in action. Probably someone had seen Eunice doing her job with care and attention, so she'd been transferred.

"Well, then." I notched up my smile to pure sunshine. "I'm here to visit Sarah."

Her brow wrinkled at me. "We have no one here by that name."

I looked through the window behind her. I could see Sarah crying in her crib.

"That's her." I was smiling and showing my teeth, fighting to keep my voice steady. "The kid crying her eyes out. If you'll just turn around, you can see her." Nurse Belt hesitated, then turned. I said, "In the pink T-shirt, see?"

She turned back, checked a piece of paper. "I have that child down as Baby Doe."

I took a deep breath. "Yes, that's right, Baby Doe. I'd like to see her."

"Are you a relative?"

"Well, no, but I saved this child's—"

"Only relatives are permitted in the children's quarters—"

"—life, so even if I'm not related to her—"

"—so you'll have to leave."

I paused and took a deep breath. "May I see the shift supervisor?"

She raised her chin, the lenses of her glasses reflecting the light, as though she were a rule-quoting automaton. Which I guess she was. "I *am* the shift supervisor. Now, do I call security?"

That's what I wanted, to fight the bastards. But this was about Sarah, so I turned around and went outside, telling myself to stay calm. I phoned Adoptive Services main number, then a recorded voice told me my call was important to them, and I heard the Carpenters sing "Close to You" for a few hours. Finally, someone answered. They told me Eunice had been transferred to Silver Hill. The Records Department.

"In Records? Are you sure? She's a nurse."

"This is the information I have. Would you like the number there?"

I got the number and the address too. Eunice had been relocated to Silver Hill. This was across the river from the federal government, and close to Congress Heights, where Shadrack Davies had been born. Congress Heights was now perhaps the poorest neighborhood in D.C. and, along with Anacostia, accounts for a disproportionately high number of the District's homicides. Shad used to take me there to visit his parents, who lived in a small clapboard house on Highview Place SE, just off MLK Avenue.

I remember Shad's parents had a bird feeder. Once Shad asked me to help him fill it. I was nine, I think. He took me to a shed and found a bag of seed, then I held the bird feeder steady while he poured.

I looked into the bag of seed, then stuck my hands into it, feeling the coolness of the seeds and the spaces between them and moving my hands through as though it were treasure. I was enjoying myself. Then I stopped, panicked that I'd let myself go. I turned quickly, a defensive move, afraid Shad might hit me for taking too long. But he was smiling, sitting beside me and watching me and smiling.

Once Shad died, his family wanted nothing to do with me. Sometimes, when I've got nothing better to do, I wonder if they cut me off because I was a white kid—or because Shad lost his life saving mine? I kind of hoped it was the second reason, but I wouldn't have blamed them either way.

The Silver Hill facility was huge, a grandiose expanse of windowless concrete, a burial place for archived records. Deep inside, I found Eunice pushing a wire cart stuffed with manila folders down an endless hallway. I caught up with her. "What happened? What are you doing here?"

She stopped the cart, eyes downcast. "What do you think? I'm a nurse, right?" Emotion choked her voice, making her Jamaican accent thicker. She picked up a sheaf of folders. "These're my patients now, okay?" She threw the folders back in the cart and pushed away from me.

I shook my head, then caught up with her again. "Why aren't you downtown?" I jammed my foot in front of the wheels. "Will you stop with the damn cart? Tell me what's going on."

"Your caseworker, Walters. Someone told her about you visiting the baby. Next thing I know, I'm transferred out." Her forehead wrinkled. "I got three years 'til retirement, I got no more patients, no more kids. Just this." She began to cry.

I stepped around the cart and hugged her. "I'm sorry, Eunice. It's my fault."

She sighed, then pulled away and dried her eyes. "No, it ain't, dear. We both know that. But now things is different." She spoke to me kindly, like a parent to a young child. "They're not gonna let you in there, not on your own, not anymore. You can still see Sarah. But now you gotta have your DCAS-appointed caseworker with you at all times."

"But my caseworker is—"

"Right." She drew the word out, giving it a sardonic edge. "So's the baby won't come to no harm, see? Walters gonna protect the baby from you."

"That's just wonderful."

"Yeah," she said, touching my cheek. "Only, I wonder who they'll get to protect you from Walters?"

CHAPTER 30

Imagine you've had no sleep, the cops have interrogated you twice, you've been pushed around by a major motion picture star, and you've caused one of your best friends to lose her job. It was only 10:30 A.M., but I was ready for the day to end. That kind of morning, you need to pick out something you *know* you can do, then do it.

Usually I'm an expert at napping. But today? It wasn't going to happen. Too many crowding images—Rush blackmailing me, Longstreet asking me questions I couldn't answer, Kane and the Elephant screaming at each other, and to top it off, the Elephant firing me. Thirty minutes of tossing and turning in bed was all I could take. I was never so glad to hear the phone ring.

"Willis, love, is that you?"

"Is this the BBC home service?"

Jones St. Pierre laughed. "No, just a terribly well-paid partner from McClure Downing. I've asked about film pirates and come up dry—locally, that is." She paused. "A local gang making illegal dupes for profit. Are you quite certain of this?"

"Are you kidding? I'm not sure if I'm on my home planet."

"Assuming you have one. I'll keep looking, but I do think I'd have heard by now."

Then the phone rang again. "Howdy, Willis."

"Ex-agent Longstreet. What can I do for you?"

"You can get your ass to work."

"Gemelli fired me last night."

"And rehired you this mornin', after I straightened him out."

"Just how did you do that? And why?"

"The why's easy—You got the stuff. Local news kept showin' the tape of you takin' down that guy with the gun. Good PR for Gemelli. What was that, karate?"

"Aikido."

"Whatever. Gemelli'd look like an asshole, firin' the guy that kept Brooks from gettin' shot. But don't make *me* look like an asshole—get some leads."

"I'll keep on it."

I got off the bed and onto the Net. With more energy than I thought I had, I started digging through Kane's name and EncryptU.com. A variety of searches and a few 404 errors later, I verified what Kane had said yesterday: when Rush left EncryptU.com, its stock price crashed. The discussion threads ran for pages and pages, but I got the gist. Apparently Kane wasn't the only one who knew that Rush was the programming talent behind EncryptU.com. But I found nothing to show motive, no hint of a reason for Rush to kill Draper Kane.

I decided to try Rush one more time, and found I had inadvertently memorized his number. How sad was that? Still, talking to him would've been nice, if only to quiz him about the Kane killing. And even if he didn't answer, I felt I was developing a fine rapport with his voice mail. Then Stayne called.

"A question, my boy—when you filled out your initial form for DCAS, to adopt this kid—"

"Sarah."

"Right, Sarah. Were you still married?"

"No. I mean yes. Hell, I don't know, I think we were separated. Karla had started the divorce proceedings, but we were still legally hitched."

"And the divorce was finalized?"

"About eight months ago."

"Well, you see, as far as the folks at DCAS are concerned, you're still married. You listed your ex on the form."

"Christ."

"It gets better. Walters wants to meet her."

"Forget that."

"I'm just telling you what Walters's boss told me."

"Did he enjoy Alice?"

"Not enough to overlook this. And your chances of adopting this girl as a single parent are the same as me winning the Kentucky Derby. So if your ex—Karla?—doesn't show, you have two options. You can bring someone and tell 'em it's her."

"No."

"Or you can get married."

"For real?"

"Oh, probably a tissue-paper bride would be fine. Of course for real. Is there anyone? How about the bag lady?"

"I'll think about it."

"My office still has hot and cold running Hooter girls."

"Don't remind me. Anything else?"

"You've got a great lawyer, that's the anything else."

I put on Tommy Flannagan's *The Cats,* Flannagan and Coltrane trading fours while I made lunch. Then I heard Lilly's soft step on the stairs. She keyed the lock, then there was the pause while she placed the keys back in her carryall. Lilly wasn't one to misplace things. I smiled at this as the door swung open.

"You're home," she said, tossing the *Post* on the table. She'd opened it to the photo of Stoddard and me. "I figured you'd be out on the town with Sondra fuck face."

CHAPTER 31

I pulled Lilly down so she sat on my lap. "Yeah, Sondra stopped by, she's in the can, trying on your clothes. Hope that's okay." I kissed the back of her neck.

She rested her head on my chest. I closed my eyes and took a deep breath and, for a tiny moment, everything was fine. Okay, my marriage had been a mistake. But maybe marriage wasn't all bad. Except that Lilly didn't want to get married. She'd told me so, repeatedly. But maybe if I asked her now, she would feel different. She kissed me, gently pushed me back, smiled after the tiniest hesitation. "What're you working on?"

"I'm researching Rush Gemelli." I showed her Rush's card.

"This the guy who's, like, paying you in cash? I hope you're getting it up front."

"Why?"

"He's a cheapie." She turned the card to me. "See the edges? They're microperfed, he printed them like a sheet of labels." She looked into my eyes. "You okay?"

"Sure. Exhausted from dealing with Sondra Stoddard and Corbin Brooks."

"Corby. We were models together when we were teens." Her fingertips massaged the back of my neck. "That lawyer—he's expensive?"

"He's not cheap."

"I've got, like, five thousand saved up."

Five thousand. This from a woman who didn't even like

babies. Her generosity, her caring, felt warm and solid. Since the day that Shad and Eddie both died, I'd had to look out for myself. Now Lilly had stirred an echo, a feeling, some type of lost sensation rushing back. "You're a frugal genius," I said.

She sat back so she could look in my eyes. "If it'd help you stay out of warehouses . . ."

I held up my right hand in the Boy Scout's promise. "No more warehouses. Besides, you need that money for your business."

"Why not take it, like a loan. You can pay me back whenever."

I touched her hand. "You keep it for now, okay? How'd your meeting go?"

She moved away, just an inch or so. "I should've known better. I'm writing software, so why do they need to *meet* me? Then, when I walk in there, they all give me the look."

"'The look'?"

Now she shifted so she was sitting beside me, her brow wrinkled. "Yeah, you know. The Look. The ritual eye fuck. I walk in, and like twenty eyes scan my whole body from head to toe."

"Did your antipheromone spray help?"

"Sent nine of them across the room right away." She should've sounded happy about that.

I said, "So things worked out."

Her face began to pucker. "Except for the last guy."

"'The last guy'?"

"The CEO, he runs the company." Her eyes welled up and tears spilled down her face.

I put my hand on her shoulder. "It's okay, Lilly."

She shook her head, her face red and pinched up like a little girl's. "You don't get it. The CEO, he offered me a job."

"That isn't what you wanted?"

She faced me, tears hanging from the underside of her chin. "Not on salary. Not in their office every day. A freelance consulting job, Willis. That's what"—and here the sobs choked her off for a moment—"that's what the meeting was supposed to be about."

I tried to put my arm around her, but she stood up and moved away. I said, "They're not—"

"I know, they're not, like, rejecting me. That should make me feel better. But it doesn't right now." She took a deep breath, calming herself. "There's something else I wanted to ask you."

This guy, whoever he was, had really upset her. "You want me to get the CEO's address? I'd be happy to torch his car."

She was still torn up, but she smiled. Then she stepped forward and took my hands in hers. "Willis?" she said, leaning close and through the tears looking lovely.

"Yes?" I wondered how on earth I could broach the idea of marriage.

"You wanna get married?"

Christ, it freaked me out when she did that. I sat away from her. "What for?"

"Well, don't you think it would, like, help things? With Sarah?"

"You're proposing?"

"Well, c'mon. Together we make a decent income. Sarah'd have two parents. Isn't that what DCAS wants?"

A woman tells you she doesn't like babies, then offers her entire savings for lawyer's fees. She tells you she doesn't want to get hitched, then proposes. And so skillfully, without saying those three words. But I guess we'd both had a lot of practice.

Now, as I looked in her eyes, I felt something wash over me, overwhelming and a bit frightening. Yet, at the same time, I felt glad. And I guess right then I figured that Lilly deserved a lot better than what I'd had in mind—a quickie marriage to appease the likes of DCAS and Florence Walters. If we got hitched, I'd want it to be because of us—how we felt about each other. In my mind there was no confusion about how much I loved her.

Yet, at that moment, I was so wrapped up in my own feelings, I hadn't thought about hers. I'd been shaking my head while she was proposing. And for Lilly, my quick refusal meant only more rejection.

Ever wish life had a rewind button? I said, "I don't think that's a good idea," and as the words left my mouth, I saw I had made a huge mistake.

Her body tensed. The color drained from her face as she pushed away. "Didn't take you long to decide."

"Lilly—"

She grabbed her carryall, and threw open my door. "I gotta go."

I reached for her. "Wait, you don't—"

She dodged my fingers. "I know I don't. That's why I'm leaving."

She slammed the door. I could hear her footsteps as she hurried down the stairs. Outside, a car door opened and shut. I went to the window in time to see her silver VW peel away from the curb.

Matthews had said I needed to get married. And now the only person in the world I'd think about asking had just walked out on me.

Perfect.

CHAPTER 32

I made a cup of coffee. Pouring the water, measuring the grounds, going through the motions—trying not to think about Lilly and thinking only about Lilly. See how easy it was to screw up everything? I watched the coffee drip. Maybe it was karma. As a kid, I'd wrecked a *lot* of homes. Was this payback? Or was it the result of my repeating an old pattern? I'd go into a home, learn what I could, then cause a big-enough problem to get sent back. If that was my idea of home, I was in big trouble.

Maybe what I needed to do was stay away from people. Especially the ones who cared about me.

I enhanced the coffee with a slug of Wild Turkey, which made the coffee better. Everything tastes better with bourbon. A great motto. Send it to the Bourbon Institute. On my table was the last disc from the warehouse break-in. No harm in looking at it, right? Then Brooks and Stoddard popped up on my screen. I almost tossed my lunch over the fence and the disc in the trash, when it occurred to me that, just maybe, there was more here than met my bloodshot eye.

So I called SatNews and asked for Vince Carruthers, a TV editor who was also a Bockman's survivor. They told me he'd be in at three. The only other lead was the list of serial numbers I had copied from the tape decks at the warehouse. The Yellow Pages pointed to Loony Lenny's, which claimed to be the biggest JVC dealer in Washington.

I called and found that their buyer, Hester Doyle, would be in around 1:30. That left me two options—go see Florence Walters, or stay home and finish the Wild Turkey.

DCAS hadn't changed one molecule since the day before. I threaded a path through a maze of offices and corridors to find Florence Walters in her cubicle.

"Ms. Walters?"

She turned to see me. "Mr. Gidney." She hefted a stack of folders—same color as the folders Eunice had been filing—and began walking the way I had come. "I hope you'll excuse me if I continue working. I'm quite busy, as you can see."

"Sure. I wanted to talk to you about Sarah."

She came to a stop by a large copying machine. She opened the first folder and placed some pages in a hopper, then pressed a green button. The pages began chugging into the machine.

"Baby Doe, yes. What about her?"

Just then, the machine stopped chugging. A light came on, flashing *Document misfeed*. Walters frowned, the lines from her nose to her mouth cutting deep in her face. "Oh, not again." She slapped the pile of folders on the ground, then grunted as she thumbed the release button, which opened a panel at knee level.

"See, Ms. Walters, I went to see Sarah. I need you there when I visit her."

At this point, I was addressing Walters's rear end, as she had gone on all fours and was halfway into the copier. I wondered what would happen if I pressed the green button now. Probably make thousands of copies of Florence Walters. I shuddered.

She backed out. "There's no way to make this work."

"So I'm wondering, What would be a good time for you?"

She looked at me. "A good time?"

"To visit with Sarah."

She sighed, closing her eyes. "Mr. Gidney, do you have any idea how many children are in my charge?"

"No, but I've seen other caseworkers with prospective parents in the nursery. I mean, it *has* been done."

"Yes, because those caseworkers are more interested in playing with our children than in caring for them. Mr. Gidney, our department is not well. We're under a court order to improve, yet we have an infestation of slackers, of people who either cannot or will not do their jobs. Incompetents who bleed the system and give nothing in return." She drew herself up. "I am *not* one of them."

Of all the caseworkers in D.C., I had to get the one who actually cared about her job. "I applaud your commitment, Ms. Walters, and wish only that more caseworkers shared it."

She sniffed at me, then opened her daybook. "Well, if you *must* see Baby Doe, we can arrange a time, I'm sure."

"That's great. Thank you."

She leafed through a few pages. "Next Friday, two o'clock."

"Next—that's a week away. I thought we could see her today, this afternoon."

She had started shaking her head before I'd finished talking. I hate that. "That just isn't possible." She turned back to the copier.

I said, "I know what this is about."

Without looking at me, she said, "And what is that, Mr. Gidney?"

"You think I'd make a lousy parent."

Still fussing with her files, she said, "I think you make a very poor candidate for this girl."

"Well, you're wrong. I'm an ideal candidate." Well, maybe

not ideal. But who better to tend the needs of a child traumatized by the system than someone who's survived it? "I wish you could see that."

She stopped with the files, looked at me. "Do you really? Wish I could see for myself?"

I didn't like the way she asked me that, or know exactly what she meant. My only choice was to say, "Of course."

"Then perhaps I will," she said. Then she smiled at me. It was the first time I had seen her smile. It wasn't what I would call comforting.

CHAPTER 33

On the street by my office a big trailer took up five parking spaces, its motor grumbling. I had to park a block over, near the American Art Museum. Walking past the vaquero sculpture, I noticed for the first time that the blue horse's eyes were wide with panic.

When I drew even with the trailer, its door slammed open like a pistol crack. A woman clutching a plastic tackle box shot past me and up the steps. Since the only other occupant on the second floor was a credit dentist, I figured she must've had a molar emergency.

I was wrong. Upstairs, five people clustered outside my office door. A different woman held the tackle box in her hands, opening the lid so the running woman could take out a brush and powder to apply the finishing touches on Sondra Stoddard.

When Stoddard saw me, she shooed the others away, then, as

an afterthought, snapped her fingers. A lit cigarette appeared in her hand. That made everything perfect. The entourage brushed past me in the narrow hallway. I walked past Stoddard, unlocked my office door. She took a long drag, dropped the butt, ground it under her red high-heeled shoe—I made a mental note to keep clear of her shoes—and brushed her hair from her face.

I stooped in front of her to pick up the butt, and the office mail. Without a word she followed me in, the shiny emerald green fabric of her pants whistling as her thighs came in contact. Her makeup was perfect. She scanned the office walls till she found what she was looking for—the mirror above the sink.

Some people steal looks at each mirror they pass, others linger because they like what they see and don't care who knows it. When Stoddard saw herself, her magazine-cover face twisted into a fleeting look of pure revulsion.

I turned so she wouldn't see that I had noticed. When I looked again, her expression was back to normal. She leaned against my desktop with her ankles crossed. She pushed out her chest. Saucy.

I took the mail behind my desk. The usual stuff—bills, a come-on in a brown envelope that looked like a check, a glossy catalog from Davidson's, which was having a fall sale on all 9 mms, "Big Savings Now!"

"What can I do for you, Ms. Stoddard?"

"I want to talk with you," she said.

"For that, you need a trailer? What happens when you eat lunch? Rent out a beauty parlor?"

She shrugged that off. "I'm waiting."

"For what?" I leafed through the Davidson's catalog. Lots of fancy firearms, laser-guided handguns, night-vision gear. Nothing to stop an actress.

"For what you did last night, at the movie house. Stunts. Cheap theatrics. You think I'm some kind of circus performer?"

"I don't think about you at all." My foot was throbbing.

"Then you need to. Gemelli told me you had to." She smiled as she said his name, as though she liked saying it. "He said you worked for him, so when I'm in town, you work for me."

"He was wrong. And your husband wouldn't like it."

"Who cares about him?"

"I do. I'm scared of him. I'm afraid I'll trip over him and break something."

She laughed, but stopped when I got up. "Time for more acts of bravado?" At the door, she caught up with me, put her arm through mine. "Then you can drop me. I'm at the Hay-Adams."

It was a few blocks away. I shook my head. "An honor."

We rode in uncompanionable silence down the elevator, but as soon as I started my car, she started talking. About herself. Going west on F Street, she sketched the details of her life. As though I were interviewing her for *People*. "I was the always the youngest, like in drama class. Even back in third grade, they saw I had talent."

Her trailer lumbered behind us. Maybe she'd smear her lipstick and we'd have to pull over. Three car lengths behind the trailer, I picked up an accordion-bumpered Acura.

"Then my agent got me an audition for a TV spot, for a regional bakery."

Four people in the Acura. Its engine roared as it closed the gap, cutting off the trailer. Now it pulled even. Vietnamese guys looking over at us with decidedly unfriendly expressions.

"There were maybe a hundred kids trying out," she said.

The front passenger—Ph'uck—lifted something. It looked like a rocket-propelled grenade.

"Jesus Christ," I said.

"Yeah, can you imagine? But they picked *me* to do the spot."

I hit the gas and cut over to Twelfth Street. If Stoddard noticed anything erratic about my driving, she didn't show it. She kept talking while the Acura sideswiped a Chevy. I hurtled down to G Street, switched to Fourteenth, hooked a left. Her trailer was gone, but the Acura was half a block behind. And gaining.

"Then, when I got to New York, I had to find an agent I could *really* trust, you know?"

The Hay-Adams was coming up fast. I had to keep a safe distance from the Dragons till I got rid of Stoddard. The Elephant might get angry if she got shot up in my car. I screeched into the Hay-Adams turnabout while reaching across Stoddard and flipping open her door. The doorman took a step toward us as I slammed on the brakes. She was still talking—I think she was a teenager in summer stock now—when I put my foot to her backside and shoved her out of the car. I hoped she would be okay. Her chances were better than staying in the car with me.

Stoddard curled into a roll that incorporated my shove with the motion of the car. Amazing. I mean, she could really move. For an instant I wondered where she'd learned to do that. Then I floored it, south on Fifteenth, shot past the Washington Monument, and angled left to Ohio drive so fast that my right wheels lifted off the ground. Ph'uck and his buddies were ten yards behind—and gaining.

CHAPTER 34

I couldn't believe it. A high-speed car chase? My car couldn't *do* high-speed. So I had to time this next part just right.

I flashed my left blinker, swerved over to the left lane, the Dragons right behind me, then I cut right across two lanes of angry drivers onto 395. The Dragons tried to follow—and instead hit the concrete divider. Behind me came squealing tires and breaking glass. I looked in the rearview, then smiled. After listening to Stoddard, I thought the Dragons' car crash sounded like music.

I grabbed the next exit, then headed back to D.C. There was street parking at Dupont Circle—so far my biggest accomplishment of the day.

Just how had Ph'uck the Magic Dragon got onto me? And how would I ditch him? With the Dragons after me, was Lilly safe? Or Sarah?

I needed to find Rush. Lilly had the technical chops to help me, but I'd managed to screw up everything. Part of me was just optimistic enough to hope I could make it up to her. But I still needed help, so I decided to call Jones St Pierre. Her office told me she was on a break. I had a hunch where she'd gone.

The east side of Dupont Circle has eight chess tables. Seven were deserted. A group of men stood around table six—the regulars, self-taught players who were nearly impossible to beat. Men in torn jackets, gimme caps, unbuttoned plaid shirts with dirty T-shirts underneath, and old blue jeans with holes at one or both knees. They had stopped their own games to watch Jones.

Her light brown eyes were clear as she looked across at her opponent, a white guy in a seven-hundred-dollar suit, gnawing his knuckle. With an almost dainty movement, she slid her knight and put his king in check. She smacked the chess clock, then saw me and winked.

The guy rubbed his chin, made a move.

"Oh dear," she said in her BBC announcer's voice. She slid her black bishop, then stood straight. "And that, as they say, is checkmate."

The regulars chuckled and fist-bumped each other while the loser gnawed his knuckles and frowned. Jones held out her hand, and the guy gave her five. Five dollars, that is. " 'Nother?" he asked.

She got up, slid her purse on her shoulder and her arm through mine. The regulars waved good-bye. She blew them a kiss. I said, "You ever let anyone win?"

"Never," she said. "And most particularly not that motherfucker. He's a tobacco lobbyist." It shocked me to hear her swear in that cultured voice of hers. "So, what brings you here?" She steered me toward her office.

I said, "I need some information."

"You didn't come by just to get your ass kicked?"

"I'm not that good at chess."

"Who said anything about chess?" We took the elevator to her office and she went behind the desk, all business. "What did you have in mind, love?"

"A client pulled a disappearing act on me."

She nodded, turned in her swivel chair to face her computer. "Name?"

"Rush Gemelli. Rushmore, I guess. I don't have his Social."

"The Elephant's son, I gather. And we're tracing him because . . ."

"He has something I want." I sat on the edge of the desk to better see her monitor. "So where're you looking?"

"You know . . . national DMV records, Equifax, Merlin, Nexus. Direct-mail and subscription lists, phone company . . . the usual." She hit the return key and sat back. "It's searching. We are too, by the way, for another good investigator." She grinned at me. "If you happen to know any."

"If anyone asks, I'll mention it."

"What about you?"

"I don't think so."

Her voice was a singsong parody of politeness. "Is it the work space, love? Too nice for you?" She sat up, as though struck by an idea. "We could bring in an art director, there's a leaky spot down by the boiler room—we could degrade it a bit for your office."

"Jones, you're sweet. But it wouldn't work out."

"Of course, the loner." She shook her head, braids dangling by amused eyes.

I shrugged. "Maybe you've got something."

"And you've got nothing."

"Excuse me?"

She pointed at the computer. "Nothing. No record of Rush or Rushmore Gemelli."

I went around the desk to look over her shoulder. She smelled of lavender. "How can that be?"

"Offhand, I'd say operator error." She saw my confused look and added, "Perhaps you have his name wrong."

I dug Rush's card from my pocket. "What it says on his card."

"Let's have his phone number."

I read it as she typed the number into a reverse directory, then hit the enter key. "No matches, not even the K Street address." She held out her hand. As I gave her the card, our fingers touched. Her fingers felt cool. "Well, that's why."

"What?" I asked.

"Cryptographic services, Willis. This fellow's a specialist, probably expunged himself from the databases."

"He can do that?"

"If he really wanted to. All it takes is talent and time."

"Look, while you're there, check out a guy I'm working with, Boynton Longstreet."

"You must be joking."

"The FBI took him."

"They must be desperate. What's his Social?"

"I don't know," I said.

She sat back in her chair. "Good lord, Gidney," she said in her Houses of Parliament voice. "You've worked with this fellow for how long? And still know nothing about him? How ever do you manage to kill a day?" Jones's hands blurred as she typed. "Well, that's better."

"What?"

"He's here, for one thing, not a cyberghost like your client. Forty-seven-years old, born in Oklahoma City, good credit risk, registered voter, no felony convictions." She grinned at me. "Which would be handy, his being an FBI man and all."

"Anything on his family?"

She scanned her screen as she typed. "No, just lists his mother as Longstreet, first name Bonnie, died eight years ago. No father of record. Your man dropped out of high school. Worked as a policeman in Oklahoma City, then got his GED, finished college, and joined the Bureau.

"And he resigned when?"

"October eleventh last year."

"Hmm," I said.

Her smile widened. "'Hmm'?"

"It's what we solo investigators say when we stumble over something interesting. October eleventh was the day after Chuck Gemelli's wife, Elizabeth, died."

"Then Longstreet turns up in Washington, working for MPAC. See for yourself," she said, pointing at a photo of Longstreet and Gemelli shaking hands. "The *Post* did an article on film piracy." She looked at me, her eyes lively. "You think it's a coincidence? The timing with Elizabeth Gemelli's death?"

I shook my head. "Anything on Mrs. Gemelli? A connection between her and Longstreet?"

More typing. "No. Just more MPAC stuff, linking Roger Franklin Quell with Gemelli senior and Longstreet. And a news release about an antipiracy conference in L.A. three years ago. That's it."

She leaned back in her chair and stretched, her hands behind her head and a lazy smile on her lips. "Your friend, whatshername, could've done all this. Lilly? You two have a row or something?" Asked in a casual way.

"She's very busy right now."

"Uh-huh."

"What's that supposed to mean?"

"It's what we large-agency ops say when we hit a nerve. But do think about what I said, all right? You could have fun here, Willis." Her eyes were bright. "If you know what I mean."

"I'm getting the general idea," I said.

CHAPTER 35

Loony Lenny's was in a town house on a short block of Eighteenth Street, just below N. You could look at the stone facade and imagine refined folk sipping tea while Debussy played on the Victrola. When I walked inside, a wall of sound accosted me—gunfire, screams, explosions. And a wall of TV sets showing a close up of Corbin Brooks, shouting and looking heroic.

There was very little floor space. I made my way through stacked boxes of phones, disc recorders, and satellite dishes that nearly edged out the customers and salesmen.

I sidled up to the counter, where a Hasidic salesman was speaking to a young woman. He was explaining the different functions of a cell phone when a second Hasidim ran up to him. "So you going to sell something this morning? You going to talk all day?"

"I'm selling, I'm selling," the first man muttered.

"You're taking forever, with a customer waiting," the second man said. He turned to me. "I'm Lenny—what can we sell you today?"

"Hi, Lenny," I said as I took out the sheet of serial numbers.

Lenny glanced at the papers. "What's all this?"

"I'm researching video decks, and a friend said you sell JVC."

"Biggest dealer in the Mid-Atlantic." Another customer came in behind me.

I handed him the list of serial numbers. "Can you tell me if you sold these? And who bought them?"

He didn't touch the list. "You gonna buy one?"

"No, I really want to know—"

But by then, he'd turned to the next customer. "I'm Lenny—what can we sell you today?"

Apparently I had ceased to exist. I left the counter and wandered into the back, where another Hasidim told me Hester was coming downstairs. I turned and saw a compact, spherical woman bounce down the stairway like a basketball, then dribble to a rest before me. She patted the faded brown kerchief tied around her black hair, of which a few black strands escaped. "You the JVC guy? What's the problem? I'm Hester Doyle."

"Doyle?"

She advanced on me. "Yeah, Doyle. You gotta problem with that?"

"No, it's just—"

"What?"

She had backed me into a stack of boom boxes. "Nothing," I said.

Now she squinted at me. "Where's Ahmed? He's the JVC guy I deal with."

I pulled out my card and gave it to her. She read it, turned it over to look at the blank side, then handed it back to me. "So?"

"I'd like to ask you a few questions."

"A few questions?" She shouted up at the ceiling, "Enough! Do you hear me?" Then she looked back at me. "Lissen, I gotta case of phones that'll only dial New Jersey, some dumbass kid blew out his neighbors' windows with a subwoofer he got here—his dad's a lawyer and says he's gonna sue us—and these meshugge dealers at Sony sent me thirty sets that are PAL standard, won't even work in this country, and you think all I got time for is *questions*?" She handed me my card. "Good-bye, Mr. Private Detective."

Lenny spotted me and came over. "Whadya talking to this guy for?" he asked Hester.

"I'm not talking to him."

"You saying I can't see five feet in front of me? You're talking to him."

"Lenny," I said.

He turned to me, his face red. "What?"

"Shut up or I'll knock you on your ass."

Hester laughed. Lenny shot her a dirty look. "This is my final warning, Hester. You get back upstairs—now." He drew himself up. "I *forbid* you to speak to this guy anymore."

She lowered her eyebrows, and high-velocity Yiddish began shooting out of her mouth, along with tiny particles of spit. Hard to tell which was more dangerous. Lenny backed up. She followed, her words like the stream of a water cannon, forcing him back, until he ducked into the men's room and bolted the door. Then she turned to me, face red, and jerked her head toward the street. We walked outside and she hailed a cab.

After it pulled away from the curb, she took the kerchief off her head, shaking her black hair loose. "I want shellfish," she said, glaring at me as though expecting an argument.

Quick on the uptake, I said, "Shellfish."

"You're buying me lunch," she said. It wasn't a question.

"Of course," I said.

Half a dozen shrimp and one margarita later, she sat back in her chair. "So, okay, Mr. Private Eye, ask." When she said "ask," it sounded like *esk*.

"Thanks. I think that someone maybe bought DVD burners from you and is using them to make illegal dupes. If I gave you some of the serial numbers, could you tell me who bought them?"

"Absolutely, if you supply the crystal ball." She reached for her glass, saw it was empty, and signaled the waiter for another. "You think it would be easy?" she said, leaning toward me. "Look, Lenny is just a distributor. When you buy a disc player, a TV, whatever, we're done. Now it's between you and the manufacturer, that's why they give you all that crap to send in, little warranty postcards, whatever. What, you think we're gonna take the time to call the manufacturers, tell 'em Joe Blow just bought a disc player? Get real. The serial numbers aren't even on our sales slips."

The waiter brought her another margarita. It was about two in the afternoon and the restaurant was dark and quiet. Hester sat back in her chair and gave me a level look. "You're not so bad-looking, you know that? You Jewish?"

"I don't think so."

"You don't know?"

"I was an orphan, a foundling." I shrugged and held up my palms. "Maybe I'm Jewish?"

"You don't look Jewish."

"Neither does Paul Newman."

"You don't look like Paul Newman, either."

"I'm taller."

"Shit, *I'm* taller than Paul Newman." She held her glass by the stem and slowly turned it. "There's another problem. Lenny, that little shit. My brother."

"Your brother?"

"Yeah, it's his business, and he never lets me forget it. See, Lenny likes to run things his way. And that means keeping private matters private."

"Sure." I sipped my beer and set the glass down carefully. "I guess he's giving you a break at that."

Her eyes got a hard look. "A break?"

"He's letting you work in the family business."

"*Letting* me work? Hey, excuse me, but what the fuck does *that* mean?"

"Nothing. It's just that a lot of men wouldn't hire their sisters."

Her pale face took on a red flush. "Lissen, Paul Newman, what I do for that meshugge, he'd need five guys to replace me."

"I'm sure he appreciates it."

She laughed without humor. "Then how come for every dollar the men get, I get sixty cents? That sound like appreciation to you?"

"Then here's your chance. Score one against Lenny and make a little extra."

"How little we talkin' about?"

"I'd pay you a reasonable amount for your time."

She lost a little tension around her mouth. "Maybe even a slightly unreasonable amount?"

"Sure," I said, "so long as it's a reasonably unreasonable amount."

"These video decks, you say they're JVC? Lissen, I like you, so here's the truth. Say I call JVC, ask 'em who bought this deck with serial number so-and-so. First thing they'd ask is, 'When was it sold?' What'll I tell them? Last year? You know how many of these things we sell in a year, boychick? When they got done laughin', they'd say, 'Fahgeddaboutit. Who's gonna take the time to look?'"

"So you can't help me?"

"Nobody can." She looked at me and shook her head.

"Too bad you're not Jewish," she said.

CHAPTER 36

He had picked a lousy place to hide—I spotted him outside my apartment as I drove past. Small, wearing a green fatigue jacket. Ph'uck again, this time alone. Why couldn't he give up? How much face did you have to lose before you called it quits? Matthews rang me as I pulled around to the back alley and parked. "What's up?"

"What's up? You are, my boy. You're up. You've traded up! It's fabulous!"

"You're calling about—"

"Sondra Stoddard, holy Christ, have you shtupped her?"

I rested my head against the steering wheel, eyes closed. "No, she's got a thing for albino lawyers." My fingers rubbed grit beneath my eyelids. "Why are you calling me, counselor?"

"You should have told me, Willis."

"About what?"

"Working for Chuck Gemelli, idiot. Don't you realize what that gives you?"

"Enlighten me."

"Credibility. Importance. Let's see Florence Walters crap on your private eye business now."

"I thought wanting to be Sarah's father made me important." I climbed out of the car, opened up the shed, grabbed my shovel.

"Oh, right. We're dealing with D.C. government, I need to explain this to you? Look, it so happens that Oscar Penny, Walters's boss, is one of sweet Sondra's biggest fans."

"So?"

"So the fact that you're with her in the paper makes you real in a way you weren't before. It's all about perception. You're a high-profile hawkshaw working for movie stars. This *has* to help your case."

"Great."

"It *is* great. Listen—whatever you do, don't screw this up. If anything in this world is going to help you, my boy, it's connecting with Brooks and Stoddard."

I decided not to tell him about pushing Stoddard out of my car. "I got it."

"Great, try not to lose it."

I stashed the phone, then closed the door to the shed. Here we go again. The shovel had a good heft. And I liked the feel of the wooden handle. Maybe I would write the manufacturer and tell them. "Dear Ace Hardware, your model 740 shovel is a champ. I used it to knock out three people in just one week! It's also great for burying possums and light gardening."

I crept up behind Ph'uck, changing my grip, grasping the shovel's handle like a baseball bat. But I didn't think about baseball. I thought about money to pay lawyers. I thought about how Rush Gemelli was blackmailing me. And I thought about Corbin Brooks, vertically challenged action star, and Sondra Stoddard, America's sweet potato. I had to stay away from them, just for the next forty-eight hours. Brooks had told me to keep away. Stoddard had spiked my foot.

I swung the shovel at Ph'uck's head. Then—in mid-swing—I saw how tight I was holding the shovel, and how hard I was swinging it. Back off, Gidney, don't decapitate the guy. Just in time I slowed the blade. It made a pleasant *bong* against his skull. He collapsed face first in the bushes, quiet as a popping bubble.

Call Haggler? Maybe. I went to the shed, hung up the shovel. When I came back, Ph'uck hadn't moved. As I approached him, I felt a low flutter of panic. Something about seeing him on the ground looked familiar. I turned him over.

Corbin Brooks.

I sat on the ground beside him. Well, Matthews had told me to connect with him.

Now I had.

CHAPTER 37

Brooks was a heavy little runt. I shouldered him up the stairs, dropped him on the couch. Sunlight streamed in. I looked where I'd hit it his head. No blood, which was good.

I got aspirin and water. Then I sat across from him. The direct sunlight made shadows on his hands. His right thumbnail had a groove that ran down the middle. The hard light made his face look haggard.

He didn't move. I grew tired of watching him. Maybe he'd come to sooner if I didn't watch him. I swallowed the aspirin. A few minutes later Brooks groaned, so I got more aspirin. When I came back, he looked up at me, squinting through the sunlight.

I handed him the pills and water. "Here."

He gulped it down, then gave me a vicious look. "Ever been sued for assault?"

"You want to tell a judge why you were hiding in the bushes outside my front door?"

He sat a little straighter. "I wasn't *hiding*. I was staking out your place." He shielded his eyes from the sunlight. "And close that fucking shade!"

"That's what you learned in the movies?" I left the shade where it was.

He frowned. "The movies?" He said it as though he wasn't quite sure what they were. For a moment, I worried about how hard I'd hit him. Then he touched his head and glared at me. The old Corbin Brooks was back. "Hey, I've been trained by experts, okay? The best stunt people in Hollywood. I can be you better than *you* can be you."

Wonderful. Next he was going to talk about the Method. "Why're you here?"

He sat up, out of the sunlight. "Part of the craft, that's all. Research. And I haven't seen much here I can use."

"Glad to hear it."

"You can laugh, but I know you've seen my movies." As if that proved him right.

I shook my head. "Sorry."

He look surprised. "Not even *Road Kill Soufflé*?"

"I'd rather iron my shoelaces."

He wasn't used to anyone talking like that. "Lots of people saw *Roadkill*—two, three times." He shrugged. "I wanted to see how someone like you does his job. I mean, you did okay last night."

This could not be happening. "You're researching me?"

"Look, I'm curious. I was a writer. I mean, I *am* a writer. I'm more writer than actor." He frowned at me, his always-onstage quality gone. "I moved from Virginia to L.A., wrote novels, peddled scripts. Some producer joked about a walk-on. I was broke and took it." Brooks started rubbing his forefinger against his thumbnail, along the groove he'd worn into it. "Well, fast-forward a couple of years and now I'm this other guy who stars in movies."

"And Stoddard?"

"Just keep your fucking distance from her."

"I plan to." I sat down opposite him. "Sounds like you really care about her."

"It's none of your business." He voice rose and he winced, then lightly touched his head wound. "Christ, this how you welcome all your guests?"

"I'm having problems with a gang. Of munchkins. Had you pegged for one of them. And my guests use the front door."

Outside there was a soft footstep—Lilly. She didn't smile when she came in. She walked as if gravity were slowing her—the atmosphere was that heavy.

"Hey," she said. She had shucked the baggy clothes, the scary makeup, figure-flattening sports bra. Which meant this was one of her "inside" days, when she knew she wouldn't have to deal with the world of men and didn't care how she looked. She was dressed in a sleeveless yellow top, olive shorts, with the kind of body that would make a runway model hang up her heels. I felt the need to reach out, touch her arm. I don't think I'd ever seen her look so beautiful, and I wondered if this meant I knew I was losing her.

She gave me plenty of space as she went past. "Sorry I didn't call first. I came to get my things, if that's, like, okay." Her head down, she walked into the living room. Then she saw Brooks. "Hey. I know you." Some of the tension left her face. "Corby."

Brooks was Mr. Cool. "Hey, Lilly. Long time."

I felt so tired, I couldn't think. A herring would've had a better shot at figuring this out. "You two've met?"

Brooks rubbed his chin. "Is that what you detectives call a deduction?"

I was ready to take him apart with my hands.

Lilly said, "I did tell Willis we were, like, models together. Maybe he didn't hear me." This last said for my benefit. My stomach knotted as she gave Brooks a sweet smile. "I saw you were in town."

"God, you look amazing." He took her in his arms and kissed her. If only I'd hit him harder. Too late now. Maybe for a lot of things. The three of us stood there, as though embedded in amber—Lilly smiling at Brooks, his arms around her waist, and me to the side, feeling dead all over. Maybe the amber was inside my brain, clogging up the works.

I cleared my throat. "This is wonderful," I said. "Let's go out, my treat."

She ignored me. "Can I give you a lift, Corby?"

"That'd be great." *Now* he looked like a movie star, the bastard.

Lilly swept through my place quickly and efficiently. Books, clothes, and all her makeup. Erasing all signs that she had ever been here, that we'd ever been together. Brooks stood by, arms crossed. For him, this was amusing.

She paused at the doorway, not wanting to look at me. "I guess it's good-bye." A kiss on the cheek, and she was gone. Brooks didn't look at me either. But I saw him smile as he passed by, his eyebrows up. Marveling at his good fortune, at the pleasure he anticipated. I went to the window, saw them drive away.

Long after Lilly's VW had vanished from sight, I stood there.

I felt like a pillar of lead. Lilly was the person who cared, who loved me. I'd driven her away. Took me a year, but I'd done it. Congratulations.

Which left only Sarah. Brooks hadn't heard about how I'd shoved Stoddard from my car. But he would. And when he did, he'd call the Elephant. I pictured Sarah, alone and afraid, maybe missing me as much as I was missing her. I hated Walters for keeping Sarah and me apart.

Then I had an idea. Maybe not the best I'd ever had, but I turned it over and it looked good. I found the Web site for Diaper Donnie's laundry service, and saw it was in Silver Spring. Maybe fifteen minutes away if I hurried. I grabbed my coat, but stopped by the window one more time before I left.

I wondered if I stood there long enough, would Lilly come back?

CHAPTER 38

Thanks to Florence Walters, I could no longer walk in the front door of DCAS. That left the loading dock. And that meant I needed my clipboard.

Now I have to tell you, a clipboard is a passport into any loading dock in the world. The only other thing you need is a bad attitude, and for me, at that moment? No problem. The dock manager didn't even want to talk to me. I was only five words into my spiel when he waved me on.

Oh, and the beat-up hamper I was pushing? The one I had,

uh, borrowed from Diaper Donnie? For now, it was just insurance, confirming what the guards already saw—I was a tired working stiff who didn't give a damn if they let me in or not. So they let me in.

Attitude is everything.

I wasn't there for quality time—I didn't need a hamper for that—but I wanted to make sure Sarah was all right. To let her know I was still around. And to be honest, there was another part to it. Hard to describe. It's just, well, I was used to seeing her. Holding her in my arms. Getting a whiff of that macaroon smell from the top of her head. I know the emotional need was part of it, but this was physical—I could almost feel my eyes ache for the sight of her.

Look, this wasn't a kidnapping. I just wanted to let her know I hadn't forgotten. Let myself know, too, and make sure she was all right. I planned to bring her back. Really.

I made it up to her floor, then threaded my way through rows of cribs. Some babies were sound asleep, while the ones next to them were red-faced from crying. I saw hungry babies who needed new diapers, babies who needed to sleep and couldn't, and a few who stared at me through the bars of their cribs, their little faces still, their eyes empty, like the eyes of dolls.

I hurried. Finally I found her crib, the pink heart with the broken plastic case on the sheet. But no Sarah. With what I hoped looked like a casual sweep, I went round and round, searched the makeshift kitchen, even the small patch of green space outside the door. I checked the bathrooms nearby, I even rolled the hamper past the administration offices. But I couldn't find her.

I couldn't find her.

CHAPTER 39

"Christ Almighty, Willis, you picked a shitty time to drop by. Ever hear of the six o'clock news?" Vince Carruthers sat in a darkened room at SatNews, viewing one of the pirated discs I'd taken from the warehouse. Once more, Corbin Brooks's too-handsome face flashed on the edit console's two monitors. Where was my shovel when I really needed it?

Vince checked the video signal on a rack of diagnostic gear. He certainly had enough of it. In addition to the editing gear, there were racks of video processors, amplifiers, scopes, and a weird-looking black box. "What's this one do?"

Vince said, "It's a fucking espresso machine. Sit down and shut up. We gotta finish before Moose Breath shows up."

"Moose Breath?"

"Tony Corona, we're on his nickel," Vince said. "He finds out I'm not cutting his show, I'm in deep shit."

It was the same action scene I'd watched at my place. Brooks playing a cop, working the mean streets and alleys of a nameless city. His clothing was artfully degraded, his tousled hair perfectly in place. "This is a pirate copy?" Vince asked.

"That's right."

Vince swiveled from the monitor to look at me. "This doesn't look pirated. The picture quality, the sound—I'd guess this was the studio release, not a bootleg." Vince turned back to the screens, rubbing the edge of his sharp nose. He had a long narrow face, thinning brown hair, and a pale complexion he referred to as his "studio tan."

Eyes on the screens, Vince said, "Pirated movies look like shit, Willis. In the old days someone with access to a film lab would make a copy of a print. The copies were crap—grainy picture, bad sound. Then comes the video camcorder, and now everyone and his mother is a pirate. We're talking morons who sneak in tiny handheld cameras, they shoot the movie off the screen, you can't hardly hear or see a thing." He gestured toward the screens. "But this is, like, perfect. Pristine."

Just then, the door cracked opened, revealing the serious brow and lantern jaw of Tony Corona. "Vince, it's showtime." Corona stuck his head in farther, then frowned at me. "Well, well, the guy who fucked up my show."

Vince said, "He's got some video from that pirate operation, we're checkin' it out."

I looked at Vince. What the hell was he doing?

"Really? A pirated video?" Corona came in and sat beside me. "Well, avast, me hearties. Which film is this?"

Vince said quickly, "Came out last year. Don't you go to the movies? My wife, she loves 'em—every time we get a sitter, we go see something." He turned back to me. "You sure this is pirated?"

"I'm sure. How did they make such a clean copy?"

Vince didn't answer. He pulled the first disc out and replaced it with the second. It was the same scene as the first, the same close-ups of Brooks trying for tough. Then a cut to his costar, the beautiful and latently talented Sondra Stoddard.

Corona sighed. I could smell why Vince called him "Moose Breath." He had some Don Diegos Coronas in his shirt pocket, and now he took one out and started to chew the end. "Jesus, look at her," he said. "Brooks is one lucky bastard, waking up next to that every morning."

The door burst open and a kid with a ponytail and glasses dropped a stack of discs next to Vince, who looked up at the clock. News time. Corona said, "Outside, Gidney." In the hallway, Corona looked both ways, then said, "I want this."

"What?"

"This story. It's big. It's big, and I appreciate your bringing it to me."

"I didn't bring you anything."

Apparently he didn't hear me. "I'll go prime time. No more weekend roundups." His eyes came back to me. "Where was that warehouse, the one in Virginia?"

"It's a crime scene, you won't get near it."

He raised his chin at me. "You're not the only investigator here. I can find things out just as good as you. Maybe better." His eyes took on a crafty look, it contrasted with his sincere, concerned shtick. "But we could pool our resources."

"'Pool our resources'? You come up with that by yourself?"

He looked hurt, then angry. "Okay, pal. I want you out of this building. Now."

I smirked at him and went back into the editing room. Vince was busy slamming discs into machines. I picked up the first pirated disc. "Thanks for getting Corona all over this. I thought you had more sense. Hand me the other disc, I'm out of here."

His eyes on the monitors, he said, "Thought I'd keep the other—as my fee."

"For what?"

"For not telling Moose Breath that this is *Explosive Rounds*."

He turned to face me. "This film premieres Sunday night. Gidney, it hasn't even been released yet. Understand?"

It meant the movie no one could steal had, in fact, already been stolen. Vince nodded. "Yeah. Figured you wouldn't care for Corona to know that."

"What will you do with your copy?"

"Watch it with the old lady. You got any idea what a baby-sitter costs?"

I was waiting at the elevator when Corona showed, flanked by two matching Ken doll security guards in matching gray shirts, black belts, and darker gray pants. They both had crew cuts, one was blond and the other dark.

"This is the guy," Corona said.

The guards gave each other a tough, satisfied look. After Stoddard, these two were cream puffs. The dark one said, "We'll have to ask you to leave, sir."

"If you have to, you have to." I showed them my back while I thumbed the elevator button again.

The blond crew cut tapped my shoulder. "He means now."

When someone touches you, it's assault. Even better, this guy wasn't Corbin Brooks. The blond said, "Why don't you take the stairs? Looks like you could use the exercise."

The three of them laughed. The blond was enjoying himself. "C'mon, tubby. We don't got all day." He reached for me and I twisted his hand away while stepping forward, then turned and punched his gut. The air *whooshed* out of him as he bent over, I brought his arm up over his head, put my other hand behind his elbow, and threw him into the second guard. The two of them went down in a heap. Then the elevator arrived with the sound of a bell and I stepped inside.

"And the man wins a cigar," I said, plucking one from Corona's pocket as the doors slid shut.

CHAPTER 40

I tossed Corona's cigar in a trash can on North Capitol Street, then cruised on adrenaline all the way to MPAC. Outside the entrance, Longstreet was leaning against a concrete planter. He flicked his cigarette in the street, nodded at me, and straightened up. "Whatcha got, Willis? Somethin' new?"

"Could be. I need to see Gemelli." After five, the guard's desk was deserted. Longstreet used his MPAC ID card to swipe our way into the building. We walked to the left, past the giant reception room that fronted Eye Street, and up three steps to Gemelli's outer office.

The hallway to Gemelli's office went twenty feet, snaked to the left, then went another thirty feet. We walked silently on the thick emerald carpet. Above us, the white ceiling was vaulted. And far ahead were double wooden doors to Gemelli's inner sanctum. It reminded me of *The Wizard of Oz*. For a moment, I felt like the scarecrow, trying to solve a case with a head full of straw.

We walked past walls covered with photos from famous movies, the faces of stars gazing out at us lovingly, as though inviting us to step inside the pictures with them. Which may have been preferable to seeing Gemelli. I had, after all, tossed Stoddard out of my car and smacked Brooks with a shovel. Gemelli might be angry about that.

Longstreet placed a hand on my shoulder, just where the security guard had, stopping our progress in the hallway. "You know, he's a total fuckwad today. Tell me what you found, I'll handle it."

"You'll probably end up doing just that. But we'll let him decide, okay?"

Longstreet shrugged A few more steps and we found ourselves at the double doors. He gave a polite rap, then opened the doors a crack and looked in. He motioned for me to follow him.

Gemelli sat in a high-backed judge's chair, tilted back, with his feet on a desk that was carved around the same time the ink was drying on the Constitution. He shouldered the handset to his ear, using both his hands to turn a silver letter opener, watching the light gleam off its edges.

We sat, waiting for the call to end. His office wasn't terribly large, and as the head of a lobby, he rated more space. Probably swapped it out for more hallway. The walls were covered with photos of the Elephant posing with Hollywood's and Washington's biggest stars—Clint Eastwood and Bill Clinton, Bruce Willis and Ronald Reagan. One shot had Gemelli in between Jack Nicholson and Cher. In the corner was a bookshelf with new-looking books. I checked to see if they were just bindings. On the floor, a pedestal held a giant bronze eagle with a six-foot wingspan. The eagle faced me, its angry beak open.

Gemelli nodded as he listened, then said, "That sounds fine, Senator. Yes, I'd like that. Fine. You too." He hung up the phone. "What an asshole." He looked up at Longstreet and me, his mask-like face a parody of wonder. "He wants to be president. Can you imagine? My left nut would make a better president." So far, no mention of Stoddard or Brooks. Good. Longstreet said, "Mr. Gemelli? Willis here's got somethin' he wants to tell us."

"I've no time for unimportant details."

"In my time with the Bureau, sir, I learned there's no such thing."

Gemelli looked at Longstreet for a full five seconds, then pointed his gray face and yellowed eyes toward me. "Go ahead."

I took out the pirated disc and placed it on his desk. "I'd like to know about this."

"What is it?" Gemelli picked it up and flipped it over with quick, agitated movements. "Where did this come from?"

"Part of the same batch you found three nights ago in Alexandria."

Gemelli relaxed. "Then it's nothing we need to worry about."

Longstreet grinned. "How'd ya get hold of it, Willis?"

"A source I know."

Longstreet said, "A source," as though it were a funny idea.

I asked Gemelli if he'd watched any of the discs. His face went from anxious to irritated. "Of course."

"Then you know these pirated discs are of an unusual quality? That they look first generation?"

"Yes." He began straightening papers on his desk. "Really, is that all?"

"Hey." That made him stop and look up. "Did you also know that the scenes on this disc are from *Explosive Rounds*? Of a movie that hasn't been released yet?"

Longstreet grunted. Gemelli said, "Yes, we know that, too."

"Then you have a problem, you and Quell. The industry's given Quell two million to protect this film from piracy. Don't you find it troubling that someone's already cracked your key code?"

Gemelli sat forward, resting his elbow on his desk and his chin on his fist. "You've been busy, I'll give you that. But no one has cracked my code, because I haven't finished writing it yet. Only two people will have it, me and Quell's man in L.A. And the only way a person could crack the key code is with key exhaustion."

"Which is?"

"Brute force, trying every possible combination of numbers, one after the next. The key code I'm writing? You'd need a quantum computer and about a hundred years to break it. And since no one's invented a quantum computer, I'd say we're safe for the time being." He was talking persuasively, like a salesman. It reminded me of what Kane had said about him. "And this disc— of course we've watched it. We created it for NATO."

"National Association of Theater Owners," Longstreet told me.

Gemelli nodded. "Twice a year, they get to look at scenes from upcoming films. And MPAC facilitates these screenings. Especially if the distributors feel that the project will generate interest and revenue."

"Revenue?" I asked.

"Of course. We give the theater owners a chance to bid on right of first refusal. So if you had a film coming out with Brooks and Stoddard, you'd distribute scenes from that new film so that the owners could place a bid. Take *Explosive Rounds*—it's got a budget of one twenty. Theater owners ponied up thirty mill, they know *Rounds* will be hot." He tossed the disc to me. "A souvenir."

"Glad it's not a problem. By the way, once the cops figure the failed-business angle, you'll be a suspect in the Kane killing. Will that interfere with your code writing?"

"We've talked about this before." Gemelli sat forward, his fists on the polished desktop. "My personal affairs. I've warned you to stay out of them. But I'll appease your curiosity one last time. Kane was a fool, and a poor businessman. I don't know which was worse. I've had years to kill him. Even if I wanted to, why should I do it now? And yes, I found his death shocking, naturally. But I had no motive." He sat back and rubbed his chin. "Still," he said, as though just discovering this for himself, "there *was* someone at EncryptU.com who wanted to see Kane dead."

I looked at him, wondering if I'd heard him correctly. "Your son?" I asked.

Gemelli waved his hand in dismissal. "I haven't mentioned anyone by name. But since you brought him up, I *did* hear Rush threaten Kane, when Rush left our business."

"Did he ever threaten you?"

"His own father?"

"But you think he did it, is that it? You believe your son capable of killing Kane."

He picked up the silver letter opener, letting it flash in his hands. "Who can say what another person is capable of?"

CHAPTER 41

It was a long drive back to Diaper Donnie's. I felt like the newspaper lining of a birdcage. Where was Sarah? Walters would know. Too bad I couldn't just call her and ask. I left the hamper, then called Haggler's office. He picked up and I said, "Working late?"

"On the Kane killing. Shooter used a twenty-two. That sound like either of the Gemellis to you?"

Here it came. "They're suspects?"

"Well, father and son were in business with Kane. So when they squeezed Rush out—"

"They did what?"

"Squeezed him out, boy. That's a business term. It means—"

"I know what it means."

"Good enough, as a motive. And you said you heard Chuck Gemelli argue with Kane."

"I *saw* them argue. When I asked him, Gemelli said they were arguing about his son."

"Could be Kane saw where Rush was coming from, maybe, I don't know, warning Chuck Gemelli. We'll question both of 'em tomorrow. Kinda funny, though."

I stopped for a light. I knew Emil Haggler well enough to brace myself. "What is?"

"Well, here you take a job with a guy, then the guy and his son're both suspects in a homicide. You know the kid?"

The light turned green and immediately a car honked behind me. "We've met." I hit the gas.

"Huh. You'd be doing him a favor to tell him to come in and see us."

"Sure, next time I see him."

"Yeah. Anything you wanna tell me?"

There was plenty. I wanted to tell him about how Sarah'd gone missing. I wanted to tell him about Rush, and his pictures. I wanted some help or, failing that, some damage control when everything collapsed in ruins. Instead, I said, "I'd like to talk with your guy, the gang expert. Neapolitan?"

"Napolitano." Haggler pronounced each syllable with care.

"Having problems with gangs?" He didn't let me answer, just transferred me. A young-sounding voice picked up. "Napolitano. This Willis?"

"Yeah, I'm Haggler's friend."

"I won't hold that against you," he said. We agreed to meet at Enrique's, across from the barbecue joint on Wisconsin Avenue, in thirty minutes. On the way, I called Lilly. Hearing my own voice talking into the phone, I felt like a man speaking words into a canyon so large, the sounds would take forever to bounce back.

I spotted Napolitano standing at the bar—black jeans, white running shoes, a tobacco leather jacket over a blue oxford shirt. As I approached him, he wrinkled his nose at me.

"You Willis?"

"Yeah." We shook hands.

He looked me up and down. "Undercover?"

"Overwhelmed."

He handed me a glass of beer. "Try to carry that across the room." We went past tables of well-dressed couples to a booth by the window. Outside, a Friday-night flow of shiny new cars honked up and down Wisconsin Avenue, but whether they were honking at one another or the string of Georgetown coeds parading past was anybody's guess. Across the street, an ancient white Buick looked out of place. As we sat down, Napolitano said, "I knew you were gonna dress like a schlub, we'da gone to McDonald's. My friends run this place."

"Sorry."

He shrugged, took a sip of his beer. "Haggler says you want gang information. I hope you don't want a lecture."

"Just tell me what you can in tiny bite-sized words, nothing over two syllables."

"Cool." He took another sip, thinking of where to begin. "Well, let's assume you know nothing."

"With you so far."

Napolitano told me about gangs I already knew—the Crips, the Bloods, the Pagans, STC, Fate's Assembly—and some I didn't.

"See, you got your Spanish franchise gangs, too. Like South American gangs—next to L.A., D.C.'s got the most. Take La Mara Loco, okay? Up-and-comers from El Salvador. Started in L.A., but now they're in New York, Chicago, Detroit, Miami, and D.C. Into car theft, big-time. They use cars the way we use cash, you know? Mostly, they swipe Beemers, Benzes, Caddies, that kinda thing. We're talking new cars here, not some piece of shit off the street. Then they swap the cars for drugs or weapons or whores."

"Sounds convenient."

"Better'n a fucking bank card. The other thing—the Locos are killers. Say they got a member who caps someone here. They put the shooter on a plane back to Latino land, we got no extradition treaty with 'em."

"At least they're gone."

"If they're good, they come back under a different ID. And if they're *very* good, they'll get recruited by the Mex or Colombian cartels. That's like getting an Ivy League scholarship for these assholes." He looked at his watch. "Hey, I gotta get going. Any of this helping you?"

"All of it. How about pirating?"

"Come again?"

"You know anything about gangs making illegal dupes of movies and software? Film pirating?"

He sat back in the booth. "Now, that's a new one."

I gave him the newspaper version of the warehouse in Alexandria, and the disc-duping operation there. "So, you don't know of any gangs into pirating?"

"None. Which don't mean they're not, just means I don't know about it." He glanced at his watch again.

I put some money on the table. "Where you headed next?"

He smiled, a little embarrassed I'd caught him looking at his watch. "A vacation. The wife and I are going to Akumal. You ever been there?"

"No."

"Me neither. But she loves to snorkel, and she set it all up. We leave Monday for a week. But tonight we're gonna start, uh, celebrating when I get home." He stood up. "Nice meeting you, Mr. Willis."

I shook hands with him. "Thanks. But the name's Gidney, Willis Gidney."

"Haggler just said Willis. What's your last name?"

"Gidney."

The smile dropped off his face. "Get up," he said. He led me to a booth in the back. "Sit down a second."

We sat down. He leaned close to me and said, "Your name's Gidney?"

"What about it?"

"Fuck, and I'm sitting in the window seat next to you?" He looked down, shook his head. "Jesus, why not just hang a fucking bull's-eye around my neck, man?"

"What's the problem?"

"You, you're the problem. The Dragons are looking for *you*, man." He raised his hands. "Hey, you shoulda fucking said something." His voice was a stage whisper, I was sure everyone in the bar could hear him. "Shit, and you got your picture in the *Post,* too." His face had an earnest look. "Gang killings, they come under *my* purview. Look—you gotta leave town. I don't want my vacation all fucked up." He shook his head. "Do not get killed before Monday, okay?"

CHAPTER 42

I had to case my own apartment before going inside. It gave me a bad attitude. I'd just put my feet up when the phone rang. Hester Doyle said, "So, I'm speaking to the shamus?"

"The same."

"What's that mean anyway? I mean, in Yiddish a shamus is like a janitor, the guy that keeps the temple wastebaskets emptied, you know? Ever read Arthur Naiman?"

"No." I was starting to like Hester.

"He's got this story. It's Friday night in the temple, okay? And the rabbi, to show how humble he is before God, cries out, 'Oh, Lord, I am nobody!' Then the cantor—he doesn't wanna get left out—also cries, 'Oh, Lord, I am nobody!' The shamus is very moved and does the same, crying, 'Oh, Lord, I am nobody!' The rabbi turns to the cantor and says, 'Look who thinks he's nobody!' Is that you, boychick?"

I laughed. "Close enough."

"Jaimie Romero."

"Excuse me?"

"That's the answer. You wanted to know who bought those

disc burners, I'm telling you it was Jaimie Romero. Guy lives on . . ." I heard her shuffling through papers. "Here. He lives at seven seventeen North West Street in Alexandria."

"North West Street?"

"Yeah, sounds like the guy who named streets down there ran outta steam."

I wrote down the information. "That's great, Hester. But you said you couldn't trace the serial numbers."

"I didn't use serial numbers to get this *goniff.*"

"Then how?"

She laughed. "Because this guy, this big-time film pirate, he sends in his warranty cards for the burners, all twenty-six of 'em. Can you believe it? Whatta schmuck."

"Hester, you did great. I really appreciate this. You let me know how much I owe."

"Yeah, well, it took a long time, but I'm only gonna bill you a hundred. You know why? 'Cause it was, well, like fun, you know? I don't usually have fun at the job."

"Thanks, Hester. And *Shabbat shalom.*"

"A goy who speaks Hebrew, great. Just don't tell anyone I called you on the Sabbath, okay?"

Sleep hovered above my bed like the rain clouds I'd seen outside, swollen, ready to burst. I put in earplugs, turned my clock to the wall. I didn't want to know the time. My determination to sleep was keeping me awake. I could feel my hair grow. I kept thinking about Kane. Both Gemellis were suspects—Rush for getting squeezed out of his own business, and Chuck for losing a fortune when EncryptU.com crashed and burned. D.C. is an easy place to get a gun. And as to opportunity, well, I had no idea where either of them had been at the time of the killing. I wondered if Romero could be a suspect. Sending in the warranty cards had been a dumb thing to do, though people do all sorts of dumb things, and the criminal class is no different. Provided Romero was, in fact, a criminal.

Then I thought about the Dragons. Could Napolitano be right? Hide 'til things cooled down? Be bad for business, Gidney running scared from kids. My heart was racing. So I tried some breathing exercises, feeling my chi rise up my spinal column as I inhaled, then back down on the exhale. I waited for sleep to come. Plate tectonics shifted the continents into new shapes. The stars overhead expanded to form new constellations. The freight train shook my bed. After what seemed like a long time, I turned the clock face and saw it was five in the morning.

Out of bed. Showered. Shaved. Dressed. That helped, a little. I made coffee, ate something though I wasn't hungry. I pictured Lilly asleep, and knew it was too early to call. The Kane killing was on the front page of the "Metro" section. It didn't tell me anything I hadn't already known.

I loaded my .38, thinking about Shad. I remember one time he strapped on a shoulder holster, and I asked him why he wore it. Why not stick the gun in his pocket or in his belt?

Shad smiled at me, said he *wanted* folks to see the holster strap, wanted them to know he was armed when they were dealing with him.

Long before I was in Shad's charge, I had a deaf foster mother, a plump, sweet woman, born without any hearing. One day she was going out to do errands, and I saw her put in a hearing aid. Now, she'd told me the hearing aid didn't help her. She never wore it at home, or visiting her deaf friends—or even friends who could hear. But she always wore it when she went on errands. I pointed at the hearing aid and made the sign for "Why?"

Her expert fingers forming the word shapes slowly so I could understand, she told me that no one looking at her would know she was deaf. The hearing aid told the hearing world they were dealing with a deaf person. It was a visual tip-off. So I guess it was the same thing with Shad and the shoulder holster. Me, I wasn't looking to tip anyone off. Just the opposite, in fact. I stuck my gun in my pocket and checked myself in the mirror. Wrinkled clothes, bloodshot eyes. I was a mess. But at this point, I didn't care.

At 5:00 A.M., I doubted Jaimie Romero would care very much, either.

CHAPTER 43

Romero's house was a mile from the warehouse where I'd glued the Dragons together. The house sat on a street by the railroad tracks, sandwiched between a Metro station and a flock of renovated town houses in Old Town Alexandria. A no-man's-land, a section of low-income dwellings as featureless as Monopoly houses and only slightly bigger.

Romero's was a one-story shack, with a fake rock facade stuck to the street-facing clapboard exterior. There were black iron bars on the window and door. One of the black shutters hung at a rakish angle.

I parked a block away and walked back. The air vibrated with a low rumble I knew well. A whistle blew and a freight train chugged past Romero's backyard, the same train I heard every night. I wondered if he ever lay awake listening to it.

Farther up the street, past rusted chain-link fences and muddy lawns, a skinny woman in a housecoat gave me a dirty look. I leered back at her.

No one answered Romero's front door, so I went to the backyard, expecting to find piles of abandoned trash, but everything was cleared away. Someone had planted grass seed, and tiny green blades poked up through the peat.

I knocked on the back door, waited, then nodded to my nonexistent friend inside the house. All the time, my picking tools were busy.

The house was empty, and it smelled of new paint. A long white hallway with rooms off to the left. Three pictures in frames on the dresser. The floors were swept, the bed was made. I wondered if Romero would mind if I took a quick nap. Somebody's been sleeping in my bed.

As to the three pictures—two were color and one was black and white. First, a guy in blue jeans, crouched and smiling, a golden retriever in the foreground jumping and catching a red Frisbee. Stock photo, came with the frame. The other color shot showed a dark-haired man with a hooked nose, he smiled in profile at a good-looking blonde next to him They wore swimsuits. The girl's was a one-piece suit that looked a few years out of date. The harsh sunlight made her face hard, like a mask. It made me think of the Elephant.

The black-and-white picture showed a teenage version of the same guy—who I now assumed was Romero—sitting at a picnic bench beside an older boy, grinning at the camera with their arms around each other. The family resemblance said they were brothers.

I took the two photos of Romero, then went through the

drawers, looked under and behind them. Nothing. His closet held a dark suit from JCPenney, a few white shirts, and a lot of empty hangers. An empty suitcase on the shelf in back. Tucked away was a spray paint setup.

Romero should have had *some* papers, even unimportant ones. But he had nothing. Had someone searched here already? The bristles of his toothbrush felt dry. So was the floor of the shower. A tiny living room barely contained the overstuffed duct-taped furniture. A small table sprouted like a weed between skyscrapers. The table was particle board and the laminated wood top was covered with a light dusting of white paint. Next to the phone was a rectangle-shaped area without the tiny drops of paint—a clean space.

The fridge in the kitchen was tight against the wall. I put my shoulder against it and heaved with everything I had. It gave two inches. Take that, Westinghouse. A few more shoves got it away from the wall, where I found nothing but a strip of dust as high as a deck of cards. So Romero missed a spot, I thought with satisfaction.

Then I saw, lodged in the grillwork, two scraps of paper. I pried them lose. One was an insurance statement from Geico with Romero's license number. The other was the crumpled bottom half of some kind of form. In the lower left, in six point font, it said FORM CJA. At first I couldn't place it.

Then I remembered—it was a parole form. Except the feds didn't call them parolees anymore, they were "supervised releasees." So when Romero had painted this room, he'd had a radio transponder attached to his phone that would electronically monitor his movements. House confinement.

If Romero kept his parole forms, where was his calendar? I mean, I've been in plenty of homes where someone's on parole. Usually they put the PO's card right on the fridge. Why not? Most of them have family and friends working their way through the criminal justice system. Romero's fridge was blank.

While I walked into the kitchen, I punched Haggler's number.

"So you're alive," he said.

"Yeah, Napolitano will be so happy. Could you pull a sheet on a parolee for me?"

"Why would I do that?"

"'Cause you're homicide, and this guy might be a witness to the Kane killing." Which was bullshit, but I needed Haggler's help.

"Shit." Some papers rustled. "Okay, who's the guy?"

I spelled the name and gave him Romero's address. He told me to wait, so, with phone to ear, I checked out the rest of the kitchen. The sink was clear of dirty dishes, the drain was dry.

"Okay. Romero was part of Mara Loco, did three years for grand theft auto, resisting. Released on parole eight months ago." More typing. "Guy's got quite the sheet. Did time at Lewisburg."

Lewisburg—that was it, the towers I'd seen on Tuckerman's chest. "Okay. Now, late Thursday or early Friday, someone dropped a body, name of Tuckerman." I tried to keep the excitement out of my voice.

"One a the Roaches. So?"

"Check his sheet, where he did time."

I heard him clicking the keys. "Huh, Lewisburg. Same time as Romero."

"So they might've known each other. Who arrested them?"

Haggler sighed. "Let's see. Detective Tony Mondano busted Romero."

"I'd like to talk with him."

"So would his widow, but his heart attack kinda put a crimp in his conversational skills. Now, as to Tuckerman. He got busted by D.C. cops working with the FBI. A cash and credit deal—we

165

spend the cash and they take the credit. Screen doesn't show the Feeb's name. And this brother officer has passed on as well."

"I'd like the FBI agent's name. The one who busted Tuckerman."

Haggler cursed me, said he'd try, and hung up. I let myself out of Romero's house, then sat in my car. The front door looked as though it were trying to tell me something. Then I stared at the windshield. It was just a windshield. Stayne Matthews called, he'd cleared my appeal with Oscar Penny, I could file my "Intent to Adopt" immediately. I could get to DCAS as early as 9:00 A.M. if I liked—Saturday hours.

I drove three blocks, stopped, turned around and went back, back to Romero's bedroom, and picked up the stock photo of the man and the dog. I pried the frame open. Inside was a thousand in hundreds and a check stub, computer-printed. In small type were an employee number, the amount, the date it was issued, and the employer's name. Which, indirectly, was my employer, as well.

MPAC, the check said.

I put the cash back in the frame. At this point, I was hoping Romero was still alive.

CHAPTER 44

I stopped at my apartment to get the forms for DCAS. Parked outside was a patrol car, with an older white cop at the wheel. A gift from Napolitano, just in case I forgot I had a gang trying to kill me. On the way downtown, all the lights were green, which had never happened to me before. An omen.

Walking into DCAS felt a bit unreal. True, I had done just what Haggler had said—I'd worked within the system, placed my trust in the folks who were in the business of caring for kids. Now it was all paying off. Shad would've been proud. So why did I feel weird?

Past the infant dorm I found the administration office—open. Further proof the system works.

"Good morning." I laid my form on the desk. A big balding white guy I'd never seen before sat behind it, wolfing down fried chicken and gravy from a plastic tray. His name tag read "Shoat." He didn't look at me, just glanced at the form, then went back to the chicken. "You're too late."

"Excuse me?"

He tapped the form with a stubby finger, leaving behind a grease stain. "This girl? She's gone."

Keep cool. "No, that's wrong. See, I spoke with my lawyer this morning, he cleared this with Mr. Penny. Please, check the file."

His eyes darted to a stack of folders on his right, then he tore into a wing, nodding his big head. "Yeah, I checked it earlier, okay? Someone's already filed on this girl." He dipped a chunk of white meat in cup of gravy, then licked his fingers.

A bureaucratic screw-up. Had to be, since once someone filed for Sarah, she couldn't be matched to anyone else. "That's not possible."

He shook his head. "Yeah, it's possible. Yesterday, around lunchtime."

Which explained why I couldn't find Sarah. "But we spoke with Oscar Penny—"

"Penny probably dint know another family filed the form."

"You sure?"

"Sure I'm sure, I was here when they came, I helped them with the baby's car seat, what a pain *that* was." Shoat made eye contact for the first tine. "Hey, you don't mind, I gotta finish eating, okay?"

"But who filed it?" I leaned over, rested my hands on his desk. I had the horrible feeling Florence Walters filed it herself, just to keep Sarah and me apart.

Shoat surveyed the chicken, then popped another chunk into his mouth. "Confidential," he said, showing me the chicken while he chewed. "What can I say? They took the baby with them."

"Hey, Mr. Shoat," I said. He looked up. "I want to thank you for being so helpful." Then I flipped his lunch tray into his lap.

"Jesus!" Shoat pushed himself from the desk, gave me a vicious look, then ran to wipe himself off. Or maybe to get more gravy. Either way, it gave me time to scan Sarah's file.

What's worse than discovering the kid you're trying to adopt is with the wrong family? It's when that family's adoption papers look better than yours. Talk about solid citizens. No outstanding debts, paid their credit card bills on time. Same with the mortgage. The type that kept their recyclables separate and never had a late fee at the library. It was sickening.

I copied down their information, then replaced the file where I'd found it. The question was, Was I too late?

CHAPTER 45

Horace and Violet Bishop lived at 614 Butternut Street NW, near the Takoma Metro. I nearly ran to my car. I had to see Sarah, make sure she was all right, that the Bishops weren't mistreating her. I floored my car up North Capitol Street, past Rock Creek Cemetery. Given time, I knew I could find evidence they were unfit to parent her. Or with more time, I could manufacture some. I left a voice-mail message for Stayne Matthews. God only knows how I sounded. Upset? Maybe just a little.

The Bishops had a small white vinyl-sided house, not far from the border with Maryland. No cars out front. I rang the bell, but no one was home. What was I planning to say to them if they answered? Hand her over? *Jesus, I thought, calm down, okay?* I had their address, I could start with that. So, okay, they probably wouldn't move away in the next few hours.

And I did have pressing business—Jaimie Romero. The pay stub meant Romero had been inside MPAC. Rush had told me he had an inside contact. Maybe Romero had set up a fake pirating operation, just so the Elephant could take credit for busting it. Hey, this was D.C., stranger things had happened.

So I went to MPAC. You'd think Saturday noon would be quiet, just right for rifling the personnel files. Instead, the place was electric. I followed a pizza delivery boy into Gemelli's office, but no one had time to eat—Gemelli was a wind-up general, issuing orders for the big premiere tomorrow night, shouting at his young women employees. The women smiled and pretended to like it. Longstreet nodded at me. Situation normal, apparently. I said, "I'm going to look at a file."

Longstreet blocked my way. "Is that right. Whose?"

"Jaimie Romero's."

Gemelli stopped talking. His eyes narrowed. "An *MPAC* employee? I'm not paying you to investigate our own people."

"Think of this as an inside job," I said.

"I know all the employees, and I've never heard of him."

"Then why did Romero have this?" I showed Gemelli the payroll stub I'd found.

Gemelli held the paper at arm's length to read the small print. "Well, this man is not an employee, just a subcontractor."

Longstreet added, "A freelancer—like you." He put the stub in his pocket. "Where'd you get it?"

"Romero's house. Look, I don't care if Romero was freelance or your personal valet, he's involved. We find him, we find who else is involved. His Social Security number—that's all I need to start."

Gemelli had that look, I was about to get canned. "You keep investigating the wrong area—you're supposed to be looking for another warehouse, local film pirates."

Longstreet said, "Just a second—maybe Gidney's right. We should check, to play it safe."

Longstreet's reversal made Gemelli hesitate. He still had the arrogant, angry look. Yet something held Gemelli back. I noticed Longstreet watching me as I watched Gemelli. Why was Longstreet pushing him so hard? Going out of his way to contradict him?

Now Gemelli gave Longstreet the same look he'd given me. "Now, are you willing to put your job on the line for this?"

Longstreet never got a chance to answer, because Roger Franklin Quell slammed open the twin doors, snatched a pizza, and threw it at Gemelli's face.

CHAPTER 46

Chuck Gemelli jerked back, but not fast enough. The pizza hit his chest, then trailed red sauce down the front of his pinstriped suit. "Jesus Christ, Roger."

I thought Gemelli might faint. Longstreet's face was carefully neutral. Gemelli steadied himself against a desk, then managed a hideous smile. His carefully tanned mask got all creased in the middle. Palms up, he said, "Roger, we both know there's a lot at stake. But I don't see why—"

"I'll explain it again, in tiny bite-sized words." The sight of Gemelli covered in sauce seemed to restore Quell's composure. "The industry—the one you're representing?—refuses to lose *another* two billion to pirates next year. We're going to fix that. How? Because we will control the movie in a way the studios can't. No bootlegs, no international black market."

"Roger, we've been through this—"

"They gave me two million for this project. I have to show results. I *have* to. So we keep to the plan. We send my show as a burst, in real time, using the NIST algorithm and your asymmetric key code. No labs, no film prints to dupe. There's only one copy, in L.A., so there's no possible way to duplicate it. Right?"

"Roger—" Gemelli seemed to weaken. Quell closed the distance between them.

"And now you have the balls to e-mail me"—and here Quell swiped at Gemelli's head with his phone—"that we should *fake* it? Ship the movie out from L.A. on a fucking hard drive?"

"A backup. So if God forbid there's a screwup—"

"That's *your* problem."

"—or interference from heavy cloud cover. For God's sake, Roger! I don't control the weather."

Quell took a step back, regarding Gemelli. "And when the press finds out? That we're a sham? We trumpet the arrival of encrypted satellite movies—then ship out the same fucking movie on a hard drive? You saying that computer files off a hard drive can't be copied?"

"No one has to know."

Quell waved his arm at Longstreet, me, and the secretaries. "Of course people will know, these assholes know already. You can't keep this secret." Quell shook his head. "We are using the NIST algorithm and your key code, tomorrow night. There *will* be no other copies of *Explosive Rounds*. Not on a hard drive, not on a disk, not on a print. Is the code finished?"

Gemelli gave a lightning-fast glance at Longstreet, who nodded. "Yes," Gemelli said.

"My tech guy wants to verify—the key code is forty digits? A random key?" Gemelli nodded again. "See how easy this is? My guy in L.A. will need your key at noon West Coast time."

"I already e-mailed it."

"You e-mailed it. So no singing telegram? No skywriter?"

Quell was enjoying himself, humiliating Gemelli in front of his troops. "I hope it won't be too much trouble to ask that the Uptown projectionist has the same forty-digit key?"

"I'll make sure," Gemelli said.

Quell started to leave, then stopped to look at Longstreet and me. "You two. Security?"

Longstreet said, "That's right." Quell asked our names and we told him.

"Anything happens to ruin my premiere, there won't be a take two for either of you. Understand?" He grabbed a slice of pizza, took a bite, and dropped it on the rug as he walked out.

CHAPTER 47

Gemelli's gray face went as red as the pizza sauce that splotched his suit. When he left to change clothes, Longstreet gave Gemelli's backside an amused look, then told me to wait while he checked the files.

He was gone thirty minutes. One thing about the FBI—they really know how to check a file. I got a voice mail from Stayne Matthews, telling me not to fret. Walters's boss was on our side, he said. Walters was just gaming the system to get Sarah away from me. Yeah, that made me feel much better.

I picked up issues of *Variety* and *Premiere,* then put them down. On the opposite wall were pictures of Brooks and Stoddard, of course. Brooks posed in three-quarter profile, beard stubble on his face, looking intense about something just outside the frame. Stoddard's was a glamour shot, with plenty of leg.

Movie people were bizarre. And Quell was a world-class pizza-throwing douche bag. I could understand Gemelli's backing down from him. But why would Gemelli back down from Longstreet? Was he deferring to Longstreet's FBI experience in piracy? I replayed the scene in my mind, ignoring the words, concentrating on the dynamic.

Longstreet came in, dropped a memo on the secretary's desk, then motioned me outside. The sidewalk was empty, except for a colorless mound of cloth that probably had a homeless person sleeping beneath. Longstreet lit a cigarette, blew out the smoke, and turned to me.

"Okay. Tell me everything you know about Jaimie Romero."

It was drizzling while we walked to the Zamboanga Café. I told Longstreet some of what I knew. I'd finished just as Chella set down our coffee. His face was calmer than it had been on our walk, but not much. When he picked up his cup, coffee slurped over to the saucer. He was trying hard to stay in control. He placed a folded paper napkin between the cup and saucer. Looking down he said, "I just went way out on a limb for you."

Now he looked up, his gray eyes cold. "I'm riskin' my job. So, first, you're goin' to tell me who your client is. Then you're goin' to tell me *where* he is. Then, maybe, I'll tell you what I found in the files about Romero." I started to say something, but he cut me off. "Hey, you know what? Fuck that. Rush Gemelli's your client. Don't even bother denyin' it."

"I'd say no, even if he was."

"And you're the guy who broke into the warehouse."

"Wow, is this like a real FBI interrogation?"

"No, 'cause the FBI wouldn't let me kick the shit out of you because I felt like it." He took another sip, looking out at the tourists on F Street. When he finally spoke, he kept his voice steady. "See, a guy like Rush could get Romero in at MPAC. Like he got you in. Then Rush expunges Romero's file, it's easy for him. Which would explain why I found nothin' on Romero. Could be that's why he hid his payroll slip. He was afraid of Rush. You see that, right? You know the Elephant screwed Rush out of a few million dollars."

"So I heard."

"So Rush has got a few million reasons to nail Daddy. Does Rush have the means? The smarts? Absolutely. He just needs someone to give him opportunity. A chump. In this case, you." His eyes were flat. "You'd best tell me where the little prick is hidin'."

Longstreet may have been right. Rush had used me to break into the warehouse, and then to find out his father's plans. I could see only one flaw in what Longstreet said. "I have no idea. What about the key code?"

Longstreet said, "*I'm* handling it, with the guys from NIST. Chuck doesn't want Rush anywhere near it. You gotta understand something—Rush is rogue. And you've been helping him."

"I hate that these aren't even questions."

"And I oughta can your ass. But I'll give you one last chance. Try not to screw it up." He set down his cup. "Willis, sincerely, now would be a real good time to tell me where Rush is, and anythin' else you know."

"Rush is not an easy guy to find. Did you see where Tuckerman got whacked?"

"Who?"

175

"The gang member I told you about. You don't like coincidences, right? Not twenty-four hours after I talk to this guy, he's dead."

"So a gangbanger gets shot. Forget about it." He signaled Chella for the check. "We gotta wrap this up before the premiere. Gemelli's tit's in a wringer."

Chella set down the tab, then walked away. Longstreet turned and grinned at me. "Nice ass on that girl. Bet you like the dark meat, huh?"

I was glad Longstreet had said that, I'd been getting dangerously close to actually liking the guy. "Chella's a friend of mine."

Longstreet shrugged. "One last thing."

"Draper Kane."

Longstreet nodded. "I can see Rush doin' it."

"I can't." That was the flaw in Longstreet's theory. Not because Rush was my client. If Rush was motivated by anger over EncryptU.com, why would he have waited years to whack Kane? Plus, I couldn't see Rush killing Kane in that way. Whoever planted that .22 was a pro. An artist. But Rush was all Haggler had right now. When Haggler found out I'd obstructed his investigation, I'd be looking at jail time. Florence Walters would love that. I said, "Problem is, the cops can't find Rush either."

"Then you better try harder. Otherwise I might think you're workin' with him. Shit flows downhill, Willis. So you better hope no one gets their hands on that show. Otherwise, gettin' fired'll be the least of your problems."

CHAPTER 48

I left a message for a friend in the coroner's office, then called Rush to tell him the police wanted to question him. I didn't envy him going up against Haggler and Marziak. And me? I was grateful the investigation had taken my mind off Sarah, if only for a few minutes. I had a hard time ignoring the growing feeling of helplessness.

I had turned onto F Street when my friend from the corner's called back. She told me Tuckerman had been killed by a single .22, the fatal wound at the base of the skull. Now, in D.C., when a gang member gets shot, it's typically not so small a caliber bullet and not so precise. A spray of slugs from a MAC-11—that's the usual scenario, taking out the target (maybe) and innocent bystanders (almost certainly). Tuckerman's killing shared the same MO with Draper Kane's.

As I walked past the vaquero sculpture, I noticed how the blue horse had its hooves stuck in the cactus. The horse's eyes *did* look a bit crazy with panic. The vaquero seemed to have trouble holding on to his gun.

I trudged up the stairs, thinking about my folding cot. I planned to unfold it. When I keyed the door, I caught a whiff of something. Not an antipheromone spray, not Lilly. Who'd ever have thought I'd grow to miss *that*? No, this was a musky scent. I swung the door open, and there was Sondra Stoddard. Or maybe, I hoped, I was simply hallucinating.

She seemed pretty three-dimensional, perched on the edge of my desk, wearing something silky and short. Without the army of handlers and makeup people, she looked different. Her red hair was tangled, as though she'd driven cross-country with the top down. A crooked line of lipstick ran across her mouth. She saw me and smiled, showing a chunk of matching red on her left front tooth. A loose bra strap peeked from the outside of her sleeveless top.

"Surprised?" she asked. Her eyes had a loopy squint to them.

"Very."

Then she grinned and lifted a glass of amber liquid and tossed off a drink. I saw my bottle of Old Overholt on the desk next to her.

"To what do I owe the pleasure?" I asked, closing the door and pocketing my keys.

"Just trying out your lifestyle. Are there women private eyes, too?" She refilled her glass.

"Sure."

"Bet they don't have legs like these." She admired her legs for a moment, then another shot found its way down her throat.

"Actually, the private eye business has an unusually high babe quotient."

She laughed, her voice running up the scale. I came around the desk. The bottle didn't show much of a dent. Her green eyes had pupils the size of hubcaps. "We're not mixing drugs with alcohol, are we?"

"Care to examine me, Doctor?"

I let that pass, returning the Overholt to the bottom drawer. She pivoted as I'd come around so that I was facing her knees. They were nice knees. When I looked up at her she was sighting me down the barrel of my Ruger.

"I found this, too." She giggled. "Kind of scary, isn't it?"

"You should try it from my side." I stood slowly, we were three feet apart.

The giggles were gone. She drew back the hammer. "You pushed me out of a moving car."

"I was trying to keep you safe, there was a gang following me. And I wanted to compliment you on the roll you did."

"Huh. You liked that. Figures, doesn't it?"

"What?"

"The cheap heroics. The Wal-Mart Galahad. So distracted and self-important."

"You're right. And it's all so simple, really. I'm trying to adopt this little girl I found, and I have to pay a lawyer to help me get around this caseworker who hates me. Meantime, I pissed off some Vietnamese gangbangers who're trying to kill me, and the woman I love walked out on me. With your husband, if that makes any difference to you." I stopped, trying to think if there was anything else. "Oh, yeah, I'm working on a case that's going nowhere for a client who seems to have disappeared."

Stoddard's head tilted to the side. "And how is any of this about me?"

"I forgot to mention the lunatic with the great legs who's stalking me."

"Better." She smiled, leveling the gun at my stomach. I wondered if she'd ever fired a Ruger. The trigger requires surprisingly little pressure.

She said, "What'll you do at the premiere? Swing down from the balcony?"

I was tired. Out of patience, out of kindness, out of everything but fatigue. I reached over and plucked the piece from her hand. "Children shouldn't play with guns."

Her face flushed as red as her hair. "You son of a bitch, I could have shot you."

"You'd need bullets, then, wouldn't you?" I put the gun in my pocket. "Time for you to go, Ms. Stoddard."

She closed her eyes, took a few breaths, and the flush left her cheeks. "Sonnie." Then she smiled again, as if we had just gone to level three of some strange game. In a breathy Marilyn voice she said, "And I've been around firearms. That's a 9 mm Ruger, seventeen-plus-one capacity, nylon frame with a steel slide." How would she know that? Maybe from the weapons master on a movie set. Her hips swayed as she came around the desk. Now she stood and stretched, her arms above her head. From weapons expert to sex-kitten in two point five seconds. "Do you have any idea how many men wanna fuck me?"

"Could you call a few of them?" I opened a window—her perfume was choking me.

"Getting hot?"

"No, but I want to sleep in this room." When I turned, she was looking up at me and out came the tears.

People cry all the time, you know. Doesn't mean you have to do anything about it. You're a tough, ruthless bastard who'd sell his mother to solve a case. Provided you knew who your mother was, of course. I held out as long as I could, watching the twin mascara trails slide down her face. Then I let out my breath. I went toward her, put my hands on her shoulders. "Hey, I'm sorry. Look, playtime's over for today, all right?"

A throaty whisper: "Why do you hate me so much?"

"I don't hate you."

She pressed her body close. "I don't believe you, you hate me, I know you hate me."

She was falling apart. She looked so vulnerable. I patted her back, saying, "Everything's all right," feeling the softness of her skin. The next thing I knew, our lips were together and her tongue was down my throat. That's when I heard a sound in the doorway.

Please God, no. I was afraid to look, but I had to. I glanced over. Lilly. I pushed Stoddard away.

"Well," Lilly said, "I guess I needed to see this." She turned and hurried down the hallway, her baggy clothes billowing as she moved. I caught her by the stairwell, taking her arm. She wouldn't look at me.

"How long were you there?"

"Long enough."

"It's not what you think."

Her eyes wouldn't meet mine. "Really?"

I took her chin in my hand so her eyes came up to mine. "No. We—she let herself in."

"Looked like she was forcing herself on you," she said quietly.

"She was."

"And you pushed her away."

I took a step back. "Well, yeah, I did."

She looked down again. "Willis, that's, like, Sondra Stoddard in there. Do you realize that half the planet wants to have sex with her? And you're not the least interested?"

"Well, no, I mean . . ." I didn't see what she was getting at. "I don't see what you're getting at," I said.

"Corby likes you," she said.

What did that have to do with anything? "Lilly, Stoddard and me, I don't—look, let's sit down and talk, okay?" I touched her arm, rested my fingers there. "You're the one I—"

"I've known Corby a long time. He *really* likes you, Willis. A lot."

"Lilly, I don't give a fuck what he likes."

Now she looked in the direction of my office, then back at me. Her faded blue eyes welled up with tears. "Is that really true?"

And on that confusing note, she sobbed, broke free, and ran away.

CHAPTER 49

When I got back to my office, Stoddard was gone. I checked the Roger, taking comfort in working a piece of machinery where everything functioned perfectly. I locked the gun in my desk, then locked the door to my office. I'd have to talk with the corset shop folks downstairs, about who they let into my office. Which would've been easier thinking about what Lilly had said, and try to make sense of it.

The thing is, losing her would ruin my life. I felt sick thinking about it, but at least I knew Lilly could take care of herself. Thinking about Sarah made me panic. As though every small, defenseless second counted.

My thoughts chased each other like mice running in a wheel. I parked outside Rush Gemelli's K Street address. I hadn't much hope. Just one more lead on the trail to nowhere. I was moving, but I wasn't getting anywhere. Walking through the lobby, my foot still smarted from where Stoddard's heel had impaled it. A fitting image—me going around in circles, my foot nailed to the floor.

Mother Hubbard's cupboard had nothing on Rush's office, a tiny room he'd rented from a software firm. I taped a message to

Rush's door, then called the Carlton for Roger Franklin Quell. Some flunky snarled that Quell was not to be disturbed. I told him I worked for Gemelli. That softened the flunky, who allowed I could find Quell at the Uptown theater that afternoon, in three hours' time.

I wasn't far from Lilly's apartment, which was on Hopkins Place NW, a narrow one-block street near Dupont Circle. I circled Hopkins, looking for her silver VW and not finding it. So I looked for a place to park and couldn't find that, either. Some detective.

Ten minutes later, I scored a space where I could see her front door. Maybe God was smiling on me. Or He might have been hoping I'd let my guard down, He has a twisted sense of humor. Hunkered down in my seat, I watched her door and sipped tiny rations of water. I rationed the water because my bladder is the size of a garbanzo bean.

Autumn leaves drifted like red and yellow snowflakes. Straight and gay couples walked by holding hands. An old white Buick crawled past. I put on Oliver Nelson, "Stolen Moments." Last time I'd heard it, Lilly was making tea in my kitchen. I'd watched her pour the water, pick up the tray. Lilly in the doorway with the sunlight behind her, steam rising from the cups. So why was I playing the same song now? Just to torture myself when Stoddard couldn't be around, I guessed.

I tried Rush and got no answer and hadn't really expected one. Haggler would arrest him, and it would all come out—including Rush blackmailing me to work for MPAC. Even worse, that I'd committed a felony for money, pure and simple.

Tucked between the front seats of my car was a spiral notebook I used on stakeouts. I tore out a new sheet, and tried writing a note to Lilly. I'd tell her how I needed her, how I loved her. I'd write something true, poetic, with all the romance she deserved.

Three hours later I'd used up my time, and had littered my car with crumpled sheets of paper. I sighed, then pointed my car up Connecticut Avenue, and the bridge that spanned Rock Creek Park. Flashes of gold and red treetops in the afternoon light. Ahead, the Uptown theater. I didn't want to go there, I didn't want to see the Elephant, or Longstreet, and I especially didn't want to talk with Roger Franklin Quell. So naturally he was standing beneath the marquee.

Quell said, "Well, the private dick."

"A minute of your time."

"Walk with me," Quell said. We entered the Uptown. He stopped at the deserted concession stand. A toady rushed to scoop popcorn. "This is your minute, Gidney," Quell said, brushing back his blond hair.

"The discs I gave Gemelli had pirated scenes. Of your movie."

"Scraps for the theater owners. Gemelli's already told you."

"So why were a bunch of hoods duping it?"

Quell shoved a handful of popcorn in his face. "Huh," he said. "A conscientious sleuth." He snapped his fingers and someone materialized with a napkin. Either Quell was doing a great job of concealing any spark of interest or he truly didn't care. He turned away, as though we had finished.

I followed him down the aisle, the huge Uptown screen seeming to expand as we drew near, Quell gazing up at it. "Beautiful. Like a young girl, a virgin with her legs spread wide." He smiled. "The company that distributes my movies—they've done very well with me. That's why they invested the two mill. To stop the piracy."

"A lot of money."

"They didn't part with it easily." He shoveled in more popcorn. Apparently no one ever suggested he chew with his mouth closed. Spraying me with tiny kernels, he said, "They're not complicated people, these men. And when they get unhappy, it happens fast. Maybe that explains the kind of shows they do—explosions, shoot-outs, that kind of thing."

I brushed popcorn off my jacket. "Does this get interesting?"

Quell picked a kernel I missed, turned it in his hand. He looked relaxed. Entitled to do whatever needed doing. "No one writes about movies and the mob." He swallowed the kernel. "You know what's funny? These mob guys, they'll decide in a second to nail somebody, I mean ruin him completely, right? But the punishment? Weeks. Months. They really enjoy stretching it out, they want to see you *rolling* on that bed of nails. And how do they do that?"

I felt a chill when he continued. "Research. They find out who you care about, then go after them. Hurt them in life-changing ways." He smoothed back his blond hair. "I may put that in my next movie."

"If you get a next movie. I think you've already been hacked."

His face went red. He threw the box of popcorn at me. "Just how fucking stupid are you? It's two mill! When they find out some hack investigator's creating a problem, distracting me, taking up my time—you know what they'll do?"

"You push people around long enough, you start to imagine you're tough." I turned and walked out, trailing popcorn behind me. Away from Quell. Away from the Uptown, the Elephant, everything. Striding down Connecticut Avenue, coming down hard on my heels, feeling like the guy in the funnies with his own personal rain cloud. So somebody steals Quell's film, so the Elephant was disgraced—who cared.

I did. I was in too deep with Sarah to do anything else. My shoulders were hunched above my ears. I felt as though I hadn't taken a breath in a hour. Ahead of me, weaving across the sidewalk, was a black-haired man in a suit and tie, a tiny phone pressed to his ear. He was having an animated conversation and gesturing with his free hand while taking up most of the sidewalk. I edged past him, dark in my own thoughts. Then something pressed into my back. "Yes, that's a gun," he said quietly, snapping the phone shut. With his free hand, he fished the .38 from my pocket.

I'd never met this man, but I'd seen his face before. I heard a car pull up behind me.

"Now get into the car. Slowly. I'm trying to go a week without killing anybody."

"I admire a man with willpower," I said.

"In the car, Gidney."

CHAPTER 50

In the backseat was a Latino pointing a Glock. He wore a work shirt and jeans and let off an odor that would put swamp gas to shame. The well-dressed man sandwiched me between them and *clunked* the door shut.

The driver glided south on Connecticut, steering the big car with two fingers on the top of the wheel. The well-dressed one held the gun very steady while shaking a black fabric hood loose from the inner pocket of his jacket. "You mind wearing this? Or I could crack your skull."

"Don't go to any trouble." I pulled on the hood. "It gives me a secure feeling, you not wanting me to see where I'm going," I said, my breath making the hood's fabric a little wet. "As though I might have a chance of coming back."

"See?" The well-dressed man sounded pleased. "A reasonable man, Luis, that's just what I said. Hey, Mickey, some music, man."

I felt the driver shift. A moment later, a blistering trumpet shot though the car, and a Latin beat picked up. "Arturo Sandoval," I said.

The well-dressed man laughed. "Not bad, man. Sort of gives a new meaning to the term *blindfold test,* huh?"

Luis grunted. My new friends settled back. Maybe they were Mara Loco. If so, I was impressed. Nice to see an aspiring, better sort of criminal. I didn't think they were going to kill me, not right away, at any rate. And the fact they'd snatched me meant I'd upset someone. I'd been making some kind of progress—but what? I still couldn't see the whole picture, which made me angry at myself. Quell had just threatened me, but this couldn't have been his work, it was too fast. All I knew was that, shortly after I'd talked with them, Kane and Tuckerman had been shot dead. I had no interest in joining them. I tried figuring the route, but it got tough once the driver hit the Whitehurst Freeway and crossed into Virginia. Still, I knew this disc. *The Latin Train.* By the time "Waheera" was playing, we'd driven about thirty minutes. We parked and I was escorted, hood in place, out of the car. The floor was cement, and there was a dampness to the air and the closed-in hum of fluorescents.

An elevator took me to a carpeted floor. I went through a doorway, and then down another hall and through another doorway. The well-dressed man said to take a seat.

They tied my hands behind me. Off came the hood, and I was looking at a room full of Latino kids, between the ages of fifteen and twenty. Smoking, drinking beers, playing cards, watching

TV. Like the dayroom at Bockman's. A blue haze hung in the air. At a table next to me, a huge kid was giving himself a tattoo. He used a needle and a ballpoint pen attached to a little battery-run motor. It was slow work. He had his tongue out and his brow furrowed in concentration. So far, he had tattooed a crude border on his left arm and the words *La Marra Lo* when I said in Spanish, "Hey, man."

He looked up at me.

"Just one *r* in *Mara,*" I said.

He was still frowning at his arm when Luis, the man with the plaid shirt from the limo, came in dragging a boy by his shirt collar. The others stopped what they were doing. Luis let go of the kid's collar, dropping him to the floor, then told the well-dressed man, "Kid did it again, Jorge."

Jorge shook his head. "Shit. Guys, over here." The Mara Loco gang members trooped over to form a circle around the kid. Jorge shot back the cuff on his jacket, revealing a gold watch. "Ten seconds. On my mark. Go." Then, as Jorge counted out the seconds, all the kids in the room kicked the stuffing out of the one on the floor. When it was over, they moved away and Luis came into the circle. He helped the kid from the floor and asked him if he was all right. The kid nodded, looking ashamed. One of the others handed him a lit cigarette, which he took gratefully.

Jorge sat beside me. "Sniffing gas—he knows that's against the rules."

"So you beat him?"

"Taught him a lesson. Discipline, that's the key. I learned that in Nicaragua."

"You were a freedom fighter?"

He grinned a wolf's grin. "Haven't heard that shit in a long time. No, Sandinista. Tomás, he's the freedom fighter around here." A small rangy guy a few years younger than Jorge opened a door. In his hand was a little bottle I didn't like the look of. He tossed it, caught it, and nodded at me.

"I'm ready. Bring him in."

CHAPTER 51

Jorge pulled me to my feet and shoved me into the next room. It was carpeted, had wood paneled walls, leather chairs, and a metal desk. Tomás sat behind it, facing me. There was a window behind him with a view of a river. Probably the Potomac, which meant we were south of Alexandria. Blue skylight highlighted the black glossy hair Tomás had brushed off his forehead. He played with the tiny glass bottle. Sodium pentothal?

Luis's odor expanded behind me. He shoved me into a chair while Tomás regarded me with calculating brown eyes. His face had small, almost delicate features. "So, you're Gidney."

Luis smacked the back of my head. I turned and looked up at him. "Don't do that again," I said. "And back off, your aroma is rotting my clothes."

Tomás said, "Hey, Gidney, worry about me, okay? You're gonna be our guest for a while." He waved the tiny bottle at me. Maybe it was some kind of poison.

"How long a while?"

"Who knows? You do like we say, you just might leave here breathin'. Consider this a chance to sample our hospitality." Just then, a door opened to his left and a woman came in. The men in the room seemed to stand a little straighter when she did. I could see why.

She was slender, with black hair down to her waist and a cool, smooth forehead. Her small breasts filled out a mustard yellow top that went nicely with her complexion, and she had sprayed on some black stretch pants. She was smoking a small cigar, chewing gum, and when her almond brown eyes flitted over me, I raised and lowered my eyebrows at her, Groucho-style. She pretended not to notice.

She walked a lazy walk to the couch, arranged some pillows, then sat down, her back against the pillows and her legs out-stretched. That's when I noticed her feet were bare. Little puffs of cotton were stuffed between her toes.

Tomás turned the top of his tiny bottle and removed a brush, then wrinkled his forehead as he bent to apply red polish to the big toe of the woman's left foot. Smiling, his eyes on her toes, Tomás said, "So, Gidney. You're makin' trouble for everyone, snoopin' around all over—how come?"

I said, "It's my job."

"I hope you get paid by the mile. No, I mean, like, why? Other ways to make a buck."

"I flunked out of the crook's academy."

"Hey, you guys clear out a moment. We wanna talk." Jorge lead the others out, closed the door softly behind him. Maybe this was my chance to escape. Maybe I could break free and overpower Tomás and his girlfriend and jump out the window. Right, and maybe the fumes from the toenail polish would knock us all out and I could just float away through the keyhole. His girlfriend stubbed out her cigar in a glass ashtray on an end ta-ble, then fooled with a fresh one while Tomás dug out his lighter.

I said, "You're the freedom fighter."

He beamed at me. "You talk to Jorge? Yeah, el Narigón and me were shootin' at each other, now we're fuckin' partners. So tell me about the kid." He lit the woman's cigar and she purred at him.

"What kid?"

"The one you're trying to adopt. Shit, we heard all about it."

"From who?"

"Don't worry about that." He went back to the girl's foot. "Y'know, I can't think of no private eyes with kids. Charlie Chan never adopted no kids."

"Didn't need to, he had number-one son."

"You dig those movies?"

"The ones with Warner Oland."

Tomás was on the second toe. "He's the best, man. But that don't explain *your* kid."

"I could say it's none of your business."

"Sure, and I could shoot you for sayin' it." He looked up at me. "C'mon, Gidney, you got me curious."

I took a breath, let it out slowly. I had tried explaining this— to the folks at DCAS, to Jan and Janet, to Lilly. No one ever got it. No reason this gang boss should get it now. "Look, it doesn't matter." I sat back in my chair with my eyes closed. I felt too tired to argue anymore. "I was working a case. I went into this house in Northeast and found a dead woman there. The police were never able to identify her. A white woman. And there was this black baby. So when I left, I took the baby with me."

I opened my eyes. "Then the cops came and took her, stuck her in D.C. foster care."

"Rough ride for a kid," he said.

"Yeah, well. Some time ago, I went through there myself, and the ride hasn't gotten a hell of a lot smoother. I thought I could save the kid a little trouble."

"A little trouble for her means a lot for you."

I sighed. "Starting to look that way."

Tomás blew on the girl's toes, then started in on the other foot. "It's like that whole Oriental, Warner Oland thing, you know? You save a life, you're responsible for it."

"Never thought of it that way."

"Sure. That's fuckin' rare, man. I really admire you takin' on that kind of responsibility."

I looked at him. "So, you'll let me go?"

"Nah, you'll stay on ice for a while, then I'll probably kill you." He grinned up at me. "You kill a guy, you got no responsibilities at all. See, that's why I like *my* job."

CHAPTER 52

While Tomás went to work on his girlfriend's toes, six Locos went to work on me. They pounded my ribs and loosened my teeth. For them, it was exercise. For me, it was the most sound going-over since my induction to Bockman's.

Then they took me to an empty room and got mad at one another—none of them had brought any rope. Two watched me while the rest went searching. It hurt to move, but I looked around. The ceiling had a grid for fluorescent lights, but the acoustic tiles and fixtures were long gone. Some feeble light squeezed in through the metal grating on the window. The floor was bare concrete, with a few scraps of carpet lying here and there. In the corner was a smashed VHS tape. An unplugged refrigerator stood on the other side, its open door gaping foolishly.

The others came back with rope. They formed a circle, then forced me down on the concrete floor while two of them pointed guns at me. The two shooters were facing each other on opposite sides of the circle. If I made a move, they'd just as likely shoot each other as me, but I was in no condition to chance it. Once they had tied my wrist and ankles, they stretched the ropes and lashed them to support beams, copper piping, and the dead refrigerator.

Then they left.

I spent a few minutes just lying there. The concrete had felt cold through my jacket at first. Then my body heat made the floor warmer. I took a few breaths, feeling my chi rise and fall along my spinal column. I was tired. I figured if I closed my eyes for a moment, I'd have more energy to get out of this mess. Sounded reasonable. That's because I was a reasonable guy. But I wouldn't fall asleep, no way. Just a little rest. Surprising how comfortable concrete could be, really. Then my eyes snapped open—I *had* fallen asleep. I slapped myself—mentally, of course—then began working the ropes in earnest.

Was the weak link the copper pipes? They'd tied my left wrist to a pipe junction that looked none too strong. I started tugging. At first I couldn't tell if I was making any headway. Then a few minutes later, I stopped and craned my head around. My eyes had adjusted to the dark. One of the pipes had bent. Good work, Gidney. Keep it up, and you'll be out by Christmas. The problem was, I needed a tiny bit more rest. See what I'd been able to do with a catnap? Imagine how many more copper pipes I could yank out with some real sleep behind me. Fistfuls of pipes, thousands of pipes, millions and billions and trillions of pipes.

A whiff of cigar smoke. The door opened. Tomás's girlfriend

stood silhouetted in the doorway, the hall lights making her cigar smoke blue. She entered, closed the door quietly. Hot damn, she'd come to untie me. Poor kid, probably smitten with my good looks.

"I am Valerian," she said in Spanish.

"A pleasure to meet you."

She knelt on the floor next to me. "Did they hurt you? Are you all right?"

"How about untying me?"

"You are different, not like the others. I am going," she said, "to read you my poetry." She produced a pile of pages—it looked bigger than *Moby-Dick* in manuscript form—and began:

> *"Rain falls between my toes.*
> *Memories bubble up from my nails.*
> *Like drops defying gravity—"*

"Uh, excuse me," I said, "but I'd be able to concentrate much better if you untied me."

She thought about it. Then shook her head. "Tomás would not like that. Just try to visualize the words. Your ropes are illusion."

Well, that was helpful. She cleared her throat.

> *"Chaotic choices stream to my portal.*
> *The Disney Channel is speaking through me.*
> *Mickey, where are you?"*

I found myself hoping the Locos would be back soon. The kicking they'd given me had been easier to take. The problem was, I needed her to leave before I could try to escape. But I was so tired. If I listened any more, I would crash.

She lit a cigar, then continued, stanza after stanza. You had to hand it to her, she really did have a grasp of the mundane. I tried to stay awake. I visualized the unpaid bills collecting in my desk, and which ones I'd have to pay first. I thought about the Elephant and Kane and Rush, about Haggler and Marziak, about Brooks and Stoddard. I visualized Florence Walters. I thought about the Dragon Boys, about Napolitano warning me at the bar, about Jorge pointing a gun at me. I thought about Lilly.

Nothing helped. Valerian kept reading. The concrete floor felt warm. Comfortable. My will drifted, along with my consciousness, drifted into the air like smoke, and evaporated.

CHAPTER 53

Sunday morning. The day of the big premiere. I felt great.

Sure, I was tied to the floor in an abandoned warehouse, at the mercy of a bunch of hoods getting ready to kill me—but why nitpick? I'd just had my best night's sleep in months. You could have elected me president and it wouldn't have killed my groove.

I pulled at the ropes that held my hands and feet. Just like the night before, I tried pulling the copper pipes with my right hand. The rope cut into my wrist. Then I stopped as I heard movement outside the door. These were street kids, it was way too early for them to be up and around. The noise passed. I went back to the pipes. After what seemed like forever, I gave it up. My heart was racing. I craned my head to see the refrigerator. I gave it a try. It hurt my arm, my ribs, my back. My whole body was on fire, but I nudged it, got the refrigerator an inch closer. I didn't know when the Locos were coming back, so I tried again. I figured if I put absolutely everything I had into it, I could buy an inch. Then a short rest. A few more attempts bought me just enough slack to work my wrist free. After that, I loosened the other ropes, carefully, so I could slip back into them.

I stood, looked around, listening for footsteps and not hearing any. Not much in this room to work with. But I used what I found. I had to hurry, get ready. Then I lay back down, slipped back into the ropes. I tried to look the way they had left me. If they opened the door and sounded the alarm, I was a dead man.

I didn't wait long. When they came in, I kept my breathing even and my eyes closed, until they started kicking me. I had no idea if this would work, but what choice did I have? Three of them, with guns in their belts. One was the tattoo artist who couldn't spell *Mara*. The other two pointed their guns while the artist undid my wrists and ankles, pulling me up on my feet. I staggered and bent over. The one on the left came to steady me as I reached into my shirt, then swung the jagged plastic from the broken VHS cassette up and across his face. Blood spurted and he screamed and backed away as I sent a roundhouse kick into the stomach of hood number two, who tumbled into copper pipes. Now I kept turning, accelerating and feeling my breath rising as I switched feet and snap-kicked the *Loco* with the gashed face. This took about three seconds.

Hood three, the tattoo artist, looked like a man whose backup parachute had failed. He ran for the door. I was right behind him, the refrigerator cord in my hands. I slipped the cord over his head and around his neck, pulling him backward and up.

Now, this kid had a gun. If he'd stayed calm, he could have shot me. Instead his hands clawed at his throat. He kicked backward, but I had my legs apart. Less than two minutes and the fight went out of him. He slumped to the floor. I took his gun and car keys, then the guns and keys of his friends. All the guns were fourteen-shot Glocks—the firearm of choice among those who can't aim.

Hood two, the one without the gash across his face, started to stir. I tapped him back to sleep with the Glock, then went to the tattoo artist, made sure he was breathing. Christ, I hadn't wanted to kill him, I'd been very careful about that. Maybe the son of a bitch had fainted. "C'mon, you idiot," I said. "Wake up." I slapped him and his eyes snapped open with a lovely bit of fright in them.

"Get me out of here," I said.

"*Yo no sé.*"

I switched to Spanish. "Look, you little shit. Tell me what I want to know and you'll live to tattoo another day. Where's the exit?" He shook his head. I pressed the barrel of the Glock against his forehead and asked him again. He didn't answer, just sat there slumped in defeat. The gun wasn't scaring him, he'd probably never been shot. But he had been strangled—recently. I dangled the loop of refrigerator cord in front of him. "This is going around your throat—again—if you don't answer. How do I get out of here?"

He shook his head. "Tomás'll fucking kill me, man."

"Worry about me."

He started shaking. Well, he was only sixteen or so. A sensitive hood. "Downstairs," he sobbed. "The garage."

I pointed him to a dusty corner. "Draw it for me."

"I can't, I don't know how." He was getting hysterical.

"What's you name?'

"Chuco."

"Calm down, Chuco, everything's cool. Now think hard. If you were going to the garage, which way would you go?"

He knelt down and made a map, his trembling finger tracing

a sawtooth path through the dust. He sniffled and wiped his nose on his sleeve. "These're the elevators."

"How about the stairs?"

He looked at me, his eyes filled with tears. "Stairs?"

Christ. "Okay, I'll find them myself."

"Hey, man," Chuco said. "Tomás finds me and I got no injuries, he gon' be fuckin' pissed." I nodded, then bent down close to him. "Quick, behind you!" He whipped his head around and I smacked him with the Glock. Never saw it coming. I left a message and my cell phone number in the dust for Tomás, then tried the door.

It wouldn't budge. Locked? That didn't fit with the overall pattern of sloppiness. I put my shoulder to it and it opened with a bang that sounded louder than the big one that started the universe. Maybe I was nervous. I scanned the empty hallway, knowing if I could only get out of there before someone shot me—or worse, read poetry to me—I'd be a lucky man.

I went down to the corner, took a right, as Chuco had instructed. Voices approached and I scrambled for an open door, found one, and ducked inside. The voices grew closer.

Jorge's voice asked, "So it's tonight?"

Tomás said, "What he wants. He's cooked some way of stealin' the movie and wreckin' his old man, all at once."

"He sure hates the old guy." Next to my door, they stopped. So did my breathing.

Tomás said, " 'Cause of what he did to his mother, I think."

"The father? What'd he do?"

"He shined her on."

Jorge asked, "And that means?"

"That he blew her off." Tomás sounded like he was enjoying himself.

Jorge blew out his breath. "*¿Que mierda dices?*"

"*La cogió y la tiró a la mierda. Bonnie le escribió y lo llamó, pero el nunca regresó las llamadas. El nunca la ayudó a soportar su hijo y por eso, el hijo lo odia.*"

"*Ya lo cache.*"

They started moving away.

"And the *hombre*?" Jorge asked.

"Said to give him a chance to talk, find out what he knows, then whack him."

"Sooner, not later. He worries me."

I got a chill as I realized they were talking about me. Their voices faded as they moved away. I waited a moment, checked the hallway. Another left, and I found the elevators, and, just a bit beyond, two doors. Which one was the stairwell? I cracked open the first door. Inside, two Locos worked over a man tied to a chair, a big white guy in a shirt that had once been blue and was now streaked red. I closed the door. The next door was the stairwell. I took the first step. I didn't know the big man. He had nothing to do with me. I was lucky to be alive. My heart was pounding. My hand on the gun was sweaty. Eddie Vermeer would've told me the smart move was to get out while I could.

CHAPTER 54

At first, they didn't see me. I slipped in, aiming the gun at them, but they were too busy pounding the big man to notice. So I cleared my throat. I felt silly doing it, but it stopped them. They turned; their faces had a nice bit of shock, which grew to sullen anger when I told them to sit on the floor back-to-back.

The clean-shaven of the two was resigned in a hangdog kind of way. The other had a beard and an attitude. In Spanish he told me my mother's favorite pastimes, and that my father was not of the human species. The kids back at Bockman's would've put him to shame.

I had them link each other's arms, then tapped them with the Glock. The clean-shaven one went down fine. His buddy needed an extra tap.

I disarmed them—why the hell did they carry guns in their own hangout anyway? I decided not to take their guns. I mean, how many of these things was I supposed to carry? So I took the clips and tossed the guns in the corner. A minute wasted trying to untie the big man, then back to the bearded kid. He carried a wicked-looking knife.

I cut the guy loose. Then I tried stopping him as he slid to the floor. Picking up the state of Montana would've been easier. In the corner were some cleaning supplies left over from the previous tenant. I soaked his shirttail in ammonia, then covered his mouth while holding his shirttail to his nose. He sputtered awake, eyes locking on mine with animal fear. "Ready?" I asked. He looked at the bodies on the ground, then nodded his bloody head. I gave him my hand.

His arm around my shoulders, we went from empty hallway to the stairwell with its seemingly endless flights of stairs, which was probably only two, then finally the garage. I fumbled in my pockets for the three sets of car keys, all the time expecting the elevator would open and the Locos would spill out, guns blazing, "as seen on TV." All the key rings had remotes. The first two did nothing. The third opened the doors to a smashed-in SUV. I unloaded the big man in the passenger seat, then keyed the engine. We pulled up to the garage door, the weight sensor opened it, and I drove away from there.

The bright daylight hurt my eyes. I squinted against the morning sun. A few blocks ahead, I saw the Potomac River glisten. The Locos' headquarters was just another building in an industrial park. I was trying very hard not to speed. It took me a few minutes to find the George Washington Parkway. With the river on my right, we headed north to D.C.

The man groaned. I pulled over at a 7-Eleven and got him some baby wipes and a Coke, coffee and three Sara Lee muffins for myself. He nodded when I handed him the wipes and whimpered as he cleaned his face. Along with some bad cuts and bruises, he'd have two black eyes, but he seemed to be okay.

"Who are you?" he asked.

"You first."

"Howell, Jeff Howell." He held up a big hand. I looked at it. It appeared he was waiting for me to shake it, so I took a hand off the steering wheel. "Willis Gidney."

Pumping my hand, he said, "Gidney, Gidney . . . I used to know some Gidneys up around Towson. You related to them? A good family." He looked around the interior of the car.

"No. Why were the Locos beating you?"

"There's also some Gidneys I knew around Chicago, brothers, into rock climbing." He looked into the backseat. "You like this piece of shit? I can get you into a Lexus for next to nothing."

"Look, I don't want to play Name That Family or Let's Make a Deal. The Locos were serious back there, and I want to know why."

He looked a little hurt. "Or maybe a Caddy, which is better 'cause the money stays in the USA."

I slammed on the brakes, swerving to the shoulder in a cloud of dust and gravel. "You've got two seconds to tell me why you were partying with the Locos, or I'm leaving you on the side of the road."

He looked at his hands. "I guess I owe you that much."

"So start talking."

"Well, I'm a car salesman."

I sighed. "No kidding."

"The Locos and I are business partners." He winced when he touched the side of his face.

"What kind of business?"

"Import/export." Spoken too casually.

I loosened my jaw muscles and took a breath. "You've lost blood, you need stitches and antibiotics. You need to be hospitalized. The cars you've just tried to bribe me with—are they the same cars the Locos are stealing and shipping south? 'Cause I want to know how the deal works."

He didn't answer. I looked over at him. His eyes were closed and he'd slumped back in his seat. "No trade-in on this heap," he mumbled. Then he passed out.

When he said he was busy, Slip Barnett had told me about a car ring. The Locos were also into cars, Napolitano had said. Now I had a Loco associate dumped in my lap.

An hour and two pints of blood later, at Sibley Hospital, Howell came to. They'd pumped him full of painkillers and sewn his face together.

Now his eyes were open. "See, cars are a big deal in Central and South America. Luxury cars, I mean. You got your Beemers, your Benzes. Caddies and Lincolns."

"And you're helping them."

"I'm a consultant, giving 'em pointers." He shrugged. "It's business. See, the tariffs to bring a car into Latin America are a killer. And we got NAFTA, makes it easier to get cars across the border. So what if the Locos pay out a few thousand in bribes? They're stealing the cars, it's more profitable than drug dealing. Sometimes they don't even take cash; they just swap the cars for guns or whores or coke." This fit with what Napolitano had told me. A nurse came and checked his blood pressure. He smiled, but she ignored him. When she left, he sighed. "I'm sleepy. Why don't you go away."

"In a second. Where are the cars headed when they go south?"

"Guatemala. Then they drive 'em over land to Honduras and Belize." He yawned. "Or they're shipped by boat to Acajutla or Nicaragua. Really, I gotta sleep awhile"

Howell's eyes closed. I nudged him and he blinked at me. I said, "Last question: Why were the Locos giving you the beauty treatment?"

He yawned. "Well, I'm the car dealer, right? I'm taking a risk, right? Fair compensation, that's what we were negotiating."

"Looks like they were winning."

He waved his hand at me in a lazy arc. "Fuck no. I was wearing those assholes down." He shut his eyes, settled back. "I woulda had 'em by now if you hadn't interrupted."

CHAPTER 55

According to the file I'd filched, the Bishops had four kids of their own, ages eighteen to twenty-three. Horace Bishop ran his own auto-body shop in an alley off Kennedy Street, and his wife, Violet, had a day-care center in their house. That part of D.C., near the Takoma Metro stop, was a working-class neighborhood. I waited in my car, watching the front door. My chest hurt from the Locos kicking me. The phone in my shirt pocket started buzzing, and that hurt too.

Hester Doyle said, "So, how's the shamus? Say, you a private eye or a private ear?"

"What're you talking about?"

"I did some more checking on where *shamus* comes from. Maybe you're not a janitor after all. See, the Yiddish term *shamus* is like a private ear, it comes from the Hebrew *shin-mem-ayin*. You ever hear a Jew say the Shema?"

"Like in '*Shema Y Israel*'? It means 'Hear, O Israel,' doesn't it?"

"Not bad, for a goy. Yeah, the word *Shema* means to hear, to listen, give heed. That's the literal meaning, but it's really closer to the concept of understanding, accepting the fact of something, see? It means a shamus is a person who hears and understands. That sound like you?"

"On a good day."

"So maybe you can hear and understand when you get a bill from me? See, I got a real clear vision of you making out a check right away. Later, Mr. Private Ear."

The Bishops had a small lot, with a little white fence around it. Houses on both sides pressed in, you'd smack your kneecaps edging through sideways. The yards and houses were old but well-kept. I got myself out of the car and walked to the front door and rang the bell. Nothing. I tried again. Next door, a black man in his fifties was painting the side of his house. I walked over to him.

"Bishops live there?" I asked.

He looked over at their house, then nodded, his face flecked with white paint.

"Know where they are?" He shook his head. "Reason I ask, they have a foster child and I'm making sure they're good parents." He kept painting.

"You have a nice even stroke there," I said. Like Tomás laying polish on his girlfriend's nails. I wondered if he'd seen my message yet. There was something nagging me about my stay with the Locos, some distant alarm bell ringing, but I couldn't figure out what. Meanwhile, the man dipped the brush and kept going. "Some foster kids, the parents take them just so D.C. gives them money. You think the Bishops are those kind of people?"

He may have shrugged as he dipped his brush again. Hard to say.

"On the other hand, they could be humanitarians. Maybe they'll get a Nobel Prize and share the cash with the neighborhood."

He exhaled loudly through his nose.

I nodded. "Well, I'm tired of you talking my ear off." I went down the block, ringing bells and hearing the birds sing, my shadow long on the sidewalk in front of me. No one answered their doors. I went across the street and tried there as well. At the next-to-last house on the block, I rang the bell, then took a step back from the door and put what I hoped was a nonthreatening look on my face. A small woman with pale gray eyes and pale skin opened the door.

"Hi, I'm with DCAS, doing a routine check. Do you know the Bishops?"

"Oh, them. Yes, I do."

"And are the Bishops good neighbors?"

"Who did you say you were?"

"Name's Quell, working for DCAS. What kind of neighbors are the Bishops?"

She took a tiny step closer. "Well, I wouldn't want them to know what I told you."

"Anything you say will be in confidence, ma'am."

"Oh, well." She seemed to be thinking. "They're terrible, terrible neighbors."

This sounded promising. "Why?"

"Well, they have these . . . *brats*, they make such a racket, you wouldn't believe it."

"You mean the day-care center Mrs. Bishop runs?"

She nodded, a small, precise movement. "Is that legal? Running a day-care center in your home? Plus their own brats. *And* they encourage unwed girls to impregnate themselves."

I leaned against the door frame. "How do they manage that?"

She looked up and down the street, then leaned closer to me, letting off an aroma of pastry and bourbon. "They took in Darius."

"Who's Darius?"

"Well, I wouldn't want anyone to know I said this, but over at that house"—and she pointed down the street—"there's a slut."

"I see."

"Well, Debbie—she's the slut—wanted to have the baby—oh dear, I probably shouldn't have told you her name, and you with the government and all." She didn't appear sorry at all.

"It's all right. I'm really interested in the Bishops."

This seemed to disappoint her. "Well, first Debbie wanted to keep her baby. But after Darius was born, she saw how much trouble a baby can be. So the Bishops offered to take him."

"For how long?"

"Well, *they* said until Debbie wanted him back. Except I don't think Debbie's going to want him back, as she's got another baby on the way." She smiled at me, nodding again. I was starting not to like her.

"Bet the Bishops are pretty steamed with Debbie."

"Them? No, they get money from the government. For keeping Darius. That's what's wrong with the District, young man, the government rewards the bad and punishes the good."

"And how did the government reward you, ma'am? With a bottle of Early Times?"

That earned me a door slammed in my face, which made me feel a little better. I went back to my car and waited. About forty minutes later, the Bishops rolled up in their Sunday best, perhaps returning from church. They piled out of their car, and there was Sarah, holding hands with a boy who had to be Darius. She was grinning up at him as the door shut behind her.

No one saw me. I started my car and drove away.

CHAPTER 56

I'd driven a few blocks west to Piney Branch when an old white Buick appeared in my rearview. I'd seen the same car near Lilly's, and outside Napolitano's restaurant. I slowed to get a good look at the driver. Then a second look. No, it couldn't be. A few quick turns and I'd lost the Buick. I got onto Beach Drive and called Stayne Matthews. "Willis, I do not have Sunday hours."

"Florence Walters is following me in her car."

"What? Why would she do that?"

"No idea." Actually, maybe I did kind of challenge her to follow me around, just to see what a good parent I'd make. What an idiot I was. "A quick question, counselor—could we try greasing the good Ms. Walters?"

"No, and you know why. She's not the type. Her boss, yes, but not her. Why?"

I told him about the Bishops, the kind of family they seemed to be. While I drove south on Reno Road, he was silent. Finally he said, "Forget 'em. If the caseworker's boss has okayed it, there's nothing Walters can do, my boy. So all it means is that the child's with a nice family until we get her to you. That didn't come out right. Well, you know what I mean, right?"

My apartment was Dragon-free, thanks to the patrol car parked in front. The driver was reading the *Washington Times*.

"Hey there," I said.

"You Gidney?" I told him I was Gidney. He nodded again. "Napolitano said don't let no one whack you 'til Monday."

"Nice of him."

The cop shrugged. "Someone'll be here 'til tomorrow."

At the top of my stairs, the door opposite my apartment swung open, revealing Dino Schwartz, a freelance writer in a ratty blue robe. "Why, it's *Willis*." He talked like a suburban housewife who'd quaffed a few cocktails before welcoming home the hubby.

"Dino." I keyed the lock to my door.

"A messenger dropped this off." He handed me a thick envelope. "What is it?"

It was four hundred double-spaced pages. I read the cover page and gagged. As if I had time for this. I shoved the pages at Dino. "It's a novel by Corbin Brooks."

He gasped and snatched it out of my hands, kissed my cheek, then slammed his door shut.

Half-hoping to see Lilly there, I keyed my door open. My phone started ringing before I'd stepped inside. "This Gidney, hulking hawkshaw and all-around pain in the ass?"

"Marziak, nice to hear your voice."

"We're at Hains Point. Haggler wants you down here to ID a vic."

I gripped the phone. "It's not Rush, is it?"

Marziak laughed, his voice sounding like a wood chipper buzzing a Christmas tree. "Naw, not him, the other guy."

"Romero?"

"Yeah, him. But if you wanna question him, you're a little late."

"Because he's dead."

He whistled. "You are one quick study, Willis."

Late afternoon, and a ridge of fast-moving clouds blocked the sun as I drove past the Jefferson Memorial towards Hains Point. Families had started gathering their kids, loading up their cars for the drive home, their Sunday picnic supplies packed away, and a few fishing rods stuck out the windows.

Marziak waved me past the uniform stationed by the yellow crime-scene tape. A cold wind blew off the Potomac, but not nearly as cold as Romero's body. The ME was fussing over him, the cameraman checking his pictures. I gave Haggler the color photo I'd taken from Romero's house. Haggler studied it, then nodded. In the gloom, with people milling around him, Romero looked small and defenseless. "He's been here all day. At least," Haggler said.

"No one noticed?" I asked.

"Hell, people saw him. Fishermen walked past him, kids were playing baseball nearby. They all thought he was a bum sleeping it off."

"How'd he die?"

"Entry wound, base of the skull."

I walked around Romero, looked at his face. "No exit wound. The shooter probably used a small-caliber weapon."

"Like Kane," Haggler said. "And Tuckerman."

Marziak walked up. "Gidney explaining the crime scene to you, Loot?"

Haggler said, "You say this guy was involved with MPAC?"

"I found a check stub, Romero had hidden it."

"Why would he do that?"

"I don't know. Did he have anything on him?"

"Nothing," Haggler said. "Could be a robbery."

"What was this guy doing for MPAC?" Marziak asked.

"I don't know."

Marziak tilted his head at Romero. "How long he work there?"

"I don't know."

"Well, he's too small for a security guard."

"I'm betting he was there for another reason."

"Like what?" Haggler started walking to his black SUV. Marziak and I turned to follow.

"I don't know," I said.

"There's a shitload you don't know," Marziak said.

"Yeah, I'm thinking of putting that on my card." I turned to Haggler. "Look, Romero bought the video decks they used in making pirate copies in that warehouse in Alexandria."

"Doesn't explain why he's napping under the stars, does it?" Marziak asked. "This more of your client's work? First Kane, now this guy? That what Rush Gemelli hired you for?"

My hands had clenched into fists. "Gemelli hired me to help his father."

We came to a stop by Haggler's SUV. Marziak's giant eyebrow came down. "For such a smart guy, you sure do some dumb things. We could make a case that Rush Gemelli's buying you off, that you're an accessory."

"Al," Haggler said.

Marziak turned to Haggler. "I'm just saying, that's all."

Haggler said to me, "You think Rush killed Kane?"

"No. What about ballistics?"

"They're both twenty-two slugs," Marziak said. "So, what do you say, smart guy?"

"Rush doesn't seem the type." Why was I sticking up for Rush? Had my involvement with Sarah, my anxiety over her, clouded my judgment? Rush told me he wanted to help his father. Did I believe him because I wanted to be Sarah's father?

Marziak snorted. "Not the type. Maybe you could teach a seminar for the rest of us."

Haggler gave him a dead-eyed look. "Get some coffee, Al."

Marziak's cheeks flushed. He shoved a patrolman aside, got in a squad car, then peeled away.

"He's crazy about me, isn't he?" I asked.

"At least he had the guts not to quit."

"Do we have to do this?"

"Al Marziak didn't graduate top of his class, neither. Shad

died protectin' you, boy. Least you coulda lived up to what he saw in you."

"You told me to give the cops a try, and I did, okay? I went through the Academy, plus a year on the force." The temperature had dropped with the light. I was glad it was dark, I didn't want Haggler see me trying to keep a lid on what I felt. "You're saying you were surprised things didn't work out?"

His jaw muscles bunched, he poked me in the chest. " 'Cause you never stuck with it. You just up and quit and never told me what the problem was." He dropped his hand. "I could've helped you."

"No, you couldn't."

"That's *your* story. But in my book, that means you never tried. You never—" He stopped and closed his eyes, drawing a deep breath. "Where's Rush Gemelli now?"

"I can't find his home address, just a deserted office."

"You tell him he's our meat?" Meaning their primary suspect in the Kane shooting.

"Give me a little credit, okay? I said you wanted to talk, that's all. How about the father? You talk to him?"

"Yesterday. He seemed open with us." Haggler looked out at lights from Bolling Air Force Base reflected in the water. "Unless you're working pro bono, Rush paid you. Where's all this going?"

"To the lawyer."

"For the kid, right? You're actually going through with this?"

"Yeah."

"You good on everything?"

I thought about the Bishops. "Sure."

"Uh-huh. No problem with the background checks?" Haggler's eyes got a half-lidded look I didn't like.

"I cleared them okay."

" 'S funny, what with your juvie record."

"Yeah, apparently that was okay too."

He took a paper from his pocket. "Look familiar?"

A copy of my DCAS clearance form. "D.C.'s a big bureau-cracy," he said. "Things can slip through the cracks."

I stared at him. "You cleared my record."

"Just made sure certain crap you pulled as a kid didn't show up." He shrugged. "But it still could."

"I'd kind of like that not to happen."

"Really? Come Monday morning, DCAS could get an amended form, listin' *all* your priors. Think you still got a chance in hell to get that kid—what's her name?"

"What do you want?"

He seemed surprised. "Rush Gemelli. Either he walks in or you bring him—I don't care which. But if I'm not talkin' to him in three hours, Florence Walters is going to get an amended form on her desk tomorrow morning. You hear me, boy?"

CHAPTER 57

It was all over. Haggler had given me three hours to do the impossible—find Rush. There were only two hours before the premiere of *Explosive Rounds*. I spent a few minutes wandering Hains Point in the dark. Circling around and around, going nowhere. Standard operating procedure.

I walked past a long line of parked cars along the water,

looking at license plates and thinking how you could use them to generate random numbers. Maybe the Elephant had done that to create the forty digit key for Quell's movie. Except it wouldn't have been the Elephant, it would've been his son. Or maybe Longstreet and his pals at NIST. Then I noticed something. I backed up and took out my notebook. I doubled checked the numbers. Unless I had written it down wrong from the insurance premium, I was standing by Jaimie Romero's car.

It was a beat-up Camry, painted primer gray. It took me a minute to nudge the locked door open. He'd kept his car clean, cleaner than mine. The only item of interest was a spiral-bound pad, wedged down into the passenger's seat. The kind of notepad that fits in your shirt pocket. It looked new, none of the spiral binding showed the compression that happens when you carry it around. Someone had written four phone numbers inside. Was this a clue? I had no idea, it'd been so long since I'd seen one.

Back at my office, I got to work dialing Romero's phone numbers. A glass of Old Overholt fortified my executive abilities.

The first phone number brought those three annoying tones the phone company lays on you when you've got a nonworking number. Same with the second. The third got me an answering machine at a beauty parlor in San Diego that had a special on perms. The fourth was nonworking. Confusing. Maybe another drink would help. It certainly couldn't hurt. I wondered if Romero had transposed any of the phone numbers, disguised them in some way. I didn't recognize most of the area codes. Then again, new area codes keep popping up, trying to keep pace with all the cell phones, faxes, and what have you. Ah, for the simple life, to live in a state with just one area code, a state where you dialed only seven numbers to make a call. Imagine the time you'd save each year. Of course, you'd have to live in Utah. More Overholt, Gidney? Your train of thought got derailed.

I called the operator, then asked if she'd identify the area codes. She came back a moment later and said the area codes were not in use. That was okay, I told her, I wasn't of much use myself. She hung up. Who could blame her? I took a clean sheet of paper from my desk and copied down the four strings of numbers. Each phone number had an area code and was ten digits long. You'd need a computer to try all the different combinations. Then I thought of Lilly. She could write a program that would not only figure out the combinations but dial them, too. Then I thought about Sarah. It was all going to end without ever beginning, and there wasn't a thing I could do about it.

So playing on that strip of grass, the one DCAS forgot to pave over, was the best it would ever get. I never would've guessed something like that would seem so important.

I wrote Romero's phone numbers again, this time all together in a long line. Maybe if you selected every other number, you'd get the right ones. Or every third number. Or alternated second and third numbers. Except it would take forever to try them all and I had to get to the premiere at the Uptown theater in forty minutes. I counted the numbers. There were forty total. A minute for each number. Egad, Gidney, you've solved the case. Quick, Watson, the needle.

I folded my work sheet in half, then in half again, and dropped it in the trash. Time to go. I was a block from my car when a woman fell in step with me—she had lots of makeup, high cheekbones, and a severe expression, all wrapped up in a tight silk dress with a fancy brocade. She said in a heavy dragon lady accent, "Beautiful evening."

"Brenda, it's me."

215

In a normal tone of voice, she said, "Oh, shit, Gidney, I'm sorry." She fished her glasses from her purse. "The street lighting here is terrible."

"You should write the mayor."

"And waste a stamp? I'll see hizzoner on Tuesday. So—you busy?" I stopped. She smiled. "Ah, a man who knows a bargain."

"Forty digits—the key code was forty digits long."

"Now you lost me."

I dug Romero's spiral pad from my pocket and looked at the numbers again. "He had the code." I looked at Brenda. "Romero had the code."

She frowned. "And that's good?"

"It wasn't for him."

I'd just unlocked my car when I heard a door slam. Across the street was the old white Buick, with Florence Walters standing in front, peering at me through those Coke-bottle glasses of hers. Christ, that woman just never quit. She started toward me, but she needn't have bothered. The next morning, it would all be over—thanks to Haggler, Walters would get my juvie record.

I'd never see Sarah again.

Screaming tires punctured the quiet, and a car tore around the corner. The Dragons. I knew it even before I saw them. I was moving across the street, looking at Walters looking at them, her face frozen, her mouth open. She was close enough to grab. Just for an instant, I hesitated. The Dragons pulled even as I lunged toward Walters with my arms out and pushed her down, my arms around her and bracing her against the pavement, just as weapon fire thundered above and bullets tore into the stone and the storefront windows, raining down glass and chips of brick and stone.

Their car squealed around a corner. Did they see that they'd missed me? I hustled Walters into my car and zigzagged through the streets. She didn't say a word. Shifting light from passing street lamps fell on her blank face. Her drivers license had her home address, which turned out to be a brick house on Varnum Street NE. An older version of Walters opened the door. When she saw us she cried, "Oh my Lord."

CHAPTER 58

We hustled Walters inside, while I told the older woman— Walters's sister—what had happened and that she should call a doctor. She wanted me to stay. I couldn't. For one thing, I had a premiere to get to. For another, if I stayed, I'd have to think about what had almost happened back there.

I drove through early-evening fog, and the air made a sound as it whistled its way through the rust holes. From overhead came the cries of seagulls. And coming up, a double string of streetlights along the Ellington Bridge, glowing through halos of fog like two lines of silver moons. Across the bridge, twin spotlights, advertising the premiere, sent their probing blue beams skyward, as though searching outer space for intelligent life. We've just about given up trying to find that down here.

White TV trucks sat with engines grumbling, their antennae

and microwave dishes bristling. A black limo crawled and stopped, blocking one of the southbound lanes. The door swung open and Chuck Gemelli staggered out like a man who'd been frozen and hadn't quite thawed. I rushed over, I thought he might fall and ruin his tux. Longstreet climbed out after him, wearing a plain jacket and tie. The crowd behind the photographers quickly lost interest. Longstreet went ahead. Gemelli's jittery eyes followed him. Stage fright?

He steadied and I took my hand away. He gave me a look that was hard to read. With a strained voice, he said, "Good to see you, son." Apparently, we were friends again. It would probably last as far as the candy counter. I wondered what I was doing there. Nobody cared what I thought. They'd disregarded virtually everything I'd said. So why stay? Because Rush had paid me to be there. It was my job, and I was hating every second of it.

Gemelli linked his arm in mine. "Step over here." I followed him to a corner. "I've got to talk to you. Kane was . . . Kane was right."

Before he could say another word, Gemelli started as if he'd been tasered. I followed his gaze and saw Longstreet heading toward us. Gemelli brushed past me to join an arriving senator.

Longstreet said, "You get canned again?"

"Not so far."

"Just remember, you're on the clock. You're gonna stick around." It wasn't a question.

"Sure. What did you tell Gemelli just now, in the car?"

He shrugged. "Rush. He's gotta make his move." We walked past the crowd at the concession stand and went into the theater. Everyone was buzzed, hungry for a Hollywood roller-coaster ride, the latest action flick, the biggest stars, the loudest sounds, the flashiest computer effects money could buy. And a story with all the intensity of a stubbed toe.

The reporters ignored the reserved-seating signs and name cards, shooting quick stand-ups before security shooed them away. Tony Corona's toothy smile for Gemelli turned to a scowl at me once Gemelli turned his back. Longstreet went to the booth, checking on projector security. When the burst came in, Longstreet had to be ready.

Then came a roar from behind us. Brooks and Stoddard making their entrance, with Roger Franklin Quell. The press photographers were crab-walking down the aisle in front of them, video lights blazing and blue flashes popping, Brooks smiling, showing lots of teeth, his arm around Stoddard's bare shoulders.

And then, behind the entourage, another face—Lilly's.

She was in her full-blown baggy clothes regalia, her carryall swinging from her shoulder. No one looked twice at her. God, she was beautiful.

As the posse swept past, I took hold of Quell's sleeve. "Yes?" he hissed at me.

I showed him Romero's notebook. "A dead man had your encryption key. Your security's blown, anyone can hack their way in. Stop the premiere right now—or your two million is down the drain."

He leaned close to me and smiled. "You out of your fucking mind? Stop things now?" He looked around the packed house. "We're about to knock 'em dead."

He pushed past me to sit between Brooks and Stoddard. Stoddard faced Brooks, but I jumped when her foot brushed mine. I tried to make the jump look casual, something I did all the time at premieres. Lilly sat a row back. I went and sat next to her.

"Hi," I said. Always the smooth conversationalist. Her blue eyes looked tentative. "I have to talk with you."

"You've done a lot of talking so far. Maybe you should just listen for a change. Do you want us to be together?"

"More than anything," I said.

"That takes commitment. I'm not sure you know what that is."

"Hey, of course I—"

"You're just listening now, remember? Like if I say to you, 'I'm not leaving your side until we work this out'—that's what I'm talking about."

"I promise. Let's go now. You don't want to see this, do you?"

She swept her dreadlocks off her shoulder. "Well, I told Corby I would. Like I kinda promised him."

I wondered what else she had promised him. The lights faded, a deafening fanfare blasted from the speakers as the studio logo flashed on, a chorus of shrink wrapping coming off packages of sweets—just so you knew the show was starting. And start it did. Did I mention it was loud? And the opening—it was so dark, I wondered if the studio had forgotten to pay their lighting bill the first day of the shoot. Brooks and Stoddard were unarmed and trapped underneath the Lincoln Memorial, a crazed killer with night-vision goggles chasing them. I heard Brooks's voice on the sound track, asking himself how he'd gotten into this mess.

Then Stoddard screamed—not in the movie, but in the row in front of me—as Gemelli stood straight up, grabbed his chest, and toppled over.

CHAPTER 59

I felt for Gemelli's heartbeat. One of the D.C. cops ran over to start CPR. "What happened?"

In the dark, red diodes from inside Gemelli's chair blinked at me. I slit the fabric—a circuit board and transmitter. "It's his pacemaker."

Longstreet grabbed my shoulder. "Someone spotted Rush outside."

Son of a bitch.

"C'mon," Longstreet said. He tore up the aisle. I followed him. I wanted to get my hands on Rush, if only to get Haggler off my back. We ran out onto the street in time to see a black Lexus U-turn and scream north on Connecticut. My feet slid on wet pavement as we got to my car. I had the door open, when I heard footsteps behind me—Lilly. "Before the night is over, remember?" She took my hand.

"Now?"

"If you're committed to staying together."

Longstreet said, "What—you're the girlfriend? Take a hike."

She told him to do something anatomically impossible, then got in my car. Longstreet shook his head. We screeched away from the curb, with Lilly sandwiched between us.

"I can't catch him," I said.

"Don't." Longstreet flashed a grin at me. "We'll see where he's headin', *then* nail him. You armed?"

"I've got a .38." Amazing, how reassuring its weight felt.

Ahead the Lexus darted in and out of Sunday night traffic. Rush ignored the lights, fishtailing over wet pavement as he dodged angry drivers. I had a hell of a time threading my way after him. Lots of drivers gave me the one-finger salute while we whizzed past, testimony to my driving prowess.

"That gizmo in Gemelli's seat," I said.

"Transmitter. It's redirecting the satellite signal."

Which explained Gemelli's heart failure—just like the time with the wireless mike. "Can't you pull the plug?"

He shook his head. "Why bother? The signal was a five-minute burst. It's all over now. Thanks to Rush." He took a quick look at me, his Norman Rockwell boy's face somber. "He used you, cuz. No way he coulda done this without you."

"Rush said he wanted to help his father," Lilly said.

Longstreet barked out a laugh. "Help him to the boneyard."

I said, "It doesn't add up. If Rush wanted to steal the movie, he could've set up anywhere in D.C. to snag that transmission. He had the key code, right? He didn't need to be at the Uptown."

Longstreet shook his head, amazed that I just didn't get it. "It's not just the theft. It's Chuck Gemelli. Uses his own kid to create a successful company, then squeezes him out and *then* tries to pin Kane's murder on him. Chuck's an animal. A few more fathers like him, and patricide would be a national sport."

I said, "So Rush zaps Daddy? And Kane?"

"His two partners at EncryptU.com." Longstreet shook his head. "Nothing that kid does surprises me now. Swipin' the film is the least of it." Longstreet had been an FBI agent for nearly twenty years, and this was his field of expertise. He sounded like he believed it. But when he spoke those last words, that nagging alarm in my head went off again, the same one as before—from my stay with the Locos. The alarm was louder now, but still unclear. It was driving me crazy.

My phone buzzed, I'd set it to vibrate at the Uptown. Just one buzz. A text message. I took a quick glance. It was from Haggler. I'd asked him to get the name of the FBI agent who'd busted Tuckerman. He'd answered me with one word: "Longstreet."

CHAPTER 60

"Everything okay?" Longstreet asked.

"Nothing important."

Longstreet. Now it began to make sense. Tuckerman was the connection between Longstreet and Romero. Which meant Lilly and I were in something much worse than I'd thought, right this second. I couldn't make a move until we got out of the car. Somehow I had to get Lilly behind me, make sure she was safe.

We crossed into Maryland, past the Beltway, where Connecticut Avenue hooks up with Georgia, heading out toward the sticks. The mist turned to rain, the streets were slick with it. We headed east on Route 32, into rolling country with few cars and fewer streetlamps. A few miles later, the ground rose to our right, forming an embankment. The breaks on the Lexus squealed. Longstreet tightened the grip on his gun.

"When he stops, pull behind, in his blind spot. I'll come up on the right and shoot out his passenger window." He grinned. "Just to get his attention, right?"

"Right." My only chance was that Longstreet didn't know I knew.

"And Miss—"

"McClellan."

"Yeah, stay in the car, okay? And keep your head down."

Good. If she stayed behind, I could get Longstreet away from the car and take care of him. The Lexus screeched to a stop on the right shoulder. I glanced in the rearview, the road was empty. I jumped out, ran at the Lexus. I wanted Longstreet right behind me, I had to make a try at him. My feet were scraping the ground, I could barely raise them, wondering if Longstreet would shoot me in the back, bracing myself for it, but it never came. Instead, the door to the Lexus opened and I was looking down the barrel of a gun, and the gun was in the hand of the Loco, Jorge.

He grinned his wolf's grin at me. For a second we stared at each other down the barrels of our guns. Then from behind, Longstreet said, "Willis."

I kept looking at Jorge because I didn't want to look at Longstreet. Something in his voice told me I'd be better off. I turned. Longstreet held his gun to Lilly's head.

He grinned. "Hey, if we were in a Corbin Brooks movie, this here's the part where the bad guy—that's you—spills the beans. How did you get onto me?"

I said nothing.

Jorge took my gun, then tossed my cell phone to Longstreet. Longstreet saw Emil's text message. He smiled, shaking his head in wonder. "Shit, you came close. So you got me as the guy who busted Tuckerman. That was the connection you were lookin' for?" He smashed my phone, kicked away the pieces. "You nearly ruined everything."

I came to a stop beside him, my hands in the air. "So the warehouse was a fake. You had Romero set it up so Rush could walk in, but not out."

"A roach motel for hackers. You shoulda heard Rush, right after you called him." Longstreet's eyes went wide. "There was a gang at the warehouse!" He laughed. "No shit. But I shoulda figured Rush would get someone to go in his place. You. Then I sicked the Dragons on you—you saw how well *that* worked out. So I had to keep you at MPAC, keep you out in front of me. Meantime, Rush has written the code where I've got him stashed."

"How about Kane? When he got shot, you were at the Uptown."

"And you were my alibi, cuz. But I still got him." He nodded toward Jorge. "With a little help from my friends." I thought about Kane and Tuckerman and Romero—all dead from a .22, shot at the base of the skull. But something was wrong. No way could Jorge have killed Romero.

Longstreet raised his eyebrows. "Ever think about it from my side? All those years in the bureau, working anti-piracy?" He shook his head. "Shit, when I resigned, I was eight months shy of my twenty. You know how that totally fucks up my retirement? It was the job, Willis. The job was messin' me up. Used to stay awake nights, thinkin' of all the schemes, all the tricks they could play. All the ways to steal a movie. Then I started to daydream about doin' it myself, but doin' it right, you know? Nothing stupid or sloppy. Just needed an opportunity, and a chump to take the heat. Then I met Chuck Gemelli."

I began to feel sick. Longstreet kept his gun on me while he touched Lilly's dreadlocks. She tried moving away but Jorge held her. "So I quit the Bureau. Then I'm workin' at MPAC, lookin' for something juicy. Startin' to feel discouraged, you want the truth. And then Quell practically hands me *Explosive Rounds*. And it's digital. So all my copies look great." He smiled at me. "Isn't that terrific?"

My heart was pounding. I was afraid for Lilly, for both of us. I tried to stay calm, use my head, think logical thoughts, but everything was jumbled. A car pulled up, Mickey and Luis tossed Rush onto the gravel. His glasses were gone, his face bloody.

"Speakin' of chumps," Longstreet said, "here's the king." He smiled at Rush. "It's easy to lie, if you're sayin' what they want to hear. Help Daddy, win Daddy's love. Kid gets squeezed out of his own company, and wants back in Dad's good graces. Go figure. And—" He stopped. Looked at me. "Hey, I'm sorry. I'm about to kill you—I shouldn't be goin' on and on. Maybe there's somethin' you want to say."

"No, I'm fine." I kept hoping he'd slip, that somehow there'd be an opening.

He shrugged. "Let's wrap it up. The Elephant hates Rush, doesn't want him near *Explosive Rounds*. I say I'll keep Rush away, and work only with NIST code writers." Rush groaned and assumed the fetal position. Longstreet nudged him with the toe of his shoe. "And Rush here—I tell him Daddy needs his help, but on the down low. It's penance. See, this is something Rush really likes. Plus a big job at MPAC at the end of the rainbow. Even groomed to take Daddy's job. Right, Rush?"

Longstreet nodded to Jorge. He shoved Lilly at me. I put my arms around her, felt her tremble. The Locos got Rush to his feet. When they popped the trunk of my car, Longstreet spun and drove a roundhouse punch into Rush's bloody face. Rush cried and fell to the ground. Longstreet kicked him, then turned and grinned at me. "I'm havin' *such* a good day."

The Locos threw Rush into the backseat. Then Chuco, the tattoo artist, held a gun on me while Mickey took everything I had, except my wallet. They wanted the cops to ID my body. After they tied my hands behind me, Longstreet motioned with his gun toward the trunk. "Time for a ride," he said.

"So there're no film pirates in D.C.?"

"Quit stallin' and get in the trunk, cuz."

I looked at Lilly, started to speak, but he cut me off. "I ain't lettin' her go, so save your breath." The Locos grabbed her carry-all. With his gun hand, Longstreet motioned Lilly toward the trunk.

I wanted to hold Lilly, protect her somehow. She looked at me, her eyes large in the dark. Jorge prodded her with his gun. She stepped into the trunk, curled into the back. Jorge motioned me in after her. With my hands tied, they had to help me. They half-lifted, half-pushed me into the trunk. I felt Lilly's body tremble. Then one of the Locos said something to Jorge, who spoke to Longstreet. He turned and smiled down at us.

"Well, shoot, you can take old Willis's car for that. He won't mind a little extra time with his sweetie. That right, Willis? Hey, don't look so glum, cuz." He put his hand on the trunk lid. "It's a nice night for a drive."

The Locos laughed as the lid slammed down.

PART THREE

CHAPTER 61

Don't ever let anyone tell you that a car trunk is the ideal place to think. Or breathe. It was hard and dark and cramped. My face was smashed against the trunk's lock. Lilly was shoved behind me, spoon-style. Her being here was entirely my fault. I was trying to come up with a way of telling her how sorry I was, when she said, "I'm sorry about this."

"*You're* sorry? It's all my fault."

"I was in the way. You couldn't do what you wanted back there because you thought I'd get hurt. Now we're locked in the trunk of a car driven God knows where by a couple of thugs who're supposed to kill us."

"You sound braver than I feel. Untie me?"

Her fingers started exploring the knots. "Why didn't they, like, tie *my* hands? Because I'm a woman?"

"It's because they're stupid."

"It's because they're men."

"Same thing."

I felt her hands move, then stop. "Hold on," she said. "Let's wait a second."

"*What?*"

"I still think there's a chance. Between us, I mean."

I took a breath. "Let's get out of here first, okay?"

"You're in a good place to listen just now. I mean, I do, like, have your attention."

"Well, would it be okay to talk *while* we're escaping?"

A pause. "That works." Her hands went back to my wrists. "Here's what I don't understand—how you think we can have a relationship when you don't talk to me."

"I talk to you all the time. Hey, behind you, up and to the left. You should find a small toolbox there."

"You're not *really* talking to me. I can't find it."

"Try behind and to the right. What's *that* mean?"

"That you're brushing me off. You clam up about your past, your childhood. There's nothing back here." Then I felt the ropes fall from my wrists.

"Let me try." It took a minute, but I managed to twist my girth around. Lilly and I were smashed together like flower petals in a book. I said, "No one likes a whiner."

"So talking to me is whining?" She squirmed against me. "Think you could get any closer?"

"It sounds like whining, talking about My Tragic Childhood." I reached behind her, trying to find my toolbox. "Son of a bitch."

"What?"

"The toolbox—I think Slip Barnett's guys took it."

"Write them a nasty note. What about you and Stoddard?"

"What about you and Brooks?"

"You first."

"Excuse me," I said, leaning over her to pull the wrench out in back.

Did I mention we were very close? I kissed her. When she kissed me back, I forgot the wrench and put my hand behind her head and kissed her again. When the driver hit the brakes, red light reflected through the rust holes and illuminated her face. She said, "I thought you were getting us out of here."

"You distracted me." I retrieved the wrench, twisted back around so I was facing the trunk lock. "I can't figure it out," I said.

"C'mon, you've done it plenty of times."

"Not the lock, us. With relationships, I'm kind of winging it." She nuzzled my neck. "Me too."

"And with Stoddard—I'm using everything but gunplay to keep her off me, and that upsets you. Meanwhile, you're off with Brooks doing God knows what."

"Maybe Stoddard is, like, more your style. Do you talk with *her*?"

The car slowed, then stopped.

Lilly said, "Willis."

"Shhh. They said they had to make a stop first, we have time."

"How much time?"

"Enough." The car shifted, as though the Locos had lifted something heavy off the backseat. Could've been Rush, but I didn't think so. Rush was riding with us till the end. In a moment, Mickey started moving again. Then sirens approached. I felt a rush of crazy hope that they would save us—that I'd see Haggler opening the trunk and looking down at me and telling me everything was cool.

Mickey pulled over to the left and stopped. The sirens and about a dozen cars went past, then the Locos pulled back into traffic.

I got the tip of the lug wrench between the sheet metal of the trunk and the lock. "Stoddard is *not* my type. She's not Brooks's type either, according to Brooks." I had just enough room to work the wrench. I gave it a couple of twists, then the lock popped out.

I grabbed the lid of the trunk to keep it shut—for now—so the Locos wouldn't see.

"She's like a movie star, glamorous. I get it." I could hear her mocking me and I smiled.

"But does she have the words *LOVE* and *HATE* on her knuckles?" I asked.

"Willis, for us—together? You'd need to be honest. You'd *want* to tell me things about yourself."

"Takes some getting used to." I couldn't shrug, the trunk was too small. "It's just that, up till now, no one in my life has been interested in my life."

"You don't share with me."

"Hey, I share. All the time."

"It's like all your emotions are all, I don't know, corroded, rusted out."

"They are not." Still, she gave me an idea. "You just gave me an idea," I told her.

"That's why I walked out, why we don't have a future. You can't say anything real."

"I can too."

"Then tell me one real thing, Willis. Go ahead."

I twisted around again so I could face her, not easy to do while keeping the trunk closed.

"How's this? Meeting you was the best, the luckiest thing that ever happened to me." I touched her cheek. "I don't care if I'm never lucky again. Meeting you is all the good luck I'll need in this lifetime." I put my arm around her. "Better?"

"A little."

The car hit a bump and we smacked our heads against the trunk. I caught it with my hand to keep it down. "I have an idea," I said. "About being rusted out. I'm not, you know, but my car is. They're going too fast for us to jump out. But if I can puncture the gas tank, they'll have to stop. Shift back a little."

"A little's all I've got."

But she moved. I started working the wrench down. The vinyl mat was glued to the floor. I tore my fingernails peeling it back. Then I used the wrench to pierce through the rusted floor of the trunk. It took a few tries, then the wet sound of the rushing road came up through the puncture.

"Doesn't explain about you and Brooks," I said.

"You're worried? About Corby and me? I was worried about Corby and you."

"Huh?"

"Well, this is, like, a secret, okay? You gotta promise not to tell anyone."

"Not tell anyone what?" We were going so fast, it was hard to get a clear shot.

"That Corby's gay."

"A gay action hero?"

"You can see why it's secret, right?"

"So when you saw me push Stoddard away. . . ."

"Well, c'mon, Willis. You gotta admit it was, like, food for thought."

"So Brooks is gay. Makes sense."

"And then, when Corby went on and on about you, it made me wonder . . . about you."

I stopped with the wrench. "What? You wondered about *me*?" The woman was messing with my self-image. "Hey, how about the time we did it in the kitchen? Or on the rooftop? No? Nothing?"

"I'm sorry, Willis." She was trying hard not to laugh.

Just then, Mickey swerved and my hand came down and the end of the wrench punctured something. "Shit."

"What?"

"I think I just skewered the muffler." Carbon dioxide fumes seeped into the trunk.

"Willis."

"Hold on." I let go of the trunk, and fresh air came howling in. Then I drove the wrench's pointed end through the rusted wheel well and into the side of the spinning tire. My arms throbbed as I angled the wrench just enough to make the tire blowout. But I hadn't expected the wheel's rotation to fight me for the wrench. I couldn't let go quickly enough, the wrench pinned my arm, a jagged bolt of pain skewered my hand. The car slewed and swerved, hit a bump, for a second the car was airborne, then rolled down a hill and the trunk slammed shut and Lilly screamed or maybe it was me and then we crashed into something and stopped.

CHAPTER 62

The smell of burning plastic.

The sound of Lilly's breathing, maybe the most beautiful thing I'd ever heard.

She was wedged in tight beside me.

"You okay?"

She said, "Can we, like, get the fuck out of here?"

"Now's good." I shoved the trunk open, then orange light flicker off the hill in front. My car was on fire. I helped Lilly out and away. Then I dragged Rush out of the back. Flames leapt out at us. I saw Mickey's head cresting through the windshield in front. Looking through the side window, I saw Chuco move. I wrapped my jacket around my hand, popped the door, then backed off as the fire singed my eyelashes. The smell of burning hair and skin made me sick. I ran in again, pulled Chuco out by his collar. I gave his gun to Lilly, saying. "If he tries something, shoot him."

Ten minutes later I flagged down a car. While the driver called 911, I came back down the hill. Chuco was conscious. He looked at the car, then at me. I put my hand on his shoulder. "Maybe you're in the wrong line of work."

The ER doctors said Rush would be okay after stitches and drugs. And Lilly didn't have a scratch, I was very grateful about that. Fifty more minutes of waiting, and they x-rayed my hand, then said I was free to go. I was exhausted, but I had to call Stayne Matthews.

Using the hospital's phone, I told him about Florence Walters tailing me, and how I pushed her to the sidewalk. He said, "Are you kidding? That's incredible! Do you know what that means? You're in, my boy, you're in. Walters *has* to approve your application. That baby is as good as yours."

"But Haggler sent her my juvie record."

"You saved her *life,* Willis. You can start painting the baby's room pink. Now don't call me again today." I hung up, then sat beside Lilly on the hard plastic bench. She rested her head on my shoulder. I closed my eyes, but my mind kept going. I didn't like Stayne saying I'd saved Florence Walters's life. I didn't like him saying she was in my debt.

I was ready to go home, more than ready to take Lilly with me. I kissed the base of her neck. Why couldn't life be simple? Then the ER doors opened and Lt. Emil Haggler came in, cracking a smile when he saw Lilly. "Well, evening, Ms. McClellan. You're looking deceptively plain tonight."

She nodded. "Thank you, Emil."

"And you," he said. The smile dropped off his face. "The fuck you doin', boy?"

"My job. Longstreet's your guy for the Kane killing."

Haggler leaned against the wall. He looked tired. "Tell me," he said.

"You found the transmitter?"

"Yeah, in Gemelli's chair at the Uptown."

I said, "Gemelli collapsed during his interview with Corona. That's what a tiny transmitter could do to Gemelli's pacemaker. As head of security, Longstreet could check Gemelli's medical files, discover his pacemaker. Then assign the seats so Gemelli was right where Longstreet wanted him."

"What about the film pirates in D.C.?"

"There aren't any. The warehouse operation was fake." I told Haggler what'd happened so far. When I finished, he said, "So Rush sends in a ringer. You."

"Hypothetically," I agreed. "Longstreet hires an ex-con, a former Loco named Romero, to buy the video decks and set up the warehouse to look like a pirating operation. Then Longstreet tells Rush, gives him the details of the alarms, figuring Rush will go for dear old dad. Meantime, Longstreet leaks it to the Dragons that someone's in their territory."

"And the Dragons show up later, at your place." Haggler's voice took on a southern edge. It meant he was angry, his inner 'Bama was showing through. "At your apartment. And that *ain't* hypothetical. How 'bout Romero?"

"Romero was the link between Longstreet and the Locos. But I think Romero was clean."

"Why?" Lilly asked.

"His house," I told her. "He'd painted it, put in furniture, kept things neat. The guy was starting a lawn in his backyard. And I bet he never missed a meeting with his PO. That sound like a guy about to cash in on a big score?"

Haggler said, "Maybe he got scared at Lewisburg." He sat on the plastic bench. "Same place you and me and Shad went, on that road trip." His face lost some anger. "And you remembered? You were just a kid, you saw those towers for a few seconds twenty years ago."

"Shad told me I might see them again if I didn't watch myself. Then I did see them, the same towers, tattooed on the chest of a knucklehead named Tuckerman."

"And Longstreet busted Tuckerman."

"He knew Tuckerman was connected, networked into the D.C. gang scene. That's the same reason I went to Tuckerman in the first place. Longstreet planned to move to D.C. and work for Chuck Gemelli, so he needed a gang connection. Tuckerman provided the link between Longstreet and Romero, and through Romero to his former gang, the Locos."

Haggler said, "Besides me, who else you tell about Tuckerman?"

"Just Longstreet. I saw Tuckerman that afternoon, then told Longstreet that night at the Uptown. Longstreet pretended not to know him, then called his friendly neighborhood Locos. The next day Tuckerman gets hit and I'm kidnapped."

"A .22 killed Tuckerman, just like Kane and Romero. I still don't get why Longstreet would shoot Romero."

"Let's say Romero was trying to go straight. So if he got wind of what Longstreet was up to, that'd make Romero a threat."

"Is that why Romero had a copy of the key code?" Lilly asked.

"Right, it was insurance," I said. "He figured if Longstreet tried anything, Romero could use the code to leverage his way clear. But he never got the chance to tell Longstreet about it."

"Well, at least it's over," Lilly said.

"Not quite." I turned to Haggler, "If Longstreet thinks I'm stuck in the ICU, I still might have a chance of nailing him."

"You want me to list you in critical condition? Why would I do that?"

"What if Longstreet had another motive, apart from profit? I think something dirty went down, years ago, that links all three killings. If I can prove it, you say I'm stuck in the hospital—just for twenty-four hours. Deal?"

Haggler shook his head. He looked miserable. Lilly touched his shoulder. He asked her, "You see now? You see why Shad wanted him to be a cop?"

Lilly looked from Haggler to me, then back to him. "You're not gonna let him do this?" Then to me, "You're safe now. It's Emil's job to get Longstreet. You have to stop."

"He's not gonna. Are you, boy?" Haggler chuckled. "Willis got the scent now." He looked at Lilly. "You just pretendin' you don't know that about him?"

CHAPTER 63

On the way to Chuck Gemelli's room, I snatched a plastic bag off a food tray. I borrowed a few strands of hair from Lilly's brush, stuffed them into the bag and shoved it in my pocket. The

Elephant glared at me with yellowed eyes, rolling his wheelchair back and forth in a fury.

"Well, Gidney, when you finally show up, you bring a police officer. Good. I want you to make an arrest."

Haggler folded his arms. "Really."

Just then, Gemelli number two rolled into the room. Rush looked pale—well, he always looked pale—and his cuts were stitched together with black thread. His eyes had a loose focus to them, probably the combination of no glasses and painkillers.

Chuck Gemelli pointed at Rush. "I'm pressing charges."

"Against your son?" Haggler didn't looked surprised.

"For conspiring to steal copyrighted material—*Explosive Rounds*."

I said to Haggler, "Chuck's feeling the wrath of Roger Franklin Quell."

"Damn straight. Tonight was a disaster." Gemelli turned toward his son. "I'm not taking the heat, I didn't want your help. You'll have to take the consequences."

"It wasn't his fault," I said.

"Of course it was. He gave the encryption code to Longstreet."

"The key code you told everyone you were writing?" I asked.

Gemelli hesitated.

"What did Longstreet say to you? At the Uptown, you were scared. You told me Kane was right. What was he right about?"

"Nothing."

"You told me you and Kane had argued about your son."

"Yes, Rush, he—"

"No, not Rush. Your other son. Longstreet."

It suddenly got very quiet in the room. I said to Rush, "He's your half brother."

"Get out of here," Chuck Gemelli said, starting to stand.

I put a hand on his chest and pushed him back into his chair. "This is Get to Know Your Father Week. Maybe you'd like to tell Rush about Bonnie."

Gemelli's mouth opened and shut, like some prehistoric fish gasping raw air.

"See, I overheard two Locos talking about Gemelli's kid. They said the kid hated his old man over what he did to Bonnie. Longstreet's record had no father listed, only a mother. Her name was Bonnie." That was the thing that'd been nagging me all along, ever since I escaped the Locos. I'd overheard Tomás and Jorge talk about killing me. But they also spoke in Spanish about why the son would want to kill the father. Tomás had mentioned the name Bonnie. And Jones St. Pierre had said Longstreet's mother's name was Bonnie.

"That's absurd." Gemelli backed his chair away.

"Do you remember? A campaign stop, in Oklahoma City." This last was a guess on my part. I was counting on the sheer number of trips Gemelli had made—they would blend together. I spoke as though I was certain. Plus, I wanted to hear him deny it.

Gemelli clamped his mouth shut.

"Kane had campaigned with you, spent time with you on the road, knew the kind of things you did. He was your damage control. So when you had—what? Consensual sex with a teenager? Kane covered it up." Still nothing from Gemelli. "You paid Kane, paid his office rent, kept him in business.

"Then Longstreet gets inside MPAC, and the first thing he does is stop all payments to Kane. Why? Because to Longstreet, that money was his. When Kane finally sees what's happening, he confronts you at the Uptown. But he doesn't tell you Longstreet's name, just that your bastard child is making waves."

I turned to Lilly and Haggler. "If the media finds out that Chuck hired his own bastard child without knowing it? Chuck would have to pack his bags. His days of hanging out with celebrities would be over."

Rush said, "Gidney, you can stop now, okay?"

Gemelli's eyes raked me over, his mouth working. "Listen. That—that *woman* had a long history of . . ." His body trembled, the words grating as though yanked out on a hot wire from deep inside. "I am *not* a rapist."

"Jesus," Haggler said.

Gemelli said, "There's no proof Longstreet is—that's he's related to me."

I pulled out the plastic bag with the strands of Lilly's hair, which, by the way, looked nothing like Longstreet's. Again, it was a bluff, the idea of the bag, and not what was actually in it. I moved the bag while I talked, making it harder for Gemelli to see its contents. "I got these hairs off Longstreet's comb. You don't mind giving us a swipe at yours, do you? C'mon, you've heard of reverse paternity DNA. Want to bet it's a match?"

That was all I had, my last bluff. Gemelli stared at the bag, then my expression. He closed his eyes, shook his head. He didn't collapse, it was more like a Gemelli-shaped balloon deflating into his chair. Nice to finally get a reaction.

I said, "So if you're thinking of putting the blame on Rush—or me—think again." I glanced at Rush. He looked like a man digesting a concrete pizza.

The Elephant contorted his face into a smile. "Well, perhaps there's something in what you're saying. I'll . . . I'll take it under advisement." He shifted in his chair, looking frail and dried out. "Now that Longstreet's, uh, gone, we'll need someone to head the security section of MPAC. Maybe you'd consider the position?" You had to hand it to him, the guy never quit.

"I'd rather have my mouth tied to a truck exhaust and be dragged naked through a junkyard," I said.

Lilly giggled as the Elephant's face hardened. "I see. Well, then we'll simply thank you once again and say good night."

Haggler, Lilly, and I were in the hallway when she gave a fair impression of Gemelli's voice. "'Well, then we'll simply thank you once again and say good night.'" She shook her head, her dreadlocks swaying. "Unbelievable."

"Runs in the family," I said.

Rush Gemelli rolled after us. "Gidney, you got a minute?"

Lilly looked at me. I shrugged and said, "Sure."

He looked at Lilly and Haggler. "In private?"

Rush rolled, I followed. "Look, I know my old man's . . . I know he's a piece of work. I mean, no one knows that better than me, okay? I never saw the guy growing up, and then our business together—" He shook his head. "A fucking disaster. I went from having a couple mil to Chapter Eleven overnight. My credit rating's still ruined. If you knew what—"

"Rush."

"Sorry, it's just, I don't want you telling anybody that Longstreet's . . . what you said before."

I couldn't quite believe it. "You still want to help your father?"

He looked down. "You probably think I'm deranged."

"What I think doesn't matter. It's up to you. You know the truth. You decide whether Chuck can stay or go. But you need to think about it."

He looked up at me. "Okay. And Gidney? Those, uh, photos? I'll destroy them, you don't need to worry anymore." I looked in his eyes. I don't know why, but I believed him.

Haggler watched him go, then said, "We gotta find Longstreet."

"What about listing me in the ICU?" I still wanted a shot at Longstreet, but I don't think Lilly wanted me to take it. She squeezed my hand till it hurt.

Haggler stared at me for a long moment, not really seeing me as he weighed it in his mind. "I gotta do an APB, I gotta cover myself here. But I'll give you twenty-four hours."

"Good."

Haggler looked at Lilly's hand in mine. She wasn't letting go, her grip was like a vise. For a moment his eyes lost their hardness. "Okay," he said.

CHAPTER 64

Lilly and I collapsed into bed. After the trunk of my car, my old mattress felt indecently spacious. So why couldn't I sleep? I lay on my back, hands behind my head, staring at the streetlight's shadow pattern on my ceiling. Thinking about Longstreet and how to find him.

I got up for a drink. The water came out the spigot and into the glass. I wondered if Sarah was with the Bishops, asleep in their house. I wondered if she was all right, if she was happy, if she missed me. I hoped Matthews was right about Walters. I was played out, I couldn't take more uncertainty. Well, I'd find out to the next morning. Or rather, this morning, which, according to my clock, was now five hours and forty-seven minutes old. Back to bed.

Far away, the freight train blew its whistle, and a minute later the apartment started vibrating as the train chugged past. I'd never hopped a freight train. How hard could it be? Joel McCrea didn't seem to have any problems in *Sullivan's Travels*. Maybe that was the solution—jump on a train and go far away, go away and never come back.

Beside me, Lilly stirred and placed her face, warm with sleep, on my chest. She sighed, then was silent. She murmured, "Take me with you."

"Promise." I held her close. The next time I opened my eyes, she had a cup of java in one hand and my phone in her other. "It's Corby," she said.

I sipped from the cup, then kissed her. She kissed me back, and that was nice. We'd almost forgotten about Brooks, when I heard a tiny voice shouting. I grabbed the phone and snarled. "What?"

"Finally. Look, I need to see you, right away."

"About?"

"Your neighbor, Dino? He got me hooked up with an agent and, well, I need to talk to you."

"Corbin." I refused to call him Corby. "I can't help you. Call the agent. Call the Writers Guild, okay? Just don't call me."

"But this is *your* fault. I didn't ask you to give him my writing, or send it to an agent." His tone softened. "Sorry, I'm being an asshole, I know. Please, Gidney, okay? Just a few minutes."

"I'll meet you at the Zamboanga Café." I gave him the address.

"Great. See you there."

I got up and showered, shaved, and put on some of my new previously worn clothes. They felt good. I walked into the living room, inhaling the last bit of toast and jam and feeling almost

246

human. Lilly sat on the couch, typing on her laptop. "What's Corby want?"

"I don't care." I walked to the window. My police protection was gone. "You have to get out of here now."

She stood, and the sunlight behind her gave her an angel glow. "You don't care about Corby, but you're gonna try to help him."

"Maybe."

"You." On tiptoe, she put her arms around me. "Wanna get together later?"

"Like maybe a nooner?"

Her eyes had that merry look. "Just what I had in mind," she said.

CHAPTER 65

I got a rental car and a new phone, then headed cross town to the Zamboanga. Chella gave me a wink as I passed the cash register. I sat at a window booth, opposite Brooks. He had on a fisher-man's cap and sunglasses, and he was tapping his coffee cup with a spoon. He was as inconspicuous as a jackhammer at a Bach recital. All the regulars were looking at him.

"What's up?"

"I'm screwed." He took off his glasses, his eyes were blood-shot. "Look at me, I couldn't sleep last night."

"Join the club."

"You ruined my life."

"You're starting to cheer me up, keep going." I leaned back as Chella set down two cheese Danish and a cup of coffee for me. She lingered at the table, her hand resting lightly by Corbin's silverware.

"Chella Galindez, Corbin Brooks," I said.

"Oh," she said a little breathlessly. "I had no idea. Pleased to meet you." Amazing how she could make "Pleased to meet you" sound like "Let's step into the back room." Brooks gave her a smile. To me, it was just a smile, but Chella caught her breath, then glided back to the cash register. I swore that if Brooks said something nasty about her, I'd pound him to a pulp.

"She's nice," he said.

"Yeah. Why am I here?"

"Your pal Dino? His agent wants my book. He called an editor he knows at Macmillan, they're excited about it."

"Great."

"No, because they'll only print my novel as part of a three-book deal. First book's an autobiography." Brooks began rubbing his forefinger against his thumbnail, up and down along the deformed groove in the middle.

I started in on the Danish. "The problem?"

"How can I write an autobiography and not tell the truth?"

My voice low, I said, "What? That you're gay?"

Brooks got a little flushed. "Lilly told you."

"You're not the first gay actor in Hollywood."

He kept rubbing his thumbnail. "Look, for the past ten years, my whole life has been a lie, okay? It sucks. Now I've got a chance to break free."

"Still don't see the problem."

"The problem, the fucking problem, is that I signed a multi-picture deal with Quell's production company. Three more films."

He held his palms out. "And I'm not playing Cary Grant roles, okay? Now honestly, how the fuck am I supposed to be an action hero if everyone knows I'm gay?"

"You could deny it."

"Deny what I wrote in my autobiography?"

"Then do like Charles Barkley—say you were misquoted." I finished the first Danish. Would the second taste better if I waited a minute before slamming it down? Worth a try.

He shook his head. "I can't go on. No way can I make three more movies with Quell."

"Well, knowing you're gay, I've got more respect for you as an actor."

"Why? For playing a straight guy? You just keep your hand gestures to a minimum, notch down the personality so you're less interesting, and don't dress as well as you'd like. It's a breeze." He looked out the window. "Especially when you read about kids who kill themselves rather than tell their folks. Or when a gay teenager gets lynched. Yeah, the closet's a piece of cake." He pushed the coffee cup away. "Truth is, I can't do it anymore."

I eyed the second Danish. It was still there. "So, the book's a way to out yourself."

"Don't you think I want to? I can't. First, I'm contractually bound to keep quiet as long as Quell wants."

"So if you *did* out yourself—"

"I'd violate the terms of my contract. Quell would sue the shit out of me." His eyes looked panicked. "What'll I do?" His voice rose. "I want you to tell me." The other customers looked at us. He put his sunglasses back on.

"You said 'First.' What's second?" I asked.

He sighed. "Sonnie."

"The substance abuse?"

He looked surprised. "You've been busy. Yeah, pills and alcohol. They kind of pave the way for some pretty self-destructive behavior."

"You're her husband."

"In name only. And besides, it's not that simple. Sonnie's problems go way back. Her dad was a stuntman in Hollywood. One of the greats. So he was always in demand, never at home. Sonnie's mother died young." I nodded. Brooks was building to something. "So the kind of guy she's attracted to is, well, kind of like you."

I didn't like the sound of that. "Kind of like me how, exactly?"

"Big. Acts tough. Knows a few tricks. That's part of Sonnie's problem." Brooks talked like a man who'd thought a lot about Sondra Stoddard's problems. "And then there's Roger's video camera. He show it to you? It's tiny, even has infrared. Do you know what that means?"

"You can shoot in the dark."

Brooks sipped some coffee. "Couple years back, Quell threw a party. Sonnie's career was just taking off. Other directors wanted her. Quell got her very polluted. Took video of Sonnie while she—" Corbin looked down at his cup. "See, last time I talked to him about my contract, and outing myself—he showed me her video. Said he'd release it to the media if I made a move. Sonnie would be finished."

I'd lost my appetite. I hate when that happens. Pushing the second Danish away, I said, "So he's got you both." Brooks nodded. "And you care about Stoddard, that's why you were acting angry, tearing into my office."

He nodded again.

"Maybe you could let it leak that you're gay?"

He shook his head. "Quell would trace it back to me."

"Not necessarily."

"Then Quell'd just hire someone to testify I'd leaked it. Quell would fucking kill me in court, and threaten to sue any publisher who wanted to touch me. He's not somebody you fuck with."

"Well, you're a writer, you'll think of something." I stood to go.

"Oh, well, thanks. I feel much better now. What are *you* going to do about Sonnie?"

"Sorry?"

Now he smiled, and it wasn't a very friendly smile. "She's very hard to dissuade, be*lieve* me."

"Well, shit," I said. "I've been as distant to her as I know how."

"You have?" He shook his head. "Gidney. Emotional abuse can be just as addictive as drug abuse. Get it? That feels like home to her."

I spread my hands in front of him. "So, if I'm nice to her?"

"It may be too late for that," he said.

CHAPTER 66

Once Brooks dragged himself out of the Zamboanga, I called Lilly and told her what he'd said. When I came to the part about Stoddard, Lilly said, "So she thinks you're her father?"

"Brooks said I'm *like* her father, somehow." I didn't like the way Brooks had described him.

"Hey, Willis? You and I, we're together. That's all that counts."

"Easy for you to say. You don't know what it's like, having

Stoddard pop up in my life all the time. I'm afraid to open a can of beans."

"So what are you gonna do?"

I told her.

"That's, like, insane," she said. "Stoddard'll never go for that."

"I think she could, under the right conditions."

"I want to see this," she said. "Meet you there."

I pointed my car north on Massachusetts, then took a left on Fourteenth. I was driving, keeping in my lane, obeying the traffic laws. I should have focused on my upcoming meeting with Florence Walters, but all my mind wanted was to figure how to nail Longstreet. Where *was* the son of a bitch? Haggler had airports and buses and trains covered. Longstreet's picture was out to all the highway cops. Odds were that Haggler would nail him. So why was I thinking he wouldn't?

When I got to the Barnett brothers' garage, Lilly was already there, leaning against her silver VW. I sidled next to her and she kissed me. We finally broke apart, each a little breathless, I said, "Hi."

"Like the moon," she agreed.

We walked into the garage, past two rows of cars with their hoods popped open like a line of alligators waiting for a chicken dinner. We found Emmet in the office, rolling a joint. He looked up at us and said, "Well, Jaysus, it's the deadbeat, walking in as brash as you please. Never mind that he owes me for my services as backup."

"Relax. I have a nice payoff for you."

Emmet looked from me to Lilly, who looked shapeless and plain in today's baggy outfit. He shook his head and looked back at me. "What payoff?"

"Sondra Stoddard. How'd you like to meet her?"

"Sondra Stoddard? No shit?" Emmet stood, the joint forgotten.

"No shit."

"Sondra Stoddard," he repeated. I wondered if he'd say it a third time and click his heels together. He gave me a suspicious look. "Are her legs really that great?"

"And her torso, even more so."

He grinned. "Hell yes, I'll be meeting her. After a wimp like you, she's probably dying for a real man." He ran greasy gray fingers through a greasier gray beard. "Sure, she reminds me of that song by the Guess Who."

Then, to the tune of "American Woman," Emmet started playing air guitar and duck-walking across the littered office floor, singing:

> *"Inflatable woman,*
> *stay away from me,*
> *Inflatable woman,*
> *momma, let me be."*

Lilly turned to me. "You're right. He's perfect."

CHAPTER 67

I thought Lilly was perfect. Outside the Barnett brothers' garage, I took her in my arms and told her so. "Hmm," she hmmed, her lips against mine. "Any plans for later?" Her smile was nothing short of luscious.

I checked my watch. "I have to see Florence Walters."

She touched my cheek. "Good luck."

"Thanks. Then I've got to find Longstreet." I'd thought about this a lot. "See, when we were in the trunk—"

Her smile faded. "Willis—"

"Hold on a sec. See, we were in the trunk and the car stopped, remember? They took out something heavy, I felt the weight shift. And then a siren and a bunch of cars went by. Like a motorcade."

Lilly said nothing.

"When the sirens approached us, the car went to the *left* and stopped. So we were on a one-way street, near the White House, I'd bet." I slumped against her car. "But where?"

Lilly looked sad. "It hurts me that you're not stopping this. Chasing after him."

"I don't want you to get hurt."

"I know." Her eyes moved as she studied my face, as though she were memorizing it. "Love sucks, you know that?"

"I'll be careful."

"You say that." She stepped into my arms. I held her, feeling her body close to mine, her dreads against my cheek. Now that I had her back, life felt whole. She locked her eyes on mine. "You're going to, like, do what you're going to do. I know that now. I know it, but I don't have to like it."

Minutes before my meeting with Walters, Matthews phoned in some last-minute advice. Told me to act as though Haggler's amended form didn't exist. Just accept Walters's thanks and bring Sarah's car seat.

I found Walters behind her desk in her cubicle, surrounded

by stacks of manila folders. When she saw me, she stood up and came forward to take my hand.

"Mr. Gidney, I'm so glad you're here. I want to thank you for . . . for helping me the way you did last night."

I felt like an imposter. A fraud. "It was nothing."

"My life is something, at least to me. And I want you to know how grateful I am."

"I'm glad to hear that."

"Well, once more, if there's ever anything I can do." She sat behind her desk and I sat in the chair in front.

"There are two things," I said. She nodded, waiting. "The first is Nurse Eunice Edgerton. I'd like her to have her old job back."

Walters drew herself up. "Nurse Edgerton exceeded her—" Then she stopped herself. She straightened a stack of folders. "All right. She'll come back where she was. And the second thing?"

"It's about Sarah. I was thinking . . ."

"Yes?"

"Well, after last night, maybe you've changed your mind."

She looked confused. "Changed my mind . . ."

She was going to make me say it. "About me being a fit parent."

"I see." She sat back in her chair. "Mr. Gidney, as long as I live, I'll never forget your bravery, and I hope you know you have my deepest gratitude."

I smiled. "That's great, because I wanted—"

"But if you think that will in any way influence my decision about that child and your adopting her—"

"—you to approve my papers."

"—I'm very sorry."

We stopped and looked at each other.

"You see, Mr. Gidney, last night convinced me that my original assessment of you was correct. When that car came around the corner, I was frozen. But you, you were moving, and moving fast." She smiled at the memory. "Faster than I could have imagined."

"But—"

She held up her hand. "Let me finish, please. The life you lead, your capacity for violence—the *occurrence* of violence." She shook her head. "There's simply no way I could ever approve of a child being placed in your care. It's just crazy to even consider it."

We stared at each other a little more. I could hear soft footsteps moving up and down the hallway behind me, the hum of the overhead lights. I stood. "All right," I said. "Fine. There are legal answers to this."

"Yes," she said. Her voice had grown quiet. "And of course you're free to pursue them. But maybe you'll think a little about what I said."

I turned and started walking away.

"Uh, Mr. Gidney?" I turned to face her. "This is hard, but I want you to know—"

"That you're grateful. Right, I got it."

"No, not that. It's just that—did you know we get over three thousand cases a year? And every caseworker has twice as many cases as she's supposed to?" She gestured at the stacks of papers on her desk. "I'm a supervisor, so in addition to my own caseload, I have to oversee all the other cases in my division."

"Life is tough." I started to leave.

"Mr. Gidney, please, wait a moment. What I'm trying to say—this is difficult for me—is that it's possible for a case to, uh, slip between the cracks."

"Ms. Walters, I grew up in D.C. foster care. I've slipped through those cracks often."

"A child like your Baby Doe—"

"Sarah."

She nodded. "Yes, Sarah. A child like Sarah could easily fall through the cracks, she has no family, no friends."

"She has me."

"She has you." Walters smiled, and something like human warmth was in the smile. "And you've done her a great service."

"By failing to adopt her?"

"By *trying* to adopt her. When I got Baby—when I got Sarah's case, and saw who was trying to adopt her, well, you got my attention."

"I still don't see—"

"There was no way Sarah would drop through the cracks—your wanting to adopt her guaranteed that. By the way, what did you think of the Bishops?"

"I haven't met the Bishops."

She smiled again. "That's not what I asked you, Mr. Gidney."

CHAPTER 68

I took Sixth Street north to Rhode Island, then onto North Capitol, thinking about the Bishops the entire way. A few minutes later I was parked across the street from their house. They'd placed red and yellow plastic toys on their lawn, plus a tiny swing set, and a slide not much more than three feet tall. Just then Darius came tearing around the corner, with Sarah squealing and toddling behind him. Must've been Horace Bishop chasing them, keeping it slow so Sarah could stay ahead.

257

My phone rang—no caller ID. "About time you called."

Tomás said, "Gidney, you killed like a quarter of my gang. I gotta put you down, man."

"You're curious, that's why you called." I told him where to meet me. "Two hours from now." I snapped the phone shut, put it away, then took it out again.

"Well, fuck me," Matthews said after I told him about meeting with Walters. "The old bitch really said that? You didn't happen to wear a wire?"

"I save that for attorney-client conversations." Now Horace was pushing Sarah on a swing. I wondered how they'd gotten the toys so quickly.

"And right now you're thinking you're screwed, am I right? Well, listen to me closely, my boy. *We're going to win this.* Do you hear me? I'm going to nail her skinny ass to the courtroom wall. It's going to cost you, though."

"How much?"

"Minimum? In the forty to sixty-thousand-dollar neighborhood." He paused, and when I said nothing, he asked, "Will that be a problem?"

I had no idea where the money would come from. "No."

"All right. I'll start the ball rolling and get back to you tomorrow with the details. In the meantime, I'd suggest that any contact you have with Ms. Florence Walters be through me. Understood?"

"Yes."

" 'No, yes, no, yes.' And they say the art of conversation is dead."

I wanted to throw my phone into the gutter, but I shoved it in my pocket. I leaned back, listening to Sarah and Darius play. I closed my eyes. I saw Florence Walters, her face frozen in the Dragons' headlights.

Across the street, Horace was joined by a short, smiling woman with a round face and bouffant hairdo. She gathered them into the house. The front door shut.

My options? I could always plant some nasty evidence against the Bishops, then ruin them financially by taking them to court.

Or I could just let the Bishops hang out with me. They'd be dead within hours, just ask Florence Walters. I was angry with myself for the scare Lilly had last night, but at least she'd had a choice in the matter. Sarah wouldn't get one. And if, somehow, I got her away from the Bishops and adopted her, I'd have to work harder, get a staff job at some place like McClure Downing. Would I be like Stoddard's dad, always gone? Would Sarah turn out like Stoddard? That was a pretty thought.

I drove to my office, took all the cash Rush had given me, and FedExed it to the Bishops. Just a precaution, in case my meeting with Tomás and Jorge left me slightly dead.

All right, it was risky meeting with them, but I'd guessed right about Tomás—he wanted to know why I hadn't told the cops about his headquarters. That's why he'd called the cell phone number I'd written in the dust on the floor.

Hains Point looked the same as it had when the cops found Romero's body. A .22-caliber weapon is so small, there's usually no exit wound. The bullet simply bounces around inside the skull, making tunnels in the brain, from which no one ever recovers. A .22 had killed Tuckerman and Kane. That was probably Jorge. But I felt sure he hadn't shot Romero.

They parked and walked toward me. If Jorge felt any discomfort about returning to the crime scene, he didn't show it. Tomás was grinning at me. "You were right," He looked at Jorge. "A reasonable man. I need to kill this guy, and now he volunteers."

I said, "You're smarter than that. You think I'd just walk in here without taking any precautions? I know the location of your headquarters, and the scam with the cars. You've seen all the Charlie Chan movies—figure it out."

Tomás leaned back against the railing as wind came off the Potomac. He wore a long black coat and a small-brimmed black hat. Jorge had black shoes, chinos, and a tan windbreaker. He kept his hands free at his sides. He looked like a contractor, which I suppose he was.

Tomás stared at me for what seemed like hours but what was probably only twenty seconds. Then he smiled. "I get it. You wrote down what you know and gave it to someone, so if anythin' like, happens to you, they go to the cops. That it?"

"Part of it," I said.

"Yeah, I figure you maybe gave a couple of copies to different friends, so even if we began torturin' you right now, we wouldn't be able to get all the names out of you in time." I hadn't considered multiple copies, but it was a good idea. Tomás was every bit as good as I thought he'd be.

Truth was, I'd taken no precautions whatsoever. I hadn't had the time. I figured if he had a chance, Tomás would come up with them for me. When he saw me smile, Tomás grinned back. "And for this you want Longstreet's location. You got a deal."

He snapped his fingers. "Hey, you could even use *us* to blackmail *him*. Like, you say, 'Gimme some cash, man, or you're goin' down like the Locos.'"

Damn, I'd never thought about blackmailing Longstreet. Eddie Vermeer would have, but not me. Tomás was even better than I'd thought. He handed me a scrap of yellow legal paper. Longstreet's location.

"Son of a bitch," I said. I looked from the paper to Jorge. "Okay to take something out of my pocket?"

"Slow," Jorge said.

I slid out a folded copy of the *Wall Street Journal* and spread it out in front of Tomás. He looked from the paper to me. "So?"

"Your scam with the cars—it's good. Very good. You think anyone else in the Locos is coming up with ideas like that? You're part of a franchise, right? It's time to think bigger."

Jorge said, "See?"

"Quiet," Tomás told him. "And I ain't followin' you, Gidney."

"You know exactly what I'm saying."

He tapped the paper. "What's this shit?"

I chin-pointed to the water behind him. He turned to look. "It's a river of money. If you can read the *Journal* and not find seven scams a day, you're not the man I think you are."

He looked down at the paper again and snorted. "A fuckin' M.B.A., man, that's what I'd need just to fuckin' talk with these people. You payin' my way through business school?"

"You need a degree? That's why God invented laser printers." I took my foot off the railing, nodded to Jorge.

Tomás said, "That's it? That's all you wanted?"

"Well," I said, leaning against the rail next to him, "there is one little thing."

CHAPTER 69

When I finished, Tomás whistled. "You got a deal. But say, how much of that was bullshit?" He started walking toward a stand of trees and the parking lot.

Jorge and I fell in step beside him. "You're a shrewd man, Tomás." I looked at Jorge.

Tomás said, "Oh, Jorge's *very* good. Problem is, the folks who find out just how fuckin' good he is aren't around to tell anybody."

Jorge's shoulders moved in what could have been a shrug. "It's a PR nightmare," he said.

Just then, from behind the trees, darted Ph'uck and a friend. They pulled out guns—MAC 11s—they were set to spray not just us but the families behind us. They never got the chance. Before I'd even cleared my gun, Jorge had shot each of them twice. His gun was silenced, no one had noticed. I bent over to look at them. Each had two neat holes over his heart, so close together that you could cover them with a business card.

"Tight pattern," I said.

Jorge nodded. "Maybe you can give me a recommendation."

I stood across from the main entrance of the MPAC building, watching the door in the fading light. The air felt moist, and I wondered if it would rain before I got inside. And since I had been inside the building, I knew the setup—the windows were connected to vibration detectors, infrared beams crisscrossed the entranceway, video cameras fed images to the security station in the basement, and a number of private guards were on patrol for good measure.

I didn't think a brick through the window would get me in.

But a plastic card with a magnetic strip would. As an MPAC freelancer, I hadn't rated one of these. That's why I stood outside, watching. Finally, someone left the building, his identity card swinging from a lanyard around his neck. I turned up the collar of my jacket.

He didn't notice me, just turned and walked toward Connecticut Avenue. A man came the other way, apparently he didn't see the MPAC employee and bumped right into him. Briefcases dropped and apologies popped out. When they finished making polite noises to each other, the employee continued toward the Metro stop and the man crossed the street to where I stood.

"You didn't learn that doing birthday magic shows," I said.

"It's nothing, really," Terry Price said, pulling the MPAC identity card from his pocket.

"We're even. Have a nice night," I said.

Once I'd carded my way into MPAC, I took the stairs to the basement. A few corridors and I came upon a thick wooden door with the words SECURITY OFFICE. I tried the knob. It was unlocked. I took a breath and turned the knob and walked into a room twenty by forty. A desk next to an array of black-and-white screens showed what the security cameras saw. And to the right of the desk, a locked door. I got through the door, and found myself looking down the barrel of a gun.

Except it wasn't a gun—it was the lens of a projector. It had the words *Julie* and *4K Ultrashow* on its side in raised metal script. There was a server next to it. Heavy equipment. So that's what had been taken from my car the previous night, before the motorcade passed. The Locos had stopped at MPAC.

I traced a set of wires from the projector to a second server, which was now recording an unencrypted copy of *Explosive Rounds*. I had the wires in my hand when something cold and metallic touched the back of my left ear. "Is your first name really Boynton?"

Longstreet chuckled. I turned, to see him shake his head. "Too bad I'm gonna waste you, cuz. You're a hoot to have around."

I held up the wires. "You sending the show to Russia?"

"Again. Those vodka-heads can't do anything right."

I yanked the wires out of the server, which beeped in protest. "How clumsy of me."

His smile disappeared. "You shoulda stayed in the hospital. Now you're gonna need one." He shoved me against the door, kicked my feet apart and patted me down. His gun in my back the whole time.

Over my shoulder I said, "Police have got the town sealed, you can't get away."

"I'm terrified. Hands up, asshole." He backed away, careful to keep a safe distance.

I chin-pointed at the projector "This was in my car last night?"

"Yeah. I cloned the Uptown's projector, copied its RMA code, then embedded it on this baby's chip. That's the great thing about computers—no loyalty."

"Must really appeal to you. When did you decide to do it?" I asked.

"Do what? Steal the show?"

"Kill your father." Longstreet looked grim. I said, "Gemelli *is* your father. How did it happen?"

Longstreet looked at me for a long time before saying, "Where'd you hear that?"

"The Locos. But I can't figure why you told them."

"They're Latino, I gave them all that soap opera shit about my mother's honor, and avengin' her. And of course I paid 'em to whack Kane and Tuckerman and Romero."

"You're lying about Romero. I can see Tuckerman was a threat. But why even bother with Kane?"

"He kept me down." He saw my confused look and laughed. "Seriously. He knew Gemelli'd had a bastard kid. Kane could've helped us, Bonnie and me. Instead, he puts himself first, blackmails Gemelli, makes him pay for the consultin' business."

"Tell me about Bonnie. About her and the Elephant."

"Jesus, you ask a lot of questions." He scratched his head. "She kept tryin', you know? Scrapin' the money together for stamps, mailin' letter after letter, makin' long-distance calls—if she'd known how, she would've tried smoke signals. It drove her crazy—I mean really. She had to be committed when I was fourteen. She died eight years ago."

"Then three years ago, you meet Gemelli in L.A."

He held his gun steady on me. "Funny, I never thought about croakin' the old guy till then. Truth is, in a weird kinda way, I admired him. Then I actually met the guy and, well, shit, Willis, you know what he's like—a fella'd hafta be crazy *not* to wanna kill him." He shrugged. "A year ago, Gemelli's wife died. I don't know why, but something clicked. I quit the Bureau. The Elephant was happy to get an FBI expert."

I looked at the cloned projector behind him. "What happened to the burst? The algorithm Gemelli told Corona about?"

"Gemelli wanted to believe it. Told him the NIST guys were really onto somethin'. Then had him ship the movie on a hard drive. A backup." Longstreet smiled and shook his head. "Now I gotta start over 'cause you fucked things up, cuz. But it's okay, seein' how it's the last time."

He backed away, the Sig pointing at me, and flipped open his phone. He punched numbers without taking his eyes off me. "He's here." Longstreet pocketed the phone. "Your buddies, the Locos? They called the minute you left them, said you were comin' here." He motioned with the gun. We went through the building without seeing a soul.

Outside it was dark. Jorge waited on the curb, holding open the door of a black Lincoln. Light rain covered his face like a cool sweat. He gave me a vicious smile. "Should I say I'm sorry?" he asked.

"It doesn't matter," I said.

We rode in silence out New York Avenue. I was sandwiched in the back seat between Longstreet and Jorge. Just past the Arboretum, New York Avenue widens and turns into Route 50. A few miles more and the driver signaled and we pulled off onto the shoulder, stopping behind a car hauler truck. On it were twelve new cars, including a long gray limo.

"That's it, isn't it? How you plan to get out of town. You're going to ride in one of those cars."

Longstreet followed my gaze. "Tomorrow," he said in his country drawl. "Today, it's your ride. You'll be crossin' the border in style."

"Let's do it," Jorge said.

We got out of the Lincoln. The rain made it feel a little colder than it was. We walked toward the car-hauler, and the driver came to meet us. Like Jorge, the driver held his gun down at his side, away from the road, so passing drivers wouldn't see. They steered me to the right, so that the hauler's cars shielded us from the highway. The driver used his free hand to pop the trunk of the limo. An eighteen-wheeler zoomed past, and the wind made me shiver.

"Let's do it," Jorge said.

"Scared?" Longstreet asked.

"Just cold."

"Well, soon all your worries'll be over."

Jorge made a movement, and suddenly there was a gun in his hand. "Should I shoot him?"

"Go ahead," Longstreet said.

"Wasn't talkin' to you, man," Jorge said, turning and pushing the barrel of the gun into Longstreet's throat. Jorge's free hand snatched Longstreet's gun. He tossed it to me.

Longstreet's face went pale, and his eyes bulged. He gulped and his huge Adam's apple jumped in his throat. "Wait a minute," he said, his hands out, looking from Jorge to me. "Wait!"

I pointed the gun and fired three shots—all hits. Longstreet doubled over and spun and grabbed his stomach. His hands twisted his clothing, then he looked up at me as though some terrible miracle were taking place.

"You missed," he whispered. "Point blank and you missed."

"I wasn't aiming at you." I went to the limo's open trunk, the lid of which I'd just perforated, and tore out the lock's electric cable. "Your turn, Longstreet. A longer ride than what you planned for me." I nodded at Jorge, who cuffed Longstreet's wrists behind him.

Longstreet said, "That kid—you need money. Willis, you

know that. And I got a partner, he's loaded, he's, he's been bank-rollin' the whole operation." He wet his lips. "How does a quarter mill sound?"

"I can't even hear you."

"Okay, half a mill. C'mon, Willis, use your head for a change. You can buy a lot of diapers with half a mill."

He was right. I'd need money to get Sarah away from the Bishops, to find a decent place to raise her. I wanted to help her, the way Shad had helped me. All I had to do was let Longstreet walk, take the money, and leave a part of my soul on the highway.

An easy choice, except for seeing Florence Walters's face, trapped in the headlights. Those same fucking lights had trapped me as well, showed me something I hadn't wanted to see, made me ask myself—why did I want Sarah? To keep her out of DCAS? To give her a safe home? She already had that with the Bishops.

No, what I realized, before I grabbed Walters, in that moment of hesitation before I saved her, was that I was a selfish prick. I wasn't doing this for Sarah, or for Shad. I was doing it for me. To get a family, I'd considered letting Walters die.

And now, my heart was beating too fast, the gun felt loose in my hand. I was like a man waking up after a drugged sleep. I looked back on the last week and saw that nearly every decision I'd made was wrong. Christ, I was lucky to be alive.

Longstreet guessed what I was going to say. "A million dollars, okay? C'mon, Willis, use your head!"

"I am, for the first time in days. And you know what it's telling me? That it's worth a million, just to see you get in the trunk of that car." I turned to Jorge. "Give him a hand."

Longstreet stood staring at me, then Jorge and the driver seemed to fold him into the trunk. The driver slammed the lid shut and, without a word, went to the cab, fired up the engine, and drove away.

Jorge and I watched until the truck disappeared over the horizon. Then I turned to him. "I'm going to take out a photo."

"All right."

I handed him the black-and-white photo I'd taken from Romero's house. He looked at it, then at me.

"I'm sorry," I said.

Jorge said nothing.

"Your brother. Jaimie Romero. Longstreet killed him." Shock, then anger distorted Jorge Romero's face. Even so, the family resemblance was there. Jorge took a step toward his car. I put my hand on his arm. "We have a deal. Longstreet rides south."

He looked at my hand. I removed it. "Your brother left some money, it's in a picture frame on his dresser. You want the address?"

"I have it." Jorge took a breath, getting back in control. Then he nodded once. "I'll be there when they let him out." He said it like a challenge. A moment later the flush in Jorge's cheeks died. He looked down the road, even though the car hauler was long gone, then turned to me, his wolf's grin was back in place. "You were good back there, acting scared."

Who was acting? I hadn't been completely sure my plan would work until Jorge turned his gun on Longstreet. "Thanks," I said, "you too. Ever think about community theater?"

He turned and looked at me for about ten seconds without expression. "Once, as a kid, I was in *Little Red Riding Hood*.

I didn't ask him which part he'd played.

CHAPTER 70

Roger Franklin Quell was in his favorite place—the spotlight—going over the teleprompter copy for his final press conference, from the rooftop of the Hotel W. The clouds had cleared, and now the sun was shining on the White House and downtown D.C. I stood near the edge, my hands on the railing, looking across the river to Virginia. Quell saw me and came over. "So you got the pirate after all. I'd never pegged you for a happy-ending type."

"Of course, it's a Hollywood story." I turned away from the view. "But I feel sorry for you."

"Me?" The notion delighted him. "Are you joking?"

"When I rousted Longstreet, you got screwed."

"Someone hit you too hard, Gidney? Or not hard enough?"

"Longstreet needed expensive gear to steal your movie. That cloned projector of his costs over a hundred grand. Even for an FBI man, he'd need help. That would be you. Plus, the business of the algorithm, the code—if that were true, you wouldn't have left anything to chance, you'd have tested everything more carefully. If you were serious about protecting your film, that is."

"Ridiculous. Why steal my own movie?"

"Blockbuster movies, there's always some piracy, it's inevitable. So you played both sides. If Longstreet succeeded, you'd get a cut from the pirate copies of *Explosive Rounds*. And if Longstreet failed, there're fewer illegal copies, so you'd make more at the box office. Either way, you win."

Quell put his back to the edge railing and crossed his arms. "A stupid theory from a stupid man."

"Given time, I can prove it. Not that I care too. In fact, I could forget all about it, if you released Brooks and Stoddard from their contracts."

"You're threatening me?" His smile got very tense. Probably upset there were no hot pizzas to throw. Still looking at the crowd, he said, "You nickel-and-dime asshole. The popcorn sales alone on this show will dwarf your lifetime earnings." He turned to face me, keeping the smile in place. "I'll tell you something else—you repeat that shit, anywhere, you can say good-bye to your friends right now." He patted me on the back, then walked away as Corbin Brooks came up. He looked like he'd been standing under a steady drip all day.

"You heard? With *Explosive Rounds*? He's gonna shoot four new scenes, a director's cut. So not only do I have three more films with him, I'm not done with the one I just finished."

Just then, Sondra Stoddard appeared, resplendent in all her Stoddardness, smiling and posing as the flashes popped, along with most of the men. "You figured what to do about Sonnie?" Brooks asked. "Work me into it, okay? If I make another Quell movie, I'll shoot myself."

I figured that could be a savvy career move, but I said nothing. Poor guy was miserable enough. He moved next to Stoddard, smiling that movie-star smile of his. I watched as the techies broke down Corona's stand-up to get ready for Quell's announcement about new scenes for his movie.

A wireless microphone had gotten me into this mess. I was

hoping that maybe it could get me out. I went past techies pointing lights and setting levels, and somehow, one of their wireless transmitters jumped into my pocket. I clipped the tiny black mic to the black lapel of my jacket.

Then something happened, a commotion from in front. Was Stoddard making a second entrance? I turned and saw Lilly walking toward me. She wasn't dressed in canvas bags. She wore something that looked like layers of forest green silk with a gold border. The wind fluttered the silk across her body. Brooks stood next to me and said, "Good golly, Miss Molly."

She put her arms around me and kissed me. When our lips parted, I said, "Nice outfit."

"Thanks." The breeze caressed her black-and-tan dreads. I said, "Lucky the wind blew the right way."

"Luck's got nothing to do with it. The forecast said the wind would be north by northwest."

"And if the wind shifted?"

"I'd still know a hawk from a handsaw."

Roger Franklin Quell approached the podium. TV lights flashed on. Then I felt dragon's breath down the back of my neck. I turned to see Emmet Barnett looking down at me. "Okay, shrimp. I'm here."

I asked Lilly for a favor. She linked arms with Brooks, who gave her a weak smile as she guided him toward the sound crew. Emmet and I approached Sondra Stoddard. "Willis, you bastard," Stoddard said. Obviously pleased to see me.

I raised shoulders and eyebrows. "Sonnie, I'm so, so sorry for how I've treated you."

Her forehead wrinkled. "You are?"

Maybe this was working. "Absolutely. And I promise to be nice to you from now on."

"It's about time," she said without conviction.

Brooks was right, she wasn't liking this at all. Meanwhile, Lilly had gotten a sudden interest in sound. She fingered the sound board while flirting with an elderly gent with glasses and a handlebar mustache. She smiled and nodded to me.

Hand in pocket, I thumbed the transmitter on and told Stoddard, "Part of me being nice to you is to introduce you to man-about-town and *mal vivant* Emmet Barnett."

He grunted. "Hey, babe."

"Emmet wanted to meet you." I saw the sound guys grip their headsets, whip their heads around. They were getting the sound, even though the PA speakers were off. Camera guys jumped behind their tripods to get video of Stoddard. "In fact," I said, "he wants to do a lot more than that, but I told him your husband might object."

"Sure, and who cares if the broad's married?"

Quell saw us. He shouted at the techs, waved his arms, but the techs were too busy recording our conversation to notice.

"Hey," Stoddard said, her index finger poking Emmet in the chest, "I am *not* some broad, okay?" Her eyes had that look I'd seen at the Uptown.

"Lady, you'll be watching that finger, 'less you want it broken." Emmet moved in close.

"Try it and you'll be walking funny," Stoddard said, pressing up against him.

A match made in hell. I took a chance and wedged myself between them. "But Sonnie, you're married to Corbin Brooks."

She looked at me as though she'd never seen me before. "Corby doesn't care. He's gay." The rooftop grew quiet. I leaned closer, pretending as though I hadn't quite heard her.

"What? Corbin is . . . cliché?"

"Gay! He's gay. He doesn't give a fuck what I do," she said.

"Oh," I said, "well, that's different." I switched off the mike, left Stoddard and Emmet, went through the crowd that now clustered around Brooks, who bathed in the lights of the TV cameras, grinning and denying everything. Smart move—nothing gives the ring of truth like denial. Roger Franklin Quell stared openmouthed at his former stars. I stuffed a dollar bill in his pocket. "Here," I said. "This should cover the popcorn sales."

CHAPTER 71

The next day they were gone. Brooks sent me a $25,000 check from New York, a small part of the advance from his publisher. Sondra Stoddard and Emmet appeared on daytime talk shows about Hollywood stars and why their half-baked boyfriends resemble their fathers. Rush went public about his father, who was forced to resign MPAC. And Quell? News of Brooks being gay had doomed *Explosive Rounds* to a DVD-only release.

Seems that Quell's key demographic—male moviegoers ages eighteen to thirty—just weren't ready for a gay action hero. This, in turn, had made Quell's investors very unhappy, very quickly. I was the least of his problems.

Lilly moved into my apartment. It was great to have her close, but I was worried. See, as a kid, I had broken up so many homes. Eddie had said it was part of my job. Then Eddie died and there were no more families that wanted me. Now here was

Lilly, trying to be a part of my life. Would I screw this up? I was afraid part of me might, just out of habit.

Lilly and I had lugged her stuff up the stairs, three times more junk than usual. A very good sign. Now we lay on the couch, Lilly on top, resting her head on my chest, and me trying to breathe without signs of distress. "I've always wanted," I gasped, "a loving woman in my life."

"*I've* always wanted a human pillow. Okay, you can breathe again." She rolled off me.

"I was fine. Where you going?"

"Be right back." And she was, with a length of rope in her hand.

"What's that for?" I asked.

"C'mon over here. I'll show you."

I followed her to the bedroom. She sat on the bed, so I sat beside her.

"I'm not sure why," she said, "but I have the distinct feeling you did something with another woman."

"Never."

She looked at me for thirty seconds or so, then nodded, as though coming to a decision.

"This," she said, indicating the rope, "will help make amends."

Suddenly, there was a wicked smile on her lips that was hard to resist.

"The only question is, Will you take your punishment like a man?"

CHAPTER 72

I'm pleased to say I did.

CHAPTER 73

An hour later, Lilly got ready to go. Back into the sports bra, the sleep-exhaustion makeup, the pillow on her butt. The whole baggy persona. Before she left, she came to the bed and set down a gift. "I hope you'll like this. And you won't have to hide it under the couch cushions."

Beneath the wrapping paper was Frank Tashlin's first kids' book, *The Bear Who Wasn't*. Long out of print. "I know it's not the same as, like, having a daughter," Lilly said. "I'm sorry it ended like this."

I thought about where Sarah was now. "I'm not. And I really don't deserve you at all." She brushed my hair out of my eyes. "You just now figured that out?"

We kissed, then kissed a little more. After she left, FedEx dropped off an envelope. Inside was a postcard of the Hollywood sign. On the other side was the block-printed message, "You should've taken the money."

I got a chill when I read it. I turned it over, looked at the picture again. When that didn't help, I took a swig from the bottle of Old Overholt. The only person I knew who would write something like that had died, years ago, the night Bockman's went up in flames.

Once I'd torn the postcard into pieces and flushed them away, I considered spending the day indoors getting drunk. Instead, I got my jacket and went driving, then found myself parked across from the Bishops' house.

A few minutes later, Violet Bishop and Sarah came around the far corner, walking hand in hand toward their front door. They went into the house, the door closed. Above me, a brilliant red cardinal let loose a chattering whoop.

"Oh, shut up," I said.

Then the front door opened and Horace Bishop walked over to me.

"You Gidney?" I said I was. He smiled, gave me his name, and shook my hand. "Well, what you sitting out here for? C'mon in. Sarah's dying to see you."

"She is?"

"Uh-huh. And Violet, she wants to meet you, too."

I got out of the car and started walking with him. He glanced at me, then said, "That Mrs. Walters, she said you'd likely be coming by."

At the front door, I heard Sarah and Darius playing, and the smell of food cooking. I stopped at the front step. Horace Bishop looked at me. "You okay?"

Good question. Here I was, about to walk through another doorway. The same as when I first found Sarah. Was I doing her a favor right now? Or the Bishops? I didn't know the answer.

Then the screen door banged open. Sarah ran and grabbed my knees. "Wiss!" she shouted. Darius hugged Sarah while she hugged me. Horace herded the three of us into their ten-by-twelve living room as Violet Bishop came in from the kitchen. She had a plate of cheese and crackers in her hand.

"So we finally get to meet you," she said, hugging me with her free arm. "I was beginning to think you were Sarah's guardian angel. You'll stay for dinner?"

"Well, I—"

"Hope you like pasta," Horace grumbled. "She got us all on a health kick."

"You hush," Violet said. To me, she said, "And we thank you so much for the money you sent. We can't keep it, but thank you just the same."

"I didn't—"

"Now hush. Mrs. Walters said you might do something like that." She smiled at her husband. "Didn't she, Horace?" She said his name as though it made a nice taste in her mouth.

"She sure did."

Sarah touched my knee and nodded once, making sure I'd stay put, then toddled over to play with Darius. He had a set of plastic animals on the floor. Horace nodded to the couch. "Sit down, man, take a load off."

I watched Violet set down dinner plates and Horace hang up his jacket. Maybe I could stay a while. Also, the couch had swallowed me whole, I couldn't have stood if I'd wanted to. It felt good to be this close to a family, even if it wasn't mine. As though I were in the company of human beings for the first time in a long time.

Horace handed me a beer. "Walters said you some kinda detective."

"That's right." I took a sip of beer.

"What sorta people you workin' with?"

I picked up a plastic elephant off the floor. "Lately," I said, turning it in my hands, "I've been with a bunch of animals."